I0684659

Also from Indigo Sea Press
Novels by Harry Margulies

The Knowledge Holder

indigoseapress.com

The Weight of the Moon

By

Harry Margulies

Deep Indigo Books
Published by Indigo Sea Press
Winston-Salem

Deep Indigo Books
Indigo Sea Press
302 Ricks Drive
Winston-Salem, NC 27103

This book is a work of fiction. Names, characters, locations and events are either a product of the author's imagination, fictitious or used fictitiously. Any resemblance to any event, locale or person, living or dead, is purely coincidental.

First Deep Indigo Books edition published
January, 2016
Deep Indigo Books, Moon Sailor and all production design are trademarks of Indigo Sea Press, used under license.

For information regarding bulk purchases of this book, digital purchase and special discounts, please contact the publisher at indigoseapress.com

Cover design by Stacy Castanedo

Manufactured in the United States of America
ISBN 978-1-63066-290-5

For my beautiful wife Joann—my love, my strength, my favorite indulgence

Acknowledgements

Writing a book is a process, one that starts with a hunch and ends many pages and many weeks later. At the center of this process lies a gratifying place where characters wait for instructions and plotlines wait for direction. If left to me, this is where I'd hang out, spend my days, maybe grow a beard.

Fortunately – or unfortunately, depending on perspective – I've had someone to coax me through this time-frittering black hole and keep me on track. I consider this individual my hero, my enabler, and, as I've been told, the mother of my two children. Thank you Joann, my wife, for putting up with my crankiness and for believing in my ability to compose reasonably intelligible paragraphs. Thank you as well for believing in my ability to replace burned-out, hard to reach, recessed light bulbs in our perilously high ceilings and for regularly prodding me to do so. The Weight of the Moon never would have been written without your relentless, yet gentle encouragement. I love you.

And to my beautiful daughters, Jessica and Jill, thanks for not rolling your eyes whenever I've asked your opinion on my writing, and thanks for being so sweet and so special. I love you both very much, and, believe it or not, in equal amounts.

I would also like to thank Mike Simpson, along with everyone at Indigo Sea Press who helped bring this book to life. Your unswerving professionalism and invaluable expertise are very much appreciated. Thanks.

Prologue

"What the hell do you think you're doing?" Tulip directed her question at the actress who was messing up the scene. "Do you like your job, honey? Can you not imagine the hundreds of girls who would die to be in your place? Maybe you'd like to get a little more into character, show a little more enthusiasm, huh? Or maybe we should just recast—what do you think Joe?"

Joe was the film's director, and this was not his first film. "I think we should just re-shoot the scene from the top. Tuley, why don't you have a nice chat with the cast, but make it a little more personable—you know, be a little nicer; could you do that for me? Alright gang, we're taking five."

Tulip didn't take Joe's comment as an affront. It was just part of her job as the film's consultant, or Assistant to the Director, as the credits would reveal. She had worked with Joe many times, and they often fell into this "good cop bad cop" bit. Tulip was a perpetually happy and friendly person, but sometimes called upon her dramatic talents when Joe needed her to.

She was still a relatively young woman, but, at thirty-one, Tulip had already played out her career as an actress. She had been such a successful performer for so many years that lots of studios sought her services as a kind of liaison between the actors and the crew. It was her job to keep things rolling, but not at the expense of quality.

Tulip really enjoyed her career. She loved the atmosphere of a film studio and the electric feeling she received from being on a soundstage. Most of all, she loved the people and the small challenges they created; it was never life and death. Films were being made, and little problems arose constantly. They never seemed to be too big a challenge for Tulip.

Tulip approached the two performers who had caused her to erupt moments earlier. "I'm sorry I got a little hot just now," she said to Jamie, the actress she had confronted. "Something seemed to be bothering you though. Can you share with me?"

"It's him," Jamie answered, nodding toward Lance, the other performer.

"And?"

"It's his dick. It tastes horrible!"

This was a situation Tulip had encountered many times in her career. Most actresses learned to handle these things themselves. Jamie was relatively new however, and had a few things yet to learn.

"Lance, is this your first scene of the day?" Tulip queried.

"No ma'am," Lance responded. "I shot the milkman scene earlier."

"Ah, and did you shower after?"

"I kind of cleaned myself off with a towel," Lance replied.

"Okay, here's the deal Lance. You're something special—I think we all know that. In fact, I can't recall anything quite as special as you in all my years in the business. But listen honey, even with that special something you have, you absolutely must take a thorough shower after every anal scene, alright? Now go jump in the shower—and don't be shy about the soap. We have cases of it in the back."

Once again Tulip had stepped in to keep the production flowing. This was her life, and she loved it.

Tulip would be a little sad an hour later when the director would call it a day. She really had no place to go after work, except to her cute little house she kept in the valley. It wasn't much, at least to Tulip, but she appreciated how her debatably ignoble career covered the million-dollar mortgage, and in California, you really needed to fork over that kind of dough just to live someplace safe and decent.

As fulfilled as Tulip was in her career, the rest of her life had always seemed empty. She was born out of wedlock to a couple destined for great things, but who didn't need or want the baggage associated with raising a child conceived before any vows had been exchanged. During one of her parents' infrequent visits, she questioned why she hadn't been aborted. Her parents' response was one of silence, accompanied by a squinty-eyed look of derision. As a young lady, Tulip herself became pregnant three times, yet chose not to expose any child to the confusion and nonsense of the self- righteous society in which she lived.

Shortly after Tulip was born, her parents took her to

California to live with her Great Aunt Rose. Her aunt did the best she could to nurture the child, but she was an older lady who had no children or experience raising them. Fortunately, she did have a very nice house and received a handsome check every month from Tulip's parents, so Tulip was never wanting—at least for material things.

When Tulip was thirteen years old, her aunt passed away. As much as she wanted to, her parents would not allow her to live on her own. They enrolled Tulip in the best boarding school they could find. She lived there until high school graduation. The Edison School for Girls did the best they could, but when Tulip was spewed out at the end, she was what she was—a product of her upbringing and her surroundings. It was about this time that she became Tulip.

When she was born, her name was Lily. She always liked this name, because so few other children possessed it. When she became an actress, she thought it best to have some sort of stage name. Not that it would have bothered her family if she had kept her legal name. She didn't even have a family, as far as she was concerned. But she didn't feel Lily was a proper sort of name for the type of actress she wanted to be. So, in keeping with the only family tradition she had been part of, she thought of some other, more suitable flower-inspired name. She came up with Tulip—Tulip Sonrod, in fact.

Tulip Sonrod became synonymous with quality porn. She was definitely hot: a lithe, tanned, silky smooth body with flowing long legs, taut, perfectly toned ass, luscious, firm breasts ignored by the surgeon's scalpel, and a permanent and radiant smile. Then there was that nose—a feature not usually considered when analyzing most adult film stars. But on Tulip, it was something you noticed. It was sharp and thin and angular, but for some reason, it oddly enhanced her appearance.

Chapter One

Evelyn carefully placed the five neatly packed grocery bags in the far back corner of the Lexus SUV, close to the hatch. She slid her Coach purse, weighty with necessities and just-in-case non-necessities, tight to the bags. There was little chance the stiff paper containers, which cradled the nibbles to be shared later with company, could now topple over. Even though evasive turns weren't part of her itinerary, the bags were very nicely secured, just in case. There wasn't anything in them more valuable than a box of basil and parmesan brittle crackers, but still they were treated with the same respect Evelyn showed everything and everyone in her life. She was brought up to be that kind of person.

Sitting properly postured in the driver's seat, Evelyn waited for the elderly couple pushing a near-empty grocery cart to pass behind. While she could have backed out of her space and re-parked six or seven times before hitting the pair, she evaluated the moment. It wasn't much of a stretch, maybe twenty years max, before this would be her and Sidney, shuffling behind a metal cart, feigning its importance as a transporter, but mostly just using it for support. Things had not gotten complicated for them yet, at least in terms of their health. In fact, they were enjoying the best years of their lives. Evelyn attributed this status to a life devoid of conflict and filled with unwavering and unquestionable values.

Seemingly minutes passed, yet the old folks were still creaking along the path of danger behind the SUV. As Evelyn's dreamlike state waned, she could feel her temper start to swell, and her stoic resolve fade. After all, she had graciously given Grammy and Grampy more than enough time to make their way to safety.

Evelyn briefly considered lowering her window to ask the sloths if they understood the concept of time, and did they realize they weren't getting any younger by spending it strolling through an asphalted parking lot. If they were lucky, they'd make it to their car just in time for their funerals. Her eyes darted back to the rear-view mirror and she caught her reflection. Who was this woman with the ruffled face? Of course she wouldn't say such a thing to these people. In fact, she truly respected her elders, and was ashamed for even entertaining these impudent notions.

Finally the path cleared, and Evelyn was free to proceed home. But there was now less time to prepare than she had anticipated.

•••

Sidney Banks peeked quickly at his watch, the sober face of the gold Movado Evelyn had given him for their thirtieth staring back at him. He had promised his wife he would be home in fifteen minutes; his office was twenty minutes from the house. Fortunately for Sidney, he was able to excuse himself from the board meeting without causing too much disruption. He hoped the Friday afternoon freeway logjam he regularly endured would have dissipated somewhat by now, and that he'd be a mere five minutes late. His wife had invited the Hanovers to the opera, which meant George and Iris would be popping by for a few minutes of socializing before leaving for the venue.

Sidney was confident that he could quickly make himself presentable when he reached the house. He continually adhered to a high standard of grooming, and little time would be needed to repair any superficial damage triggered by the stress of his day. A quick change of clothes and he'd be ready for the evening.

Always having maintained a certain conceit regarding his appearance, Sidney hadn't allowed the decades to muddle with his body the way it had with many of his contemporaries. He ardently resisted the notion that he looked different than he did when he was a much younger man. Even at sixty-two, he wore the same size slacks as the day he was married. He could not be considered slight by those who gauged such things, but was properly dimensioned for a man precisely six feet tall. His black hair was the one feature, however, that had ripened noticeably with time—still crowded across his scalp, but now interspersed with strands of silver. With the help of the shimmering pomade that he used, his hair imparted a distinguished look he did not mind. He had great confidence in his appearance, but very little in his ability to make it home on time.

Sidney pictured Evelyn laying out an assortment of delicacies about now, which usually amounted to an array of fine, unique cheeses complemented by appropriate pâtés. She was a flawless hostess, and had made Sidney a proud husband the last thirty years. As much as he appreciated her assets though, being married to her was a little like being married to the school librarian—distractions of any sort wouldn't be tolerated. Some of these were gentlemanly traditions that Evelyn just didn't grasp.

Only at certain social gatherings was Evelyn amenable to Sidney's desire for a swallow of liquor. Even though she adored crystal glasses, sterling ice buckets, and unbuttoned conversations, she never quite followed the allure of alcohol. On the rare occasion when Sidney would partake, she would turn a blind eye as if something more consequential, such as a tired dish of cashews in need of freshening, was calling to her. She was also unaware of the quantity of drink being consumed on these occasions, and Sidney meant for it to stay that way. The later Sidney arrived home, the less time he and George would have to inconspicuously slug down the appropriate amount of beverage to bear three hours at the opera. Evelyn would insist on being the driver for the evening anyway, as she refused to give Sidney the honors if he so much as glanced at the stuff. All would be well if he could just make it home without delay.

•••

Evelyn reviewed the checklist she had created earlier in the week, confirming she hadn't forgotten anything. The carpets were impeccably groomed, as if the greens keeper from Pebble Beach had something to do with them. Perfectly aligned swaths of alternating nap flow gave the floor a pristine appearance. In fact, it wasn't a greens keeper, but rather the maid, Louisa, who was responsible. Evelyn was pleased that she had finally landed quality help after Eatoy retired. She had gone through so many maids since, none of whom had made the grade.

Shortly after she arrived home from the market, Evelyn unwrapped the cheeses she purchased and set them on the coffee table in the living room. If they weren't given time to rest, there would be no purpose in eating them. The aroma, texture, and ripeness of the cheese needed to arrive before company did. Fancy crackers of all sorts were painstakingly arranged to balance out the cheese boards. Normally, she would have supplemented this presentation with crudités and maybe thick slices of pâté, but with reservations at Dominick's after the performance, too lavish a spread would certainly have been inappropriate.

After patting the outer reaches of her russet hair, Evelyn confirmed that it was arranged as her stylist had intended. She hadn't the time to trek back to her dressing area off the master to verify her appearance in a mirror. Of course there were plenty of mirrors within yards of where she stood, but she couldn't risk being caught in a moment of vanity; the Hanovers might walk in any time. In her mind's eye though, she was looking pretty good.

Evelyn was proud of her poise and of her assets, both above and below the waist. Everything seemed to still be defying gravity. She attributed at least part of her youthful appearance to the lack of wear and tear on her body. She kept her best assets fresh and only slightly used—the car was always garaged so to speak. She didn't consent to Sidney putting his key in the ignition very often. Typically, he was only permitted to open the door and touch the upholstery. On the occasion that Sidney was allowed in for routine maintenance it would be straightforward, without any tugging, pinching, or biting of any of the delicate mechanics. Evelyn didn't really have to fight the ravages of time, as long as Sidney stayed on his side of the garage.

As Evelyn was giving the room and herself a once over, she heard the doorbell. Her dress, hemmed below the knees, prohibited her from moving too quickly. She eventually reached the front door.

"Iris, don't you look wonderful!" Evelyn cackled to her guest as she opened the door.

Iris did look pretty good for a woman a week from sixty-five, so Evelyn's sincerity would not be doubted. She had striking features, some of which she was born with. Although her nose looked as if it could serve well as the pointy bow of a small ship, with its angular precision and ability to cut through any surface with ease, it did not diminish her attractiveness in any way, and somehow oddly enhanced it. Her auburn hair, which had obviously been coiffed and colored that day, was short and neat and framed her heart shaped face and bright brown eyes nicely.

Iris was a good three inches shorter than Evelyn, but the Cole Haan skyscrapers strapped to her feet more than erased that deficit. Her new finely tailored charcoal suit completed the picture.

"As do you, my dear, as do you!" Iris replied.

"And George, how nice it is to see you," Evelyn countered as she angled a small part of her face to George's right cheek. "Won't you please both come in and make yourselves comfortable?"

Evelyn led her guests to the living room, assuring George along the way that Sidney would be home momentarily.

"He must have been trapped in that dreadful board meeting he was forced to attend this afternoon," Evelyn continued. "He used to be so dependable. Now look, he's going to be at least five minutes past the time he was expected. Please do make yourselves comfortable."

Once the Hanovers were situated in front of the cheese trays, their fingers nimbly poking around the spread laid before them, Evelyn excused herself. She was growing furious over Sidney's delinquency, and her frustration was becoming quite evident. What bothered her most perhaps was that Sidney wasn't keeping just anyone waiting; it was the couple Evelyn idolized more than any other—the Hanovers.

When Sidney and Evelyn moved to Arizona from Baltimore twenty years ago, the Hanovers befriended them. Almost instantly, they became very close. The Banks could not have had any more respect for their newfound acquaintances. George and Iris always lived so properly, doing and saying the right things and forever exhibiting the essence of grace. Neither couple had children, which made the bond between them even more pure. Although Iris was only three years older, Evelyn aspired to be just like her, as if she wished to be her when she grew up.

Now Sidney was late, and Evelyn was dreadfully ashamed and terribly distressed that she had fallen short of the standards set by her good friends in the next room. As she was bemoaning her inadequacies, Sidney pulled up the drive. Evelyn took a deep breath, allowed her blood to settle and her nerves to calm, and then opened the door for her husband.

"Sidney dear, you're almost ten minutes late! I hope everything is okay with you, but no time for that now. The Hanovers are in the living room, and you must change your jacket, at the very least!" Evelyn's voice grew higher in pitch and faster in pace as she spoke.

"Okay darling—I'm so sorry. Traffic wasn't as light as I'd hoped, and it was difficult finding the proper moment to excuse myself from the board meeting. I almost considered calling you from my car, but you know how I feel about that." Sidney not only regarded the act of phoning while driving a potentially perilous distraction, but a distinctly flamboyant display of bad manners.

"Of course, dear—now scurry off to the bedroom and change that jacket. I'll inform George and Iris that you'll be down in a minute!"

Evelyn made a quick retreat back to the living room where she found her guests sitting comfortably with their legs crossed and a cloth napkin in George's left hand supporting exactly half a cheese laden cracker.

"Sidney will be down shortly—my apologies," Evelyn announced. "Oh my goodness, I've left you without offering a beverage!" With that, Evelyn turned a shade of red and scrambled for a recovery. "Iris, I found a special new tea at the store today. May I get you a cup, or do you prefer a club soda?"

"That tea sounds lovely, but I'd prefer the soda thank you. Let me come with you to the kitchen, doll."

"Of course! George, Sidney will want to make you something special, I'm sure."

"George my old friend!" Sidney bellowed, as he passed the

girls and made his way into the room. “Come with me!”

Sidney led George to the mahogany bar on the far side of the room. The bar was a highly polished and very elegant example of classic furniture carved in a serpentine shape, adding a pleasant dimension to the square room. It provided the decorator touch Evelyn was seeking for the space. The fact that it was a bar was totally irrelevant.

“We will catch up on each other’s lives in a minute, but first I want to show you my latest acquisitions,” Sidney whispered.

For a man on such a short leash, Sidney had quite a selection of single malt Scotch. He proceeded to introduce his friend to a thirty-year-old Macallan Fine Oak and a twenty-one-year-old Balvenie Portwood. Though not extremely rare, the two bottles had set him back over $1,200.

“Neat, as usual?” Sidney asked George as he uncorked the Macallan.

“Naturally!” was George’s exaggerated, yet muted response.

Sidney poured his friend a finger of the sainted liquid, and then doubled the amount for himself. As much as he knew George wanted to scale away the strain associated with a night at the opera and the wives, he also appreciated the man’s fervent self-control; the chap could walk past a roll of bubble-wrap without touching it. He was almost inhuman in his behavior. Sidney had never witnessed his friend in an obvious state of intoxication, and doubted he ever would. Perhaps, Sidney thought, he might be able to coax George into a drop of the Balvenie before they departed for the opera, but odds were the man would still be nursing the Macallan when it was time to leave.

On the other hand, Sidney required Novocain level numbness to survive an evening such as this. He was determined to reach that place located just below sloppiness, and stay there as long as he could. After splashing an almost reckless serving of Balvenie into his now empty tumbler, he turned toward George, who still cradled his smooth, heavy glass in his palm, contemplating his first sip.

“George, I can appreciate you, but I sure don’t understand you, my friend.” Sidney was starting to loosen up. “We have but a minute to prepare ourselves for a long evening of tenors and sopranos and such. Not that I don't value the talent these entertainers possess, but if you haven't noticed, we have third row seats—very close to the source, so to speak. I don't want to rush you, but wouldn't you be better prepared if you were to have another?"

"Sidney, what can I say?" George responded. "I'm very pleased at the sixty-six years I've been given so far. If I were forced to rate my life, I'd say it's been more than wonderful. But I'll let you in on a secret of mine—I'm most comfortable when I'm doing the right thing. I avoid most vices, and, of the rest, I partake in moderation. I have no worries, really. I've never knowingly lied—with the exception of some government business many years back. I don't smoke, I don't curse, I have a chivalrous passion for proper etiquette, and though mostly not my decision, I have quite a modest sex life; any sexual release I experience transpires on the date of my birth, or on my wedding anniversary. I have sexual relations so infrequently that it feels promiscuous sleeping with my wife! All in all, this lifestyle seems to work very well for me. It's not necessary for me to be inebriated my friend, although I do enjoy a taste now and then. Thank you so much for offering though."

"George, I must admit you are something special. If I could be more like you, I would in an instant."

"You are like me Sidney. You are perhaps the most upstanding gentleman I have acquaintance with. There is nothing inappropriate about an occasional waltz with the bottle. As far as I can tell, you only drink when you're in my presence! The level of Scotch in those bottles of yours never varies from visit to visit. Of course I'm not privy to your bedroom activities, but knowing how close the girls are, I can't imagine Evelyn is much more generous in that department than Iris."

"You know me quite well my friend. And I'm afraid your analysis of my wife has hit the target straight on. When we do have intercourse, it's quite the scene. Seconds after I ejaculate, she's off to that bidet of hers as if I've deposited Satan's seed!"

Sidney realized the Scotch was doing its job and silently regretted his outburst regarding his sexual standing with Evelyn.

Without looking up to catch George's reaction, Sidney swirled the remaining drops of liquid gold around the bottom of his glass, then tilted his head back and drained the remnants.

"Boys! I hope you're ready to go!" It was Evelyn's voice, excitedly intimating their departure.

The timing couldn't have been better for Sidney whose skin had flushed with his last comment to George. He had also reached that plateau of bliss from the alcohol he had hoped to achieve, and now prayed he'd retain.

Evelyn pulled the SUV around to the front so her guests would not have to see, touch, smell, or experience in any way, her garage. Not that it was filthy or cluttered. It just wasn't the place for company.

After everyone had channeled into the car, they were on their way.

Chapter Two

The seats were as Sidney promised—third row from the stage. The theater itself was nothing classic, but a predictable representation of mid-eighties architecture. Modern, clean lines defined the arena, giving the expansive space an impressive feel. Still, there was something missing.

Evelyn had enjoyed the timeless, ornate stages of New York and Baltimore, and this experience was far removed. Living in Scottsdale did not offer as many opportunities to revel in historical culture as living Back East did. When it came to the arts, seemingly nothing existed before the seventies. Of course this wasn't the case, but to Evelyn there was a level of sophistication missing that she yearned for. After twenty years, she had not fully evolved from the East Coast woman she was raised to be. As much as she loved her "new" home, her roots defined her.

The two couples settled into their seats shortly before the orchestra began tuning their instruments. There was a typical measure of muttering traversing the restless crowd as they awaited the start of the performance. As most of the clatter came from behind the third row, it was more bothersome than usual to the foursome. After a brief spell, Iris could no longer suppress her judgment of the insolent audience, and whispered cursorily to Evelyn who was seated to her immediate left.

"It's rather embarrassing, the social skills our neighbors possess."

"They have deteriorated over time, haven't they," Evelyn responded, a hand coyly cupped over her mouth as she spoke. "Last season, in this same theater, a man seated in front of us was flatulent—audibly flatulent. He obviously had no manners and no control."

"Goodness," Iris sighed in response.

The lights dimmed, and the string section came alive. The audience calmed to an appropriate stillness, and the girls settled deeper in their seats, a modest grin crossing their faces. Sidney was grinning too, the result of well measured dosing. George had a complacent look about him, which he would maintain throughout the performance.

La Traviata was beginning. This mid-nineteenth century Verdi classic had always been one of Iris's favorites. It was not the happiest of stories, but it did feature the soprano voice, and Iris could listen to a quality soprano all day long. Tonight's featured artist would be a good one—there was no doubt in her mind. This was due to the fact that Iris, in a roundabout way, knew this performer. She had not shared this special tidbit with the Banks yet, because it was part of a much bigger surprise she had planned for them later. A cozy smugness embraced her as her somewhat friend Alicia Cavaloni took the stage.

Although Iris had never actually met this woman, she was determined to create a bond with her. After all, she and Alicia had a mutual friend in New York City. Per Iris's interpretation of social hierarchy, Alicia would therefore be considered her friend-in-law.

Iris had been reviewing her upcoming social calendar with this shared acquaintance, Winnie, during a recent call, which all told amounted to a slugfest of who had the busiest, most impressive social schedule. As Iris was itemizing the arts functions she would be attending, she mentioned this performance of La Traviata. Winnie, only too happy to one-up Iris, was aware that her dear friend Alicia was starring in the touring company that would be performing in Arizona, and brought it to Iris's attention immediately.

Several days later, Winnie called with some wonderful news: Alicia would love to receive Iris and her friends in her dressing room after the performance. Although this gave Winnie the upper hand socially speaking, Iris was delighted to cash in this chip for a chance to mingle with an operatic luminary. Not wanting to appear boastful at all, she held off on mentioning this exciting encounter to Evelyn, saving it as a special surprise.

The opera was in full swing now, and the large crowd was fully captivated by the emotional story. The Banks and Hanovers had never experienced an opera as exquisitely performed as this one. Even Sidney, who at this point would have been just as easily entertained by a plate spinning on a stick, was impressed with the talent set before him.

Intermission was a minute away, and Sidney was aching for another beverage. He did not want to press his luck and possibly be caught only one sheet to the wind with the second act just ahead. There was a bar in the lobby, which would be very busy moments after the lights came up. If Sidney was not efficient in exiting his third row seat and quickly maneuvering to the back of the theater, the line would be insufferable. Another obstacle standing, or, more specifically, seated, in his way was Evelyn, who at this point decided to hold Sidney's hand, a strategy she employed from time to time to keep her husband in place. It wouldn't have been proper for her to tell her husband to stay put, but by using her deceptive strength, she could keep him where he was for the duration of the intermission.

As the theater brightened signaling the start of the break, Sidney reached with his free hand into a pocket of his jacket, removing a clean white handkerchief. He excused his other hand from Evelyn's embrace by indicating a need to cover his nose for an impending sneeze. Certainly Evelyn would release her hand for that, which she did. The sneeze did not arrive, but the free man stood and asked his friend George if he would like to stretch his legs. The ploy worked well, and the two men were quickly in the lobby. They stood in the brief line at the bar, Sidney fishing a fifty from his trouser pocket.

"Well then, what do you make of it so far?" Sidney asked his friend.

"Highly entertaining; I'm very impressed with the entire troupe!" George replied. "I must say, they made an excellent casting decision when they chose that fantastic soprano for the role of Violetta. I don't believe I've seen her before."

"I think you would have remembered her, my friend," Sidney countered. Sidney was in enough control to know it would have been improper to continue this thought. He was also dismayed that George had replanted the image of this woman in his head, after he had fought hard to suppress it. The woman they were discussing was not lacking in talent. She didn't seem to be lacking for anything, in fact. The first five minutes of her performance had been nothing but distracting to Sidney. He had been so absorbed trying to calculate this woman's weight that he hadn't noticed the quality voice she possessed. He eventually settled on somewhere between four hundred and five hundred pounds, then tried his best to re-focus his attention on the other players, or at least the magnificent set. Still, he couldn't help but think that if he saw this woman on the street, he would assume her voice to be like that of a large frog, not of an angel.

"How do you mean, Sidney?" George had given it a moment's thought, and had obviously given up.

"Well, she does stand out doesn't she!" Sidney replied in as lighthearted a manner as he could muster. Now that he was thinking about her again, he wasn't sure if it *was* possible for a five hundred pound woman to have the necessary dexterity to waltz around the stage as she did; maybe there were wires somewhere. He made a mental note to check for them in the second act.

"I see," said George. "You're referring to her girth, aren't you?"

"Well, it is an impressive dimension. George, what may I order you to drink?" Sidney was anxious to change the tack of the conversation.

The two gentlemen eventually returned to their third row seats, both smiling. Sidney's double Scotch hurriedly swallowed by the bar accounted for his. George was just happy the second act was about to start. Fortunately for Sidney, the theater prohibited taking any food or beverage past the lobby, so Evelyn would be forced to guess whether anything beyond leg stretching had taken place.

The lights dimmed, and Evelyn reached for Sidney's hand once again. This time, Sidney knew the reason for this action wasn't to hold him in his seat, but rather Evelyn's play at that perfunctory bonding ritual practiced by women everywhere. He was pretty sure Evelyn didn't have any magician's talent that could help her determine by this act whether he had consumed anything he should be ashamed of, but he made certain to breathe the other direction, just in case.

The second act was as good as the first, if not better. The emotional struggles, the romance, the tragedy—the audience was together on this ride, and when it was over they demonstrated their appreciation by uniformly rising and presenting the players with seemingly incessant rounds of acclamation.

Evelyn and Iris turned toward each other wearing broad smiles—applause ringing in their ears—tears shimmering in the corners of their eyes. Iris was very excited to tell Evelyn her big surprise, but needed a moment first to recover from the overwhelming waves of sentiment coursing through her veins. After the curtain was lowered the final time, she gathered herself so she could tell Evelyn the news.

"Evelyn dear, what did you think?" It was a rhetorical question, but still warranted asking. After all, it wasn't polite to share one's thoughts until others had shared theirs first.

"My goodness!" Evelyn replied, her left hand flat against her breastbone as if to keep her chest from falling to the ground. "That was such a striking performance! I have not seen such a polished and talented troupe of performers in quite some time. And that Violetta! What a magnificent voice!"

"Well Evelyn Banks," Iris responded, "I have a bit of a surprise I'd like to share with you. We are not going to leave the theater quite yet."

"I'm afraid I don't follow, Iris. Whatever do you mean?"

"The four of us are invited to Alicia Cavaloni's private dressing room… right now!" Iris couldn't help but notice the mixture of expressions building quickly on her friend's face as she stood speechless. She could sense confusion and excitement all balled together, producing a contorted look Iris had never seen on Evelyn before. Iris knew that Evelyn had mixed with privileged society on many occasions, and assumed she had brushed shoulders with celebrity, but this was something special and unexpected. Iris quickly summarized the story of her relationship with the star, and then the eager pair grabbed their mates to head backstage.

The girls forged ahead trying to locate the luminary's dressing room, while the boys lagged somewhat behind. Sidney had a most pleasant reaction when informed by Evelyn of their new plans, though privately wishing they were now in the car, closer to food and beverage. In spite of the recent surge of emotion and activity, he was still feeling mellow from the drink he had at intermission. He decided that if he could maintain appropriate conduct in this woman's dressing room, he would reward himself with one more swallow before dinner.

"Sidney, may I have a word?" George pulled his friend to the side of the hallway as their wives endeavored to locate the correct door.

"What is it George?" Sidney replied. "Are you okay?"

"Of course I'm okay, Sidney. I just want to be sure that you are. Those comments you made to me in the lobby at intermission. They have me concerned that you are behaving loosely, and may say something inappropriate to our hostess."

"If you're referring to my comments regarding Ms. Cavaloni's dimensions…" Sidney paused to collect his thoughts before continuing, "Certainly you know my regard for others feelings would not allow me to even whisper anything demeaning. My conversation with you earlier was meant as cordial banter, nothing more. Of course I shall be on best behavior!"

Sidney's last words were slightly slurred, causing George a small amount of concern. He knew Sidney was about to see something up-close that he wasn't sure he had the gut for. Be that as it may, George was confident the girls would occupy the lion's share of time spent with the diva, and that there would be no awkward situations.

"This is it!" Evelyn exclaimed in a discreet, subdued hiss.

The two couples gathered outside the door, and, after exchanging hurried, furtive glances at one another, elected Iris to have the honors. Evelyn, Sidney, and George watched as she knocked firmly, but not too abrasively, on the dull gray metal portal. Iris stood closest so that she could introduce herself first, then her husband and friends.

Inelegant lumbering noises emanating from the room could soon be heard from the hallway. The portentous sounds intensified at a tedious pace. The suspense was almost too much for the girls, whose breathing had become almost embarrassingly audible.

"Well, good evening everyone!" Alicia Cavaloni remarked,

opening the door with a dramatic *whoosh.* "I must be looking at Iris Hanover, am I not?"

"Why yes you are!" Iris responded, extending her hand with polished grace.

Alicia welcomed the two couples inside as Iris formally introduced everyone. There were congratulations and bravos all around, directed toward Alicia and delivered by each of the four. Alicia gestured toward a loveseat, a narrow piece with thin, dullish-green cushions. By a hair's breadth it was able to accommodate Iris and George. Evelyn and Sidney sat in two chairs that angled off the loveseat. For some reason Alicia remained standing, even though there were two more chairs available.

Sidney was grateful that Alicia had extended her hand when they were introduced. He had no idea how he could access that cheek of hers with his lips, and he was concerned Evelyn was expecting him to plant a peck somewhere about the sizable canvass. She seemed even larger to Sidney than when she was on stage. He had hoped being on stage was akin to being on television, where the performers were actually smaller than they appeared on the screen.

Sidney noticed from his vantage point a broad table on the far side of the room, laden with assorted morsels. He could detect from his seat all manner of cakes and sweets. His mental reflex was to assume the diva was expecting family members, or maybe some true, non-groupie friends, to join her for a meal, and he breathed easier for a moment. After mulling it over, he realized this probably was not the case, and that this was simply her post-game snack, so to speak. He hoped she would wait for them to leave before indulging.

All in all, Sidney was behaving himself nicely, at least from his perspective. If he wasn't, he knew he would receive earfuls later.

Iris and Evelyn continued to chat up the opera star, as if they were long lost sorority sisters. Once they were done showering Alicia with praise, they moved on to discuss the "four f's": fashion, friends, and fine art. They left out the fourth f, fitness. They didn't deem this a necessary topic to cover at this time.

George was busy soaking in everything. He kept a pleasant smile on his face, appearing legitimately interested in the girls' conversation. He was nestled very close to his wife on the loveseat, as it was barely wide enough to accommodate two adults. Not that he minded; he was always proud to be associated with Iris. He admired her in every respect. Sitting this close just reinforced his attachment to her. He had never known another woman who was so proper, and yet so beautiful.

With this unanticipated proximity to his wife, George could easily inhale her ordinarily out of reach, subtle, provocative fragrance. He found himself calculating the weeks until his birthday, when he would be granted access to the treasured blooms behind this intoxicating bouquet.

The group had been gathered in Alicia's dressing room for more than fifteen minutes, when the star offered her guests a bite to eat from the spread across the room. This caught the four of them off guard, as they each privately assumed Alicia would be attacking the fare herself the minute they were gone. Evelyn and Iris locked eyes, searching for each other's encyclopedic grasp of manners and proper protocol in this instance. There was clearly enough food laid out for a dozen guests or more, but if the diva wanted to share, why hadn't she made the offer sooner? Both George and Sidney were clearly staying far from this one, deferring instead to one of the girls. As Iris was the official connection to Alicia, she understood it was her duty to respond.

"My dear Alicia, you are so kind to invite us to break bread with you! Unfortunately, we have but a couple more moments before we must excuse ourselves. We had previously engaged a table at a beloved restaurant, and would feel dreadful if we showed up behind schedule."

"But of course," Evelyn chimed in, "you are most welcome to join us—in fact, we insist!" Evelyn beamed with pride at the quick rejoinder, reasoning that her offer would mitigate any bad feelings Iris's response may have caused.

George's expression remained unchanged: a pleasant smile and hopeful eyes. Sidney was praying his outward appearance mirrored George's, as inwardly he was about to explode. He found the woman personable enough, but dinner? His numbness was dissipating, and this meal could derail an otherwise well managed evening. He was even having a hard time visualizing a strategy for wedging the woman into the car. Sidney realized this was an inappropriate thought and forced a feeble attempt at pinching his leg through his trouser pocket.

"How nice you are," Alicia replied, "that is such a thoughtful offer! I am a stranger in town, and to be escorted to a delightful restaurant by such a wonderful group of friends…I would love to join you!"

Alicia was still standing in the small space between the two couples, facing Iris and George when she accepted the invitation. In a theatrical move, she rotated her torso and humbly bowed in the direction of Evelyn and Sidney, expressing her appreciation. Sidney was incredulous that she had accepted the invitation, and was momentarily flustered. In an attempt to cover any horror he may have been displaying, he overreacted and stood to grab Alicia's hand. His thinking was that he would be confirming her welcome with this gesture. The timing couldn't have been worse.

Sidney's momentum was carrying him up and toward the diva. As he reached for her, she was in somewhat of a twisted position, bowing toward him. This maneuver by Sidney caught Alicia off-guard. The couples watched as her already precarious balance began to falter. Still holding his hand in hers, Sidney's body wrenched forward from the pull of the swaying tonnage, his arm stretching until it could extend no further. And then she released her grip. Evelyn sat in absolute horror, her right hand moving to cover her mouth, which was unable to emit any sound. She could see Alicia slowly descending backward, but was helpless to do anything about it. The entire scene seemed to present itself in slow motion—very slow motion.

The most unique and terrifying perspective on this impending tragedy would come from directly behind the slow falling songstress. The loveseat, with its fast grip on Iris and George, was precisely in her path. George wasn't quite sure how to react. His instincts encouraged him to flee, that this was not the place to be. The gallant response however, would be to stay, and soften Alicia's fall as much as he could. Although it seemed an eternity from her initial loss of balance to impact, there wasn't enough time for George to make the right decision.

Iris was also glued to the loveseat due to her indecision. It wouldn't have been proper to jump out of the way and let her new friend descend to a most certain injury. On the other hand, what good would it really do any of them if she remained seated? As Iris's mind raced toward the proper solution to this conundrum, time ran out.

Chapter Three

Sidney was still facing the falling Alicia, his mouth agape, watching her eyes grow larger as the inevitable drew closer. He was helpless to do anything at this point. He could only imagine the expressions on the faces of his friends, the Hanovers. When the collision finally occurred, it resonated like an accident at a construction site. The bulk of the sound was created by the loveseat as it splintered into dozens of pieces, as if it had been thrust into a wood shredder.

Evelyn sat in a state of semi-shock while Sidney rushed forward to do whatever he could to extricate the now possibly injured opera star from her predicament and his friends. The expression on Alicia Cavaloni's face was quite unique; Sidney had never seen anything like it. Her eyes were bulging as if she were a hamster being squeezed by a python, her cheeks were flushed and her mouth appeared unhinged—as if she were preparing to swallow a large hoagie in one bite.

There was little Sidney could do to shift the singer even a smidge. He tried to remember any sort of leverage formula or tactic he could. He had taken a course in physics while at the University of Pennsylvania; it wasn't part of his major—just a class he picked to fulfill the science requirement he needed. At the time, it sounded easier and less complicated than chemistry or biology. After all, he would never be using anything from a science textbook later in life—not a businessman. Now he was struggling to come up with something, anything that might work to pry this woman off the mess beneath her.

"How do you get yourself out of bed in the morning!" Sidney screamed at the flailing songstress. He assumed she did sit down occasionally, and figured she must lie down at least once a day. "How can I help you get up!"

Alicia could only respond like a large captured fish, flapping on the dock and gasping for air. In the meantime, Evelyn had officially become a basket case. She started rocking back and forth, one hand over her mouth, her eyes staring into space.

"George! Iris!" Sidney called out to his friends loud enough for them to hear, knowing their ears were certainly muffled by the substantial load surrounding them. There was no response.

After making this attempt twice more, Sidney shouted to Evelyn, pleading with her to find a phone and dial 911. His wife remained seated, her eyes fuzzy puddles of horror-spawned disquietude.

Sidney rushed to the door of the dressing room and threw it open, hoping to find some sort of help in the hallway. About thirty feet away, a young man who Sidney recognized as one of the performers was leaning against an open door, apparently having a conversation with someone inside the room. He was no longer in costume. By the look on the young man's face, he was flirting with the other person. Sidney raised his voice, intending to be loud without affecting a scream. He called out to this person for assistance, assuming the young man would leave the girl he was seemingly trying to seduce, and come help Sidney. Perhaps two men would be able to leverage the woman to her feet.

The young man hurried down the hallway, closely followed by his friend who apparently was also a young man. Sidney realized he had made a mistake assuming there was a seduction taking place, but was more than glad to have the extra assistance.

"I need your help please, and quickly!" Sidney started. "There are two people beneath her, and I'm afraid they may be injured!"

The two cast members stared in awe at the scene. Sidney at first regretted spending the time recruiting these two instead of calling emergency. They stood like male versions of Evelyn—hands over their mouths, a look of disbelief glazing their ashen faces. Suddenly, they sprang into action, each reaching for one of Alicia's fluttering upper limbs.

Sidney moved behind the fallen star, hoping to use his strength to push while the others pulled. At the count of four (one of the performer's ideas, not Sidney's), the trio attempted to raise the diva from her position. The smallest progress was being made, when suddenly an extremely loud bleating sound filled the room.

"My ass! My fucking ass!" It was the diva, sounding very diva-like. "Let go—now!"

Sidney and the two cast members released her at once, and she slumped back into her previous position.

"We need to call 911 right away!" one of the two young men cried out. It wasn't that Sidney hadn't thought of this before; he had checked the hallway for help first, thinking that might be quicker. He didn't want to take the time to explain this to the men, so he scanned the room instead, searching for a phone. He found it, just to the side of what used to be a loveseat.

Sidney must have explained the situation three times to the dispatcher before she called for assistance. She couldn't understand how one person falling backwards could so severely be impacting the lives of two others. Sidney was not about to give the dispatcher his estimate of Alicia's weight, not with her lying in front of him and within earshot. After all, he felt she was suffering enough at the moment—why embarrass her like that? Plus, George would have words with him when this was over, as Sidney had pledged not to be offensive in any way.

While they were waiting for help to arrive, Sidney thought he would apologize for instigating this calamity, even though he really didn't believe he was at fault. After all, his only mistake was offering to shake Alicia's hand. She should not have put herself in the position she had, if she did not possess a proper sense of balance. Regardless, it was the gentlemanly thing to do, and so Sidney looked into the eyes of the fallen beast and pleaded forgiveness.

Alicia did not respond to Sidney's petition, as she was obviously smarting from the fall. Her face was even more bloated than it had appeared moments earlier. She did not seem to care, or appreciate, Sidney's attempted apology.

Sidney turned his attention toward the two young men who had come to the rescue. They had not yet left, but were lingering like two helpless flowers in a field of dust. They were probably waiting around just to see how the emergency team planned to fix the situation, or at least to see the expressions on the crew's faces when they entered the scene.

Sidney, mindful of his manners, offered the two helpers a bite to eat from the spread that somehow remained intact through the experience. The two men looked at each other briefly before turning to Sidney and saying: "sure, we'll have a little something."

As Sidney redirected his interest back toward the problem, the emergency crew arrived. There were two men, both of whom appeared to be exceptionally fit, wearing navy blue polos and slacks. One of them was carrying a case like a traditional doctor's satchel, but much larger.

Somehow they remained poised; they gave no indication this wasn't something they encountered on a regular basis.

Evelyn, who had remained speechless throughout the ordeal, was finally able to speak, praising the medics for their speedy arrival and asking if there was anything she could do. Before she received a response, she rushed to the medic closest to her and whispered to him: "There are two people beneath her. I wasn't sure if you were aware." She briefly removed her hand from around his ear, and then put it back as she thought of more to say. "They may very well be injured. We haven't heard a peep from them."

The emergency team didn't appear disturbed after receiving this information, but neither did they seem to be displaying much sense of urgency. They stood relaxed, perhaps analyzing the chaos, perhaps trying to formulate a strategy.

Sidney, not hearing his wife's comments, assumed she had apprised the medics of particulars she considered significant enough to share, but too rude to verbalize in front of their hostess, Alicia. He thought it best to give the gentlemen important information as well.

"She hurt her ass," Sidney screeched in the direction of the medics. "You'll want to be careful about that." Sidney felt he wasn't being impertinent, and in fact thought his comments would be welcomed by the fallen colossus. Based upon the look Evelyn shot him however, he might have been wrong.

Just then, four more rescuers marched through the doorway, two of them wheeling a stretcher. Apparently, this is what the first two men were waiting for—help to arrive. Immediately, the six heroes set about to remove Alicia from her situation so they could tend to the Hanovers.

Alicia shrieked in an octave that must have been in the soprano range, though sounding nothing like an aria, as the six rescuers rolled her to her feet and on to the stretcher. Two of the men started to wheel her from the room as the other four set about on their search and rescue for George and Iris.

When the medics who were rolling Alicia reached the door, they realized she would not fit through the opening—at least while she was lying on her back. They summoned the others, who were preparing to unearth the Hanovers, for assistance. It was necessary, they discovered, to position Alicia on her side in order to facilitate the move. The opera star had never belted out a sound as piercingly forceful as she did while she was being manipulated into this position.

By now, a small crowd had gathered in the hallway outside the diva's dressing room. The group was comprised, in great part, of chorus members and stagehands. The featured players had long ago left the theater. The director of the opera was in the hallway witnessing the debacle, and seemed to be in tears. As the two medics made their way out of the room with Alicia in tow, one of them closed the door behind him to isolate the gawkers.

The four that were left immediately started prying pieces of broken furniture away from Iris and George. Evelyn hugged her husband tight while the rescuers set about their task. As the couple watched the liberators at work, Sidney started to become aroused. He couldn't explain it, as his friends were certainly in some degree of peril—but with Evelyn's heaving breasts pressed against his chest, and her warm breath punching at his neck, his seldom-serviced genitals spontaneously reacted.

Evelyn sensed her husband's cane nudging her thigh and responded by smacking him across the cheek with the back of her hand. It wasn't a particularly rough slap, but the message was clear. Evelyn recalled her mother once alerting her to the fact that men were the strangest creatures; they served their purpose she supposed, and for that reason they must be tolerated—to an extent. Evelyn knew all too well what her mother meant.

By now, the rescuers had Iris and George spread out cleanly on the floor. The couple was obviously unconscious. Sidney assumed this was why they had not responded to him earlier.

The emergency crew remained quite active, murmuring

strange commands to each other, and frantically passing exotic equipment back and forth; they used some of it directly on Iris and George. Everything was happening so fast, and it was all very scary to Evelyn and Sidney. Sidney recognized what the men were doing to his friends; they were performing cardio-pulmonary resuscitation. About two years ago, his office manager organized a CPR class, which Sidney mandated all employees attend. Of course, Sidney couldn't be seen fumbling around a pliant and possibly alluring mannequin's open mouth, and so he failed to obtain the knowledge these rescuers apparently possessed.

Evelyn could not watch anymore, electing to relocate to the now vacant hallway outside the dressing room door. Since Sidney was fused to his wife and her unyielding, vice-like grip, he went too.

"Dear lord," Evelyn exclaimed to her husband as she closed the door behind them, "what on earth do you think is the matter with Iris and George?"

"I'm sure whatever it is my dear, they'll be fine. Those men assisting them are professionals."

"It looks bad—it looks very bad, Sidney."

"Now now, don't you worry at all my darling. It looks to me as if they've passed out, and the nice gentlemen are stimulating them back to consciousness. I'm afraid they will probably need to spend a few hours in emergency. We will do the right thing, as they would for us, and accompany them to the hospital." Sidney's comforting words seemed to relax Evelyn somewhat, and she released him from her clinging embrace.

The couple had slowly paced the hallway for what seemed an eternity, but in reality amounted to ten minute's time, when they saw four men approaching. They were dressed the same as the men helping the Hanovers, and had brought two gurneys with them. The Banks signaled to the men, swinging their arms high above their heads in an exaggerated fashion, then toward the door as if they were directing a large jet to its parking space. A more modest gesture would have sufficed in the otherwise empty hallway.

The men entered the room and Evelyn turned away, not

wanting to glimpse the work that was being performed on her friends. Sidney was very curious, but also looked away. The last thing he wanted was a permanent visual fixed in his head of either George or Iris sans clothing—especially in their condition.

A minute later, two men wearing suits and ties approached from the far end of the hallway. Neither Evelyn nor Sidney immediately understood who these men were or what their purpose was, and so they did not motion to them as they had the previous group. The men seemed to know just where they were going however, drifting past the Banks and into the room, volunteering only a cursory tip of their narrow-brimmed fedoras.

Evelyn and Sidney slumped awkwardly against the unadorned, ecru-colored wall by the door, wondering what was happening inside the room. Sidney was now certain that dinner would be out of the question. His head was starting to pound slightly from his earlier abuse of alcohol and his failure to follow up with more. He hoped that some angel at the hospital they'd no doubt be visiting would compassionately supply him with at least some quality aspirin.

While Evelyn scanned the hallway for any sort of chair to rest on, the door to the dressing room groaned open, drawing her and Sidney's attention. The two suited men caught the Banks' eyes, and shuffled toward them with a ponderous gait.

"May we have a word please?" the shorter of the two asked.

"Of course you may," Sidney replied. "But may I first ask to whom I'm speaking?"

Both simultaneously reached inside their jackets, removed their wallets and flicked them open, revealing shiny badges.

"I'm Detective Jeff Dach, Phoenix police. This is my partner Larry Hollahan. We'd like to ask you some questions."

Sidney was confused as to why the police were involved, but assumed records needed to be made in the event of future legal action. He realized he needed to carefully craft his responses to any questions he might be asked. If he mitigated his involvement in this fiasco, he could avert being a defendant in a lawsuit.

"Ask away," Sidney responded.

"I'm assuming you were acquainted with the deceased?" Detective Hollahan asked.

With that question, any blood that was near Evelyn's head quickly migrated somewhere else, transforming her appearance to that of an anemic specter.

"What do you mean, deceased?" Sidney replied. "Are you telling me that Alicia Cavaloni has passed on?"

"No sir," Detective Dach chimed in, "we're referring to the deceased, as in plural. There are two of them—on the other side of this door."

"Excuse me, Jeff," Detective Hollahan interrupted, turning toward his partner, "I think what you meant to say is 'decedents', and not use deceased as a plural. You can't use the word deceased to refer to more than one deceased person."

"I beg to differ, Larry," Detective Dach countered, "why don't you look it up? The term is used to refer to one or hundreds of dead people, if need be."

Sidney was torn between throwing up and taking a swing at both Abbot *and* Costello. "My God—they're dead?" Sidney asked incredulously. "Iris and George are dead?"

"We found identification in the deceased's wallet," Detective Dach answered as he threw a sideways look toward his partner. "His name is George H. Hanover. There was no identification we could find for the female. Maybe you could help us."

Sidney heard a loud thud and turned to find Evelyn flat on her back, spread out on the floor.

After calling for assistance from the medical attendants who were busy wrapping up the Hanovers as if they were giant salamis at a deli, and receiving assurance from one of them that his wife would be fine, Sidney proceeded to give the detectives all the information they wanted.

A half hour later everyone was gone, except for Evelyn and Sidney. Evelyn had responded well to the smelling salts and was now sitting on the floor in the hallway next to Sidney. Sidney knew she was feeling better when she asked if he had cancelled their reservations at Dominick's. The two of them looked like kids hours after their high school prom, pasted to the floor and loosely dressed. They weren't kids though; they were a couple of sixty somethings, dealing with the loss of contemporaries—and good friends.

Chapter Four

The Banks had never attended a double funeral before, and weren't sure if any special etiquette would be called for under the circumstances. As two of the Hanover's closest friends, they were not about to dishonor them by making any social faux pas. Certainly, they did not want to bring embarrassment upon themselves. Iris would have been able to answer any of the questions buzzing through Evelyn's head, but of course she wouldn't be able to help this time—or ever again.

Sidney received a call from the Hanover's good friend and attorney, Mark Dean, asking if he would serve as a pallbearer. Of course he agreed, accepting without question. Sidney and Mark were shy of being good friends, but were quite familiar with one another, having shared many occasions with their mutual friends. When he told Evelyn of the honor bestowed upon him, she immediately queried as to whom he would be bearing—Iris or George. Sidney didn't understand why this mattered at all, but Evelyn didn't want Sidney having to inquire at the last minute.

Then there was the matter of who was in which box, since the boxes themselves would be kept closed for maximum privacy. Iris had told Evelyn several years earlier that when it was her time, she did not want anyone glaring at her in that state, and so she had made explicit arrangements to keep the lid of her casket secured once the mortuary was finished tidying her up. She said that she just didn't trust anyone else to get her makeup right, and if she couldn't check it herself, she did not want anyone getting a glimpse. Evelyn couldn't have agreed more, but was concerned she would be directing her personal thoughts and prayers toward the wrong friend and wouldn't be able to discern who was who. She thought it appropriate to have tasteful portraits of her friends propped behind their respective caskets, and wondered if someone had thought of this. If Iris had known both her and George would be buried at the same time, Evelyn was sure she would have enlisted Allison, the party planner on whom she constantly relied, to make certain it all ran smoothly.

Aside from these significant details, which occupied Evelyn

and precluded her from a proper night's sleep, the last several days had been truly dreadful. Not only were Sidney and she mourning their dear friends, but they had the unfortunate experience of witnessing their demise at close range. If not for the grace of God, it would have been their funerals today. The impact of this incident was weighing heavy on their hearts and on their minds.

Sidney had not bothered to follow-up on the status of Alicia Cavaloni. Based on her condition the night she collapsed onto his friends, he assumed she would be laid-up for a while. He imagined her anguish, lying in the hospital, forced to ingest only modest portions of pedestrian quality food. This thought brought a slight smile to his face. Evelyn noticed his sly grin and dismissed it, assuming her husband had passed a little gas. With the grim reality of the past several days diminishing Sidney's spirits, she couldn't deny him this pleasure.

Sidney could still picture Alicia's moon sized—no, Jupiter sized face as it lay atop the pile that sealed his friends' fate. He felt some sort of legal action should be taken against the monster, but understood that this would not bring back to life the people he respected most in the world. He also knew Alicia was sharp enough to hire a quality attorney who would cleverly spin the blame, pinning it on the man who pushed the otherwise graceful singer off her feet. Sidney was surprised he hadn't yet received any correspondence from Alicia's legal representative. He briefly considered that she may have eaten him.

•••

The funeral was both lovely and terribly sad at the same time. The crowd of mourners had arrived with befitting punctuality, and, using polite form, had wedged themselves into the limited rows of pews at the large North Scottsdale chapel. To the last one they were neatly manicured, as if Iris had groomed and clothed them all. Everyone seemed to have a tear drifting somewhere between eye and cheek. Of course, any life that was touched by Iris came away a little more polished, and this crowd exhibited that fact well.

Iris and George had only associated with like minds over the years. They were never snooty in the sense that their friends needed to have, or display, a certain amount of wealth. But those who did not project a genteel air were never part of their circle. Iris and George were very consistent in the way they conducted their lives, and the way they collected their friends.

After the graveside service, all who remained were invited to Mark Dean's home. Evelyn estimated forty or so mourners would be gathering at the attorney's house to commiserate and pay their respects.

When the Banks left the cemetery, just a handful of people were still milling about. Evelyn had not wanted to appear anxious to leave, although the cemetery was her absolute least favorite place to be; she would have preferred spending an entire afternoon in a cigar bar. As uncomfortable as Evelyn was puttering about a field filled with hundreds of dead people she didn't even know, she certainly did not want to be the first to arrive at the Dean's home. When she determined it was the proper time, she looped an arm through one of Sidney's, and they walked at a proper, solemn pace to their car.

•••

Mark Dean and his wife Lindsay resided in a quite spectacular home. Located in an upscale, gated community, the structure seemed to sprout from the caramel-colored, boulder-laden mountain it was pressed against. It sprawled east and west along the jagged rock face to which it seemed married, oozing more than a subtle proclamation of exclusivity. Evelyn had always admired the Dean's home, despite its status as a sharp pin in her closet of envy-charged balloons.

The Banks parked on the massive tumbled-paver drive, which easily accommodated the arriving crowd. Evelyn and Sidney inched by the planked, South American Walnut double front doors, and looked about as couples stood in small groups speaking softly, drinks and plates in hand. At first glance, it appeared to be a lovely cocktail party just under way.

Although the Banks and the Hanovers had been close friends for many years, there were very few people that Evelyn and

Sidney recognized. They leisurely made their way through the gathering, hoping someone would invite them into their circle.

Negotiating their way through bands of heedless, chattering mourners, they came upon the buffet. Sidney gathered two small china plates, passing one to his wife. They each selected several interesting looking hors d'oeuvres before advancing to the end of the table to select a beverage. There was a young server with a pleasant smile positioned behind the makeshift bar taking drink orders. Evelyn requested an iced tea with one lemon wedge, and then turned her head toward Sidney, who was eyeing the expansive array of single malts. Sidney sensed his wife's cool glare, turned toward the server, and requested an iced tea as well.

Sidney wasn't sure if he would ever again hold a tumbler of his only vice, the magic elixir that Evelyn held at least partly responsible for her friend's deaths. If Sidney had been someone other than Evelyn's husband, she would have assigned full blame to the drunken fool that had toppled her new friend onto her old ones. Now Sidney's collection of fine scotch was nothing more than a crowded gun rack to his wife. He was certain that he would check on it one day, and it would all be gone—replaced by small objects d'art that Evelyn had tired of displaying in more prominent locations.

As the Banks searched for a suitable place to stand and pick at the food on their plates, they were approached by their host, Mark Dean. After handshakes and hugs, there was an awkward silence, everyone struggling for the right words. Mark broke the stillness by speculating on his wife's whereabouts, visually scanning the room. Evelyn countered by sincerely lamenting the reason for the gathering. Sidney's eyes were wandering, as he still had nothing of value to contribute to the conversation. Taking in the clustered assemblage, he noticed a stunning young lady of about thirty standing alone in the middle of the room, sipping some tea. Although she wasn't conversing with anyone, she appeared to be enjoying herself. Between sips, she'd smile broadly while looking over the crowd. Sidney couldn't recall seeing this winsome treasure at the funeral, and thought she must be hired help placed to keep the gathered from falling into an even more depressed state. It was unquestionably working—at least for Sidney. Sidney had lost focus on the conversation that had continued without him. At the first lull, he decided it was time for him to chime in.

"Mark, I'm afraid I'm not familiar with many of the people in attendance. I would imagine most are relatives of the Hanover's who made the trip to pay their respects."

"I believe you're right, Sidney," Mark replied. "To be honest, I'm not sure who most of these people are either."

"Take that one for instance," Sidney remarked, nodding toward the lovely young thing he had his eyes on. "Must be a cousin's daughter."

"Actually, her I know," Mark responded. "It's a very sad story."

"Do tell," Sidney countered, downing a gulp of his iced tea as if he were at a bar about to approach his prey, "who might she be?"

"Let me introduce you."

Mark walked over to the young lady, and Sidney turned slowly toward his wife, who he was sure was some shade of red by now. As luck would have it, she had been shanghaied into a conversation by an old acquaintance who happened by. Sidney swirled his tea in his glass, again as if it were something more, and waited for Mark to return with the enchantress. When he did, Sidney considered darting away, or at least joining Evelyn's conversation. He briefly looked over his shoulder at his wife and her old acquaintance, a literally old friend who must have been ninety, and decided to stand pat.

"Sidney, this is Lily—Lily Hanover."

"I'm charmed," Sidney stated as he reached for her hand. "I'm so sorry for your loss." Sidney made the assumption that the common name made her some sort of relative to George.

"I appreciate that, Sidney was it?"

"Yes, absolutely—Sidney." Sidney felt he could now look directly at Lily; he was talking to her after all. She was something: her skin radiated warmth as if her occupation were lying on a beach all day, and from the quick glimpse Sidney allowed himself, her legs were perfectly shaped and perfectly long. What struck him immediately though was her nose—thin and sharp, but somehow very stunning. It reminded Sidney very much of Iris's.

Lily stood with her hands cupped in front of her, wearing an adorable smile and an innocent look that indicated she wasn't ready to walk away, but wasn't sure what to say next. Sidney helped her out.

"So, I suppose you are a relative of George's?"

Lily gave a half giggle as her eyes shot up and to the right. "I guess you could say that, Sidney. I'm his daughter."

Sidney's mouth suddenly became paralyzed, unable to form a response to Lily's statement. He was sure he hadn't heard her correctly.

"George Hanover…the man we put in the ground today. You're his daughter?" Sidney asked incredulously.

"He wasn't keen on letting people in on my existence," Lily replied.

"Oh my gosh," Sidney was searching for his next words, "I suppose Iris never knew?"

"Of course she did, silly. She was my mom."

Sidney looked over his shoulder once again, confirming that his wife was still heavily involved in her conversation with Methuselah. He was pretty sure Mark was playing some sort of practical joke on him, but the timing was very inappropriate and Sidney was not appreciative.

"Excuse me Mark, may I have a word please?" Sidney asked as he captured the host's eyes, motioning him aside. "What sort of hoax are you trying to pull here?"

"You didn't know about her, Sid—nobody knew about her. Iris and George had been hiding her in California since she was an infant. She was born out of wedlock and Iris and George—well, you know how they were. They did an excellent job of containing this huge secret all these years, huh?" As Mark finished, he tapped one hand on Sidney's shoulder hoping to convey a non-verbal message, as in: now now, you don't really think you know everything, do you?

"You knew though, Mark," Sidney stated.

"Well, of course. I've been George and Iris's attorney for a good number of years, Sidney."

"I guess that would make sense. What doesn't make sense is why they wouldn't have taken the child in after they were married. You could have at least offered to prepare illicit adoption papers."

"Somebody would have figured it out, Sidney. Believe me; I made a number of attempts at reuniting the Hanover's with their daughter. They wouldn't have it. They were two of the most upstanding, yet stubborn people I have ever known. And besides, take a look at her—is she not the happiest thing you've ever seen?"

"I suppose she is, Mark. I would also imagine she's about to come into quite a bit of wealth. That smile of hers looks like it has eight zeros after it. It's not proper at all for her to be so cheerful, just two hours after her parents were lowered six feet beneath the sod."

"Actually Sidney, George and Iris bequeathed a majority of their estate to various charities. The daughter gets almost nothing."

"My goodness," Sidney responded, "you think you know people... I suppose the only person you ever really know is yourself."

"The Hanover's weren't bad people Sidney—you know that. They just insisted on carrying out this questionable charade past their demise."

Sidney looked over at Lily, who was still standing where Mark had left her, smiling as if she were oblivious to the occasion.

Now that Sidney had been apprised of her heritage, he could see the resemblance more clearly. Not only did she possess Iris's elegant beak, but he could see a bit of George in her as well. In spite of this, she was spectacularly attractive to Sidney. He thought that if this were his daughter, his pride would have overridden any sense of moral obligation to keep her closeted.

Sidney was torn between approaching Lily once again, coming to her rescue somehow, and running to his wife, who could not possibly imagine the juice he had to share. Noting that Evelyn was still trapped in a conversation vortex, he thought it would only be proper to finish the dialogue he had started with Lily.

"I'm so sorry Lily, please forgive me. I had some loose ends to tie up with Mark, and I wanted to grab him for a minute before he slipped away—my apologies."

"You are so polite Sidney. You don't need to apologize to me; you are too cute!"

Sidney wasn't certain how to interpret Lily's comment. He was pretty sure she didn't really think of him as cute, but he wasn't about to abandon the young lady as he had moments earlier.

"Why, thank you Lily. You make an old man feel appreciated." Sidney was now figuratively scratching his head, hoping to come up with any meaningful thoughts he could share or questions he could ask. "You seem so happy, Lily. I can't help but wonder, and please don't take this the wrong way, but…" Sidney abruptly experienced the remorse he felt every time he opened his mouth when he shouldn't have. "Never mind—please forgive me."

"Sidney, come on. You can ask me anything you want! If you're questioning my happiness, it *is* sincere. Was that what you wanted to know?"

"Well, I'm afraid I was about to say something dreadfully rude and…why yes, that's what I wanted to know—if that smile on your face is real."

"Seriously now Sidney—please continue your question. I'm not going to leave this alone until you do!" With that, Lily reached for both of Sidney's hands, taking hold of them in what Sidney considered a "ring-around-the-rosie" stance. Sidney did not want to turn around to see if Evelyn was witnessing this spectacle, but he could feel his blood rising and the sixteen inch collar of his starched, white shirt seemingly shrinking to fifteen inches.

"Okay Lily, I shall complete my question for you," Sidney stated as he attempted to nonchalantly dismiss the enchantresses' hands from his own. "I suppose I was going to ask if you feel some sense of relief now that your parents are gone. It must have seemed as though they abandoned you, right?"

"Oh no, Sidney—I never really considered myself spurned by them. They provided a very nice life for me—they just weren't a part of it. It's the one piece of my existence I've been missing I guess—having parents. I suppose I'd be a whole different person if they had raised me."

"I'm most sure you would," Sidney replied, in a tone he hoped hadn't come across as too sarcastic. "So, I imagine you're in town only a short while?"

"Actually," Lily replied, "I haven't booked my return flight yet, but I thought I'd stay a week or so before heading home. There's some stuff Mark needs me to deal with. Plus, I'm staying at my parent's house—I never knew them very well, and I'm thinking I might learn a thing or two just by doing a little exploring."

"Well then, it would be an honor if you would accompany my wife Evelyn and me to dinner one evening—I insist!"

"That sounds wonderful, Sidney! So you're married?" Lily sighed, as she placed both hands flat against Sidney's chest. "That's one lucky lady you have, mister."

Sidney wished he could run away before his physical reaction to her proximity became obvious, or before he said something inappropriate. Unfortunately, running would draw too much attention. His only hope was to turn his thoughts toward the reason they were all gathered today, or some similar source of melancholy.

"Would you like to meet her, Lily? She's right over there." Sidney lifted his arm in the direction of his wife, who looked as if she'd reached her limit with the nonagenarian.

"Of course I would, Sidney!" Lily's upbeat demeanor seemed indefatigable.

Sidney guided the Hanover's grown daughter toward Evelyn, who seemed quite relieved and pleased to have her conversation interrupted.

"Evelyn, I beg your pardon for interrupting, but I have someone here you must meet!"

The old bag Evelyn had been conversing with took the brazen hint and slouched away.

"Thank you Sidney," Evelyn said under her breath. "Such a pillar, that lady, but enough is enough! Now, who have we here?" Evelyn asked, employing the slightest rise of one eyebrow.

"Evelyn, I would like to introduce you to Lily Hanover."

"What a beautiful and poised young lady you are. I must offer my most sincere condolences, Lily." This time, it was Evelyn who reached for both of Lily's hands.

"The pleasure's all mine, Evelyn. And thank you."

"Now, you must tell me how you are related to Iris and George."

"Evelyn my dear, we shall discuss that later," Sidney interrupted. "Lily is in town from California, and I've asked her to join us for dinner one evening this week."

"I'm sure you have, darling," Evelyn responded. Turning toward her new acquaintance she asked: "What evening would work best for you Lily?"

"Oh, I'm totally free all week. If you'd like, tomorrow would be great!"

"Of course, dear. Sidney, why don't you get Lily's hotel information so that we can pick her up tomorrow evening—say about seven?"

"She's already told me where she's lodging," Sidney replied. "We shall see you then at seven, Lily?"

Lily agreed, cordially embracing both Evelyn and Sidney before walking away, the ever-present smile secured to her face.

Chapter Five

Sidney and Evelyn did not live far from the Dean's, so it was a fairly brief drive home. It was also a very quiet drive. Sidney had thought Evelyn would be dying to learn of Lily's ties to George and Iris and would be prying for information as soon as the car doors had closed.

Apparently, Evelyn was not thinking along these lines. She wasn't quiet because she was exhausted, as was the case frequently; she remained in her muted state due to Sidney's disappointing behavior. Of all the mourners in attendance, Sidney had selected some smiling tart to mingle with. In Evelyn's mind, Sidney had invited her to dinner because of her beauty and availability, not because she was related to her dear, deceased friends.

Sidney maintained that he was only being social, and that he would have conversed with Lily regardless of her appearance. The fact that she was well put together and had spoken the words "cute" and "Sidney" in the same sentence had nothing to do with his interest.

Now Sidney was bursting and could not wait to tell Evelyn of his discovery. He didn't want to lose the little game Evelyn had started, but he couldn't hold out much longer before spilling the beans. He decided it was best that he not say anything till they arrived home, as he was certain Evelyn would need to lie down upon hearing the news.

After they entered the house, Evelyn quietly skulked away, acting as if despondency and disappointment were all she had anymore. Sidney called out to her saying he had something very important to discuss and to please come back.

Evelyn thought she had perhaps gone a little too far, and hoped that Sidney had not suddenly acquired some stones. She returned to her husband quickly, yet still holding firm to her taciturn posture.

Sidney proceeded to diagram Lily's startling genetic makeup, giving Evelyn all he had on the young woman. Evelyn asked her husband to repeat everything several times, looking for some flaw in the story—something that might refute Lily's claim.

Eventually Sidney tired of trying to convince his wife of the young lady's parentage, his rolling eyes conveying his frustration. It was about this time that Evelyn accepted her husband's unimaginable story as genuine, acknowledging that the girl must be the daughter of her deceased friends she thought she had known so well.

Evelyn was now anxious to see Lily again. She wanted to look into her eyes, gaze at her face and listen to her speak. If this were a child of Iris and George, then Evelyn supposed she must possess many of their qualities. She wanted to observe Lily and scrutinize firsthand the traits that she hoped were inherited, and which had endeared Evelyn to her good friends for so many years.

"We shall take her to Mastro's Ocean Club for dinner tomorrow," Evelyn exclaimed. "I'll make reservations right away."

Sidney was grateful that Evelyn was now embracing this meeting. With her by his side, he would be able to enjoy Lily's company for at least one full evening—without fear of saying or doing the wrong thing.

•••

Evelyn and Sidney barely spoke on their way to pick up Lily. The uncomfortable silence was not a holdover from their previous day's journey; it came from a different place and for a different reason. Less than three weeks earlier they had traveled this same path on their way to retrieve Iris and George for a lovely evening at the ballet. But the Banks were transporting different passengers on this drive. It was anguish and heartache that rode with them now, stabbing at their souls and prompting the swelling despondency that floated through the cabin like a noxious gas.

Halfway to the Hanover's house, Sidney broke the quiet by activating his car's stereo system. Normally, he kept the volume at a modest level—just loud enough to mask the noises of the road. But both he and Evelyn required a greater distraction than merely the scent of a sound. Sidney rotated the volume control on the Mercedes' Harmon/Kardon fourteen-speaker system until Rossini's *Thieving Magpie Overture* reached the intensity of a live performance. The familiar notes somehow calmed Sidney as well as Evelyn, who was desperately attempting to remain stoic.

Evelyn maintained an emotionless façade as Sidney rolled their car across the wide, circular drive that fronted the Hanover's house. The thought of entering her old friend's home was too much for her to handle. She turned in her seat to face Sidney and caught him staring with wooden, glazed eyes into the darkening sky.

"Aren't you going to retrieve the young lady?" Evelyn asked.

"Of course, dear; I wasn't planning on honking the horn to see if she'd respond. I'm just waiting for you to compose yourself. Let me know when you're ready."

"I may not be ready for a month," Evelyn replied. "Just go get her so we can get on to dinner."

Sidney didn't have a problem with his wife's request, but he was a bit uneasy approaching the house by himself. It didn't have anything to do with the surreal aspect of the situation. His friends who once resided at this address were gone; Sidney could deal with that fact. He was just a little concerned that Lily might greet him at the door with something more than a polite handshake. He knew that Evelyn would be watching, and he didn't want to hear about it later.

The couple had been sitting in front of the Hanover's house about four minutes when Lily opened the front door, wearing the same smile she had on the day before.

Without looking at his wife, Sidney could sense steam percolating from her nostrils. Before Lily had reached the bottom step of the entryway, he was out of the car and on his way to offer an arm. There was little he could do at this point to reduce the sentence Evelyn was calculating for him in her head, even though his intention all along was to be nothing less than a gentleman.

Sidney gently placed their guest in the back seat behind Evelyn, and they were on their way. The banter exchanged in the car amounted to nothing more than meaningless and fallacious assessments of California and Arizona weather patterns. Evelyn wanted to save all the spicy conversation for when they were face to face in the restaurant.

•••

Mastro's Ocean Club had a lovely table set aside for the Banks, as usual. Evelyn was never the sort to settle. If there had been a more appropriate establishment for the night's engagement, they would presently be walking toward that even more suitable table at that even more suitable restaurant.

Although a dark and contemporary vibe oozed through the sprawling place, Mastro's was never crowded with fussy and formal dressers. Still, diners were always expected to put at least one of their best feet forward. Only the naïve, or the unrefined stubborn, would risk subjecting themselves to an evening of derisive once-overs from the more polished regulars.

Evelyn had some concern that the Hanover's daughter might not possess her parent's unparalleled measure of class. She didn't think it likely that the girl would clothe herself in revealing shorts or a bawdy top, but the selection of a more rustic eatery would have possibly encouraged that sort of dress.

As it turned out, Lily looked stunning. Her trim, black, cocktail length dress was belted at the waist with a black, faux eel skin band accented by a chunky, brushed silver buckle. The low-cut garment was held in place by quarter-inch straps, which prevented the dress from yielding to both the laws of gravity and Lily's determined, robust assets.

If Evelyn didn't know better, she would have thought Lily had spent the afternoon at a quality salon. Her shoulder length dark brown tresses had highlights Evelyn was sure she had not seen the day before. Her hair was perfectly shiny, straight, and luxurious. Her makeup was flawless, indiscernible, and complemented her refreshingly smooth and tanned skin. Evelyn was not in the least embarrassed by her guest's appearance. Sidney was glowing, as if his connection to Lily was more than it really was.

Evelyn quickly and strategically arranged seating assignments at the square table. She positioned herself between Lily and Sidney so she could easily converse with the young Hanover while establishing a sensible and prudent distance between her husband and the beauty.

Michael, their waiter for the evening, approached the threesome almost immediately. Evelyn ordered a bottle of sparkling water to share with Sidney. Lily requested a glass of chardonnay. Sidney asked the waiter if he would bring for the table an iced seafood tower stacked with plenty of king crab legs, oysters, shrimp, and anything else in the kitchen that looked particularly succulent. Sidney had ordered this starter previously and remembered it being quite delicious and quite tall. When the dish arrived it would be centered on the table, interrupting Sidney's direct view of Lily's scantly sheltered breasts, which were fearlessly parading through his field of vision. Although he was hesitant about this move, it was a necessary tactic to keep his eyes from straying impolitely.

Michael finished reciting the daily specials, confirmed he would return quickly with the beverages and the appetizer, and then, as he bowed graciously to the table, grabbed an eyeful of Lily and some of her conspicuous qualities. His lascivious behavior did not go unnoticed by Evelyn, who could do nothing but roll her eyes. Sidney noticed as well, and immediately regretted ordering the towering hors d'oeuvre.

"Lily darling, you are such a striking young lady," Evelyn started. "It must be disconcerting to be visually mauled by vulgar men wherever you go."

Sidney moved the menu he was holding higher and closer to his face, hoping to disassociate himself from the conversation.

"Really Evelyn, I find it flattering," Lily replied. "Goodness knows—a girl in her thirties needs to savor those moments. This is such a beautiful restaurant, by the way. Thank you so much for inviting me to such a lovely dinner."

"It's our pleasure," Sidney interjected, briefly lowering his menu.

Based on Lily's response, Evelyn was relieved that some of Iris and George's genes had rubbed off on their displaced daughter. This was very comforting to Evelyn, for she was already dreadfully alone without her good friend. Perhaps, she thought, this girl was a gift sent from heaven, a sort of replacement.

"You are truly welcome," Evelyn added. "Tell me dear, is everything okay with you? I know it must be difficult staying in your parent's house."

"It has been a little awkward," Lily replied. "It's been interesting though—just walking through their house, seeing what type of art my parents collected for instance. I want so desperately to know them better, discover what they were like. I feel that just by being in their home, I'm getting a much clearer sense of them."

"That's wonderful Lily," Evelyn remarked. "Aren't you harboring ill feelings toward your parents though, darling? Keeping you at such a distance and all..."

"I tried to explain this to your husband yesterday," Lily said, nodding toward Sidney. "I feel like I've had a very fulfilling life to this point, and I wouldn't want to trade it for any other set of experiences. But I have an empty spot in my heart, a void that could only be filled by having had real parents—living with them, understanding them. This may be hard to comprehend, but I loved Iris and George. I just wish I knew them."

"That's so sweet dear and also so sad," Evelyn responded. "I'm sure if things had worked out differently and you had grown up in your parent's house, you would have found them to be very special people. Why, Sidney and I had nothing but the utmost respect for them. There have not been two people on this earth that have maintained as high a standard of behavior as they did. They set the bar, and then they lived above it...Lily, we would be delighted to tell you all we can about Iris and George. Their only daughter deserves that at the very least!"

"That's very kind of you Evelyn. You are something special as well—I can tell."

The dinner was moving along nicely, with Lily becoming more endearing to Evelyn with each of her spoken words. Sidney was behaving like a gentleman, keeping his eyes mostly on his food and any mischievous thoughts mostly out of his head.

As they were contemplating dessert, an older man who had been dining a couple tables away abruptly appeared by Lily's side. He wore finely tailored clothing and a lopsided grin. Lily seemed startled by his sudden emergence and let out a small gasp. The man evidently had no intention of frightening anybody, and quickly apologized for alarming the group.

"I'm sorry for the disturbance everyone." The man pivoted toward Lily before continuing, his bouncy and distinguished voice discomfiting, yet mesmerizing. "I just wanted to personally thank this beautiful young lady for many memorable evenings." At that he reached for Lily's hand, and she allowed him to hold it briefly.

"I beg your pardon sir," Sidney snapped brusquely as he stood. "I believe you have the wrong lady."

The man looked into Lily's eyes and replied, "I don't think so. It's Tulip, is it not?"

"I'm afraid you have the wrong flower sir," Lily responded. "My name is Lily."

"Please forgive me then," the man said, squinting at the Hanover's daughter. His gaze remained fixed for another few seconds before he repeated his apology and walked away.

"My goodness!" was Evelyn's reaction. "The man must be suffering from dementia! He thought *you* were an old flame of his? These are the people we must share the roads with too—hmmpf."

"It's okay," Lily said, maintaining her platinum smile. "These things happen to me from time to time."

With all the attention being directed her way, Sidney could no longer resist the urge to take one brief peak at Lily's obvious valuables. He grabbed a fleeting glance when he sensed it was safe, and then reached for his water glass as if that were his intention all along. Seconds later, his left foot received a nasty spanking from the pointy spear that otherwise served as the heel of Evelyn's shoe. His initial reaction was to scream from the unexpected stab, but knowing that it was his wife who had caused his distress, he decided to keep his emotions bottled. Besides, it would have been embarrassing to explain his outburst should Lily query him out of concern. As his foot begged for an anesthetic, Sidney contemplated slashing Evelyn's unlimited shoe allowance, or, better yet, no longer subsidizing her cache of weapons at all.

The dinner wrapped up without any further interruptions or complications. After a pleasant drive, the Banks dropped Lily at her parents' address, promising to be in touch before she returned to California.

Chapter Six

Lily pressed against the door to her parent's house until it clicked shut, then peered out the peephole as Sidney marched back to his car. It was courteous of him to escort her into the house she thought. He had patiently lingered in the entryway while she illuminated enough lights to feel safe.

Lily wondered if her father would have been as kind. She appreciated the gallant behavior Sidney consistently demonstrated. He was very caring and thoughtful it seemed. It was just a shame that this sort of behavior was so often accompanied by the self-righteousness she despised.

The men Lily had loved in her life were poles apart from Sidney. They were sweet, yes, but they thought chivalry was a joke. They would have dropped Lily off at the curb, not at the door or inside the house as Sidney had. It wasn't that they weren't considerate—they had been taught their whole lives that women were their equal. Would a woman walk their man to the front door? This is something Lily wanted to ponder.

Lily looked around at the large lonely space that was her parent's house. It was not a hollow shell, but still, she could sense the emptiness. She guessed it must have felt the same when Iris and George were alive, moving about the place. The furnishings were beautiful, the house decorated immaculately. She couldn't recall seeing any home more perfectly embellished. Yet it was cold and remote.

Lily had spent all morning and afternoon exploring the house. She searched every room like a detective working a case, but she wasn't looking for a smoking gun—just enlightenment. She ached to learn more about Iris and George and hoped the house, and its contents, could be her teacher. Their possessions would certainly reveal something about them.

As thoroughly as she scoured the place, and as hard as she tried to unearth a nugget that would further her quest, her search ended in futility. There was not even a periodical or a book to be found that could provide insight to her parent's passions or obsessions.

It made no sense, Lily thought, that her parents could have as many friends and loved ones as the significant gathering at their funeral implied, and still lead such a sterile existence. There was either more to Iris and George than met the eye, or less to them than met the eye, and Lily had no clue which.

The time she spent with Mark Dean, both on the phone and in person, was almost worthless. The man wasn't interested in talking about Lily's parents much. Although he was their close friend, he treated Lily as the Hanover's attorney always had: professionally and matter-of-factly. He informed her of his clients' passing, making a point during the same conversation to define her limited inheritance.

Lily hated when her mind was occupied by ignorance. The fact that she knew so little of the people that gave birth to her was starting to bring her down—and it took an awful lot to bring Lily down.

Understanding her options were limited, Lily decided to take the Banks up on their offer to help. Evelyn actually seemed giddy at dinner when talking about Iris and George, and Lily assumed the woman would go on forever if she let her. She also thought Sidney might have some good stories to share as well, and she was anxious to hear them.

The downside for Lily was that she would actually have to spend time with these people. They were nice enough, but they were so full of themselves that Lily wasn't certain how much more of them she could stomach. She was convinced that they would not have been able to tolerate her either, if it weren't for their fascination over her existence.

What if her parents were much like the Banks? Lily knew that they had a problem confronting their shortcomings. After all, she was perhaps their finest example of disassociating themselves from their mistakes. It was shamefully obvious that her parents desperately wished to be perceived as perfect people.

Maybe Iris and George were just like their friends Evelyn and Sidney after all. If that's the sort of people that might have raised Lily, then she knew she wasn't discarded—she was spared.

Lily was feeling the load of the day's endeavors, and decided it was time to turn in. She drifted through the sprawling home's labyrinth of hallways toward the guestroom she had chosen as hers for the week, stealing glances at all the exquisite furnishings she passed along the way.

While hanging the dress she wore that evening in the room's expansive closet, Lily noticed for the first time a box tucked to the end of the shelf above the clothes rack. She thought she had already discovered and scrutinized the few storage containers secreted in the house. Evidently, there was one more it would surrender. Lily determined based on its round shape, colorful striped cover and twisted rope handle, that it was a hatbox. Her interest piqued, she lifted her arms, stretched hard, and walked her fingers along the bottom of the box until it tumbled to the floor.

The box was much heavier than Lily had anticipated, and she quickly ruled out the possibility of it containing only a hat. Excited at the prospect of stumbling upon something irregular amidst her parent's faultless, hermetic environment, she coaxed the container to a wide space on the plush carpet and sat before it, legs splayed. Wearing nothing but her stubborn smile, she hunched over the curiosity and peeked inside.

At first the box appeared to contain some sort of green packing material stuffed into two large plastic bags, wedged fast against the wall of the container. It took some finger prying for Lily to remove them, but once they'd been freed, the riddle was quickly solved. Lily wrenched open one of the bags, and instantly the aroma from scores of luscious, dusty, cannabis buds jumped straight to her beautifully angular nose.

Lily pawed through the first bag, her unshakable grin broadening as she pictured her parents doing the same. She was assessing the quantity and quality of her find when she noticed at the bottom of the box a soft leather satchel. She pulled at the buttoned flap, exposing a small black pipe made from an exotic looking piece of stone. Along with the pipe were about a dozen tiny brass screens, engineered to fit perfectly into the bowl.

By Lily's estimation, her parent's stash of pot weighed somewhere around two pounds. It was the most premium looking marijuana she had ever seen: rich, green, heavy buds powdered with gold from the sun—no stems, sticks, or other useless greenery at all. Thousands of dollars' worth of pot buds huddled in the two bags before her. Lily had smoked her share back in the day—which as she defined the term covered her formative years and ran up until two days ago—but it never looked like this.

If Lily didn't know better, she would have thought she had stumbled across a dealer's inventory. Her parents had no reason to be peddling illegal drugs. Their significant lives could have been permanently diminished with one badly managed transaction. No, this was the way wealthy people handled underworld materials. They bought only the best—paid a pretty penny for it—and purchased in quantity so they wouldn't have to run back for more after a few evenings of amusement.

Lifting the second bag from the box, Lily noticed another satchel. Inside this one was a heavy, gold, butane lighter. Iris and George had everything they needed for a good time right here—right inside one of Iris's old hatboxes.

Lily realized that her parents weren't in fact at all like the Banks. They may have shared the same zip code and the same gardener, but they had another side—a more human side.

Snatching one of the large buds from its bag, Lily brought it close to her nose and drew in a deep breath. The richly layered spicy essence of the plant smelled so good to her, she was tempted to toss it in her mouth and chew it up. But instead, she used the tools her parents had unintentionally left her, breaking off a small piece from the bud and sparking the delicate flower till it glowed like heaven.

Lily was still sprawled on the floor when the impact of her first toke hit. She became heavy and weak and giggly and happy—all at once. She lay immobile, enjoying one of the most intense and euphoric highs she had ever experienced. Her call to the Banks would have to wait until morning. She blessed her parents' souls for the first time and fell fast asleep.

Chapter Seven

Evelyn positioned herself outside the kitchen door, peering stealthily at Louisa as she washed the breakfast dishes. The plates and silverware always seemed clean enough, but Evelyn wanted to make sure that no shortcuts were being taken. If it were feasible, she would relieve herself of this stressful endeavor and engage a county restaurant inspector to make a surprise visit every week or so. She'd thought of this before, but considered the potential for disaster. Employing an off-duty government worker would probably cost her a maid. Evelyn wasn't one hundred percent sure Louisa was a legal citizen, and she wasn't about to let anyone deport the best housekeeper she'd had in years.

As Evelyn leaned in for a better view, the phone rang. She regarded unexpected interruptions as unforgivably disturbing, but thought it best to answer promptly in the event it was someone important. Even if it was an unwelcome solicitor, it was only proper to answer prior to the fourth ring. She quickly straightened her Ralph Lauren blouse as if the caller would be able to perceive this detail, and picked up the phone.

"Evelyn, it's Lily. I hope I'm not disturbing you."

"Lily! Of course not, dear. I hope you had a peaceful night's sleep."

"I can't recall ever sleeping as well, Evelyn. Listen, I don't want to intrude on your busy life, but I was hoping to take you up on your offer—of telling me more about my parents?"

"Oh Lily, I could go on and on about Iris and George all day; and I'd love every minute of it! I would be delighted to get together. What works best for you, darling?"

"I'm available anytime you are Evelyn. You're the one with the busy schedule. Please don't change any of your plans, but I am in town for a limited time."

Evelyn didn't want to sound as if she had nothing on her calendar, so she asked Lily to hold just a second while she feigned thumbing through some papers. "Would this afternoon be okay with you, Lily?"

"That would be absolutely wonderful, Evelyn. I really do

appreciate this. I'm just so curious—I hope you understand."

"Of course, dear," Evelyn replied. "I will pick you up about two o'clock if that's okay. Plan on dining with us this evening—we'll stay in." Evelyn thought this a brilliant strategy: to see if Lily would dress and behave for this casual get-together with the same refinement she displayed in public, at the restaurant.

Seconds after she was off the phone with Lily, Evelyn speed dialed Lena's Catering, ordering duck for three with all the trimmings, to be delivered at six.

Seconds after she was off the phone with Evelyn, Lily hit her parents' beautiful stone pipe hard, cluttering her lungs with sinful amounts of the spicy-sweet clouds they had dispatched from heaven. She was determined to make the most of her day.

•••

Evelyn collected Lily promptly at two, as promised. The brief ride to the Banks' home was filled with provocative conversation—as far as Lily was concerned. Evelyn spoke endlessly about the crisped duck she had ordered, breaking only to detail the unblemished credentials of the caterer who would be accountable for the feast.

As they approached the Banks' home, Lily attempted an awkward swipe across the edges of her mouth with the back of a stiff hand, certain some amount of drool had made its way there. Her tongue darted skittishly around numb lips as she examined her hand for residue, like an old woman scrutinizing age spots.

Evelyn navigated into the garage and noticed Sidney's car parked slightly askew, a clear deviation from his typically deft driving skills. He had been at work when she left to retrieve Lily, and now here he was, home early and parked higgledy-piggledy, as if he'd been in a tight race to the toilet. It then came to her what was going on, and she quickly regretted informing him of her schedule for the day; she should have just surprised him with their guest instead.

This reminded Evelyn that although she had taken a cursory survey of Lily's attire when they had greeted each other at the Hanover's, she'd be wise to give it a more thorough review. In case some body part—or pair of body parts—called for a little more cover, this would be the best time to delicately mention it. She had given some thought to this possibility earlier, gift-wrapping a conservative Calvin Klein outfit to present the young lady. She would insist it be tried on, and of course it would be so darling that Evelyn would be adamant about it being worn at dinner. Sometimes she was so proud of herself and her well-mannered little schemes.

As soon as they entered the house, Evelyn commenced a head-to-toe evaluation of her guest's appearance. Her eyes toured the landscape as she served up some ambiguous compliments, such as "my, my, let's take a look at you!" and "it's just wonderful what they're doing with fabrics these days." She wasn't sure she approved yet, but the ruse gave her an opportunity to stop and stare. As she gazed up and down at the young Hanover, she decided that she did approve. Lily's black pants were more or less a second skin, although Evelyn noted the Armani logo and so found them acceptable—at least for a member of the younger generation. The white gauze top she wore was very pretty, and Evelyn could sense a designer—she just wasn't able to identify which one. What relieved Evelyn more than anything, however, was that Lily was wearing a bra. She finished awarding the semi-faux praise, and released the young lady to the house.

Evelyn understood that Lily's motive for wanting to get together was to learn more about her parents. But this afternoon and evening was to be a learning experience for her as well. She wanted so desperately to replace her lost friend Iris, and who better to fill that void than the daughter she had spawned. Evelyn was far from certain whether the girl's credentials could stand up to such a comparison, but she hoped so. Lily's fine taste in clothing was already signaling her status as Iris's potential surrogate. Everything was going well so far.

•••

Lily was trying very hard to maintain a mature demeanor. She had established a wonderful relationship with her parents' stone pipe earlier in the day, handling it like a favored old boyfriend.

About sixty minutes before Evelyn was to pick her up, Lily's foggy mind stumbled upon a window of clarity, and she sensed trouble ahead. She wasn't sure what to do about it, but she was sure she would be spending the afternoon on Evelyn's hardwood floor, rolling about and laughing uncontrollably.

Lily wanted to keep her robust high right where it was rather than suffer soberly the torturous priggishness of Evelyn all evening. But she also wanted to be conversant and acceptable company, for she truly wished to learn as much as she could about Iris and George. This would have been panic time if she weren't feeling so mellow.

Lily's fear of snickering the day away at the Banks' house compelled her to ponder her options. She wished there were some magic elixir stashed in the guestroom closet that would allow her to maintain the buzz she had while keeping a lid on any potential childlike outbursts. She was so high that she actually spent five minutes searching the mostly empty closet shelf for such a potion.

Giving up, Lily retreated to the still well stocked walk-in pantry. Her serious appetite required something satisfying, like a sleeve of cookies. At the back of one of the shelves, she noticed a gift-wrapped box that showed some potential. She took the box from the shelf, and saw that it had a gift tag at the top reading: "To Iris and George—With Love, the Hendersons." Lily wasn't sure who these people were, but she was positive that neither Iris nor George would mind if she unwrapped it.

Under the fancy gold paper and inside a hinged wooden box, Lily found a bottle of Remy Martin Cognac—Louis XIII. She deliberated for about ten seconds before removing the cork and searching for a glass. What she tasted was better than any cookie she might have found. She allowed herself about two fingers of the stuff before stashing the gorgeous glass bottle next to the hatbox in the guestroom closet. Lily was now mellower than ever, prepared for whatever Evelyn wanted to say.

•••

Evelyn led Lily into the living room and excused herself almost immediately to gather some tidbits from the kitchen. She returned carrying a serving piece crafted in etched crystal and burdened with a broad selection of appealing crudités. She placed the assortment on a round table perfectly centered between a stoutly cushioned leather armchair and its sofa-sized sibling. Lily had been staring solidly at a Sandor Bernath desert landscape hanging by the fireplace when Evelyn had left the room. She was still fixed on the watercolor when Evelyn returned.

"I see you have an appreciation for American landscapes?" Evelyn asked hopefully.

"Sure," Lily replied, not really understanding the question but not wanting to sound wasted by asking Evelyn to repeat it.

"It's an original Bernath, dear," Evelyn stated.

"Of course it is!" Lily responded, thinking instead it was a mountain and a few cacti.

"I haven't even asked what you'd like as refreshment, Lily. I'm so sorry. What may I bring you?"

"Oh, a glass of water would be wonderful please." Lily was actually dying for something wet; her mouth was doing a spot-on impersonation of a cotton field at harvest time.

Evelyn was in the kitchen fixing a soothing pitcher of iced water with lemon wedges when Sidney found his way to Lily. She seemed lost in the Bernath watercolor Evelyn insisted they purchase two years ago.

"A big fan of American landscapes, I see," Sidney blurted out, taking Lily by surprise.

"Oh my goodness," Lily screeched seconds later. "Sidney, how nice to see you—I do appreciate your having me to your home."

"Well, any daughter of our dear friends Iris and George is welcome any time!" As Lily turned to greet Sidney, he noticed she was wearing slacks that appeared to have melted to her skin. His eyes surveyed downward and he couldn't help but spy the defining lines of her female structure. When he looked up, he was ensnared by Lily's bright, perpetual smile. Sidney's face flushed crimson as his blood was surging there, as well as somewhere else. Evelyn pranced into the room and Sidney's mind stumbled into disarray, trying desperately to grasp an image that could offset his physical state.

"I see you've greeted our guest, dear," Evelyn announced to Sidney, who was shuffling sideways toward the sofa. "Lily, please make yourself comfortable as well—and don't forget the crudités. My goodness, we have so much to talk about!"

Evelyn's encouragement did not fall on deaf ears. Lily edged the crystal plate of splendid raw vegetables closer to her, plucked a dewy carrot, and drowned it in the most fabulous chive dip.

Sidney was anxious to initiate the conversation, wanting to assure Evelyn that he was present purely for intellectual purposes. "So Lily, I don't believe we've asked what line of work you're in." Sidney knew this was a good question, as his stirring erection immediately began to subside. He also received an approving nod from his wife, which, to Sidney, was a bit unexpected and unsettling.

"I work in the film industry, Sidney. I'm a consultant of sorts," Lily replied while groping a broccoli floret covered in soft cheese.

"How interesting!" Evelyn chimed in. "What sort of consulting work do you do, dear?"

"I work on set—kind of a liaison between the actors and the behind the camera people. It's not as glamorous as it sounds, but it pays the bills."

"Fascinating!" Sidney kicked in. "Evelyn, I bet we've seen a number of films that Lily's been associated with."

"I'm certain you are right, Sidney," Evelyn said. "Lily, please give us a few titles; ooh, this is exciting!"

"Well," Lily responded as she dipped a glistening celery stalk in something that looked French to her, "I'm afraid I only work on industrial films. You know—safety in the workplace, corporate training, that sort of thing. Everything is released straight to DVD. Evelyn, do you mind if I have some more water?"

"My marketing department orders those sorts of films all the time!" Sidney interrupted. "What's the name of the studio you work with?"

"Actually, I work with several. Hey, I've never asked what

sort of business you're in, Sidney. I'd really love to know!"

Evelyn turned toward Sidney and shot him a stern look, indicating that this evening was not about him, and to keep his reply brief.

"Thank you for asking, Lily," Sidney replied in a humble murmur. "My company is involved in all types of financial matters—everything from general accounting to commercial investments—boring stuff really."

"It sounds interesting to me, Sidney," Lily said, chomping wolfishly on the best carrot stick she had ever eaten.

"You still didn't mention any of the studios you have affiliations with," Sidney queried with sincere curiosity.

"Actually, I really only work on films for the retail industry, so I guess you wouldn't be familiar."

"Try me."

"Sidney!" Evelyn about jumped out of her seat. "Please don't torture the poor girl. I'm sure your company's little film ventures have nothing to do with Lily's work."

"Um," Lily appeared to be thinking hard. "Have you heard of Quick Release Studios? That would be one of them."

"No, I'm afraid I have not," Sidney responded. "Sounds like they have a fast turnaround time though—I'll have to check into them."

"Sidney, the girl would love to learn more about Iris and George. Maybe we can move on?" Iris asked.

"Of course, dear. What marvelous people, your folks. Is there any special information you're after, Lily?"

"Whatever you can share with me Sidney—and Evelyn. I saw them rarely. I'm pretty sure they weren't anything like I pictured them to be. In fact, I'm certain of it. I don't mean to be rude, but did you mention what time dinner was going to be served?"

"Not for a few hours, darling," Evelyn replied. "Now, I for one could not have had more respect for anyone than your parents. They were the pinnacle of propriety, the essence of elegance."

"I could not agree more, my dear," Sidney added. "Just days ago I mentioned to your father that I wished I could be more like him—the man set a standard which we should all strive to reach."

"Their demise is not just our loss dear," Evelyn nodded toward Lily, "It's the world's loss." After she spoke these words, Evelyn's emotions got the best of her and she excused herself to wipe away tears in the next room.

"You'll have to pardon my wife," Sidney said to Lily, "She was always so passionate about your parents. Your mother was Evelyn's guiding source."

"The four of you must have been much alike then?" Lily asked.

"Well, I can't say we have lived up to the high standards of Iris and George Hanover; goodness knows we've tried. But we did get along quite well, Lily. I'd say if you were looking for a representation of your parents, it would be egotistical of me to put us in their league. But Evelyn and I have tried to model our lives after theirs. Yes, I would have to say we were much alike."

Lily appreciated this answer from Sidney, although she really didn't comprehend much of it. While Sidney was speaking, Lily's mind was floating about, contemplating loud music and tasty food. She was pretty sure the implication was that he and Evelyn were a lot like her parents. Lily wondered if that meant there was another side, a hidden side to the Banks that she had not seen.

Evelyn returned to the room, apologizing for her uncontrollable behavior. Lily sat fixated on the woman, trying to picture her with a joint between her lips. As hard as she tried, she could not conjure this image. She wondered if maybe her parents weren't aware of the stash secreted away in a closet of their house after all. Maybe it was left by a guest who forgot it, or wasn't comfortable taking it when they left. It was all a little much for Lily to digest currently, so she let the thought fall away.

"Sidney, did you share a good Iris and George story with Lily while I was out of the room?" Evelyn asked.

"I can't say that I did, dear. Why don't you go first?"

For the rest of the afternoon, Lily got earfuls of Hanover adventures along with tales of their virtuous deeds. Evelyn recalled two of the vacations they shared with Iris and George: one was to Mexico, the other to the Caribbean. On both trips the couples found time to shop in open-air markets for local trinkets. Evelyn never thought of spending money at such a place, as there was never any assurance of quality—and, as Sidney semi-joked, Evelyn has always had a phobia about touching anything that doesn't display a Saks Fifth Avenue label. Iris, however, always made some acquisition or other, and most astonishingly, never once haggled over the price. The item may have had an extra hundred dollars built into the markup, but Iris always took the vendors at their word that she was receiving an excellent value. Evelyn knew that Iris understood the game, but she could afford the generosity and was happy to help those less fortunate than her.

Sidney complemented Evelyn's narratives with several yarns in support of his friend George, and his honorable existence. One of his favorite anecdotes took place before he came to know the man, but Iris had told the story many times over the years, and Sidney was quite familiar with it. What it boiled down to was the fact that George did not even have one alcoholic drink at his own bachelor party!

Lily sat dazed, not sure what to think of all this. She wanted to enjoy the history ride and glean what she could from it. Her buzz was starting to wear down, and she was able to focus enough to understand what Evelyn and Sidney were saying to her; but they were such bizarre stories. As far as she could tell, her parents might have been the real Beverly Hillbillies—except they were more educated and lived in Arizona.

Something was wrong with the portrait Evelyn and Sidney were painting of her parents. It didn't jive with the snippets of their lives she had been privy to over the years, and their one-sided perspective did not allow for the great box of hooch her parents had tucked away.

Lily needed to know more. She was pretty sure that either the Banks were not acquainted with her parents at all, or they were covering for them, hiding Iris and George's abscessed morals from their ignorant little girl. She could see them doing this as one last benevolent gesture to their dear friends.

What Lily really wanted right now was to fire up some of Iris and George's pot. When Lily was stoned, she found Evelyn to be quite a trip. She seemed otherwise to be a strange, affectedly arrogant woman.

Lily had the forethought to drop a fat bud into her purse earlier in the day, along with the small stone pipe and gold lighter. As the Banks were blathering, Lily contrived a plan to steal a couple hits; unfortunately, the plan involved being left alone for a minute or two. Her hosts had no one else to focus on but her, and they barely blinked, so she was pretty much cornered. If only they had a dog that Lily could volunteer to walk, but no.

Lily was pretty certain she wouldn't be followed into the bathroom, so she waited for Evelyn to take a breath, then gathered her purse and excused herself.

Sidney escorted his guest to the closest toilet, which was just around the corner from the living room. After Lily closed the door behind her she realized that it wasn't actually a bathroom, but something more like you'd find on an airplane. She was quite startled by the diminutive size of the space, given the otherwise extraordinary dimensions of the house. She abandoned her plan to light up, as she was definitely within hearing and smelling range of the Banks. She briefly wondered if anyone ever had the moxie to relieve themselves in this room.

Lily wanted to ask for larger accommodations, but couldn't think of a proper way to do so. What made matters worse is that she did not have to pee. There was no fan to mask any sounds, and Evelyn and Sidney were only a few feet away on the other side of the wooden door, waiting silently. Lily could picture them pricking up their ears in some discreet, unassuming manner. They would be expecting to hear at least a small tinkle. Lily thought maybe she was still a little high, as this wasn't the sort of thing that normally concerned her. She flushed the toilet and hoped for quality insulation.

When she stepped out of the tiny washroom, Lily noticed that Evelyn had disappeared. Sidney informed her that dinner had arrived, offered an arm, and escorted her to the dining room.

Evelyn had already pre-set the table and somehow managed

to have the food laid out by the time Sidney and Lily entered the room. Lily's mouth pitched open when she spotted the dressed table, replete with a silk covering and matching folded napkins, two sleek silver candlesticks—each holding an impossibly tall pillar of intoxicating light—and what Lily assumed to be the good china and good silver. The ambiance Evelyn had created was more how Lily imagined the White House dining room would appear when heads of state were visiting. Somehow it didn't seem fitting for a casual meal with a former porn star.

Lily could smell the delicacies, which lay curtained within the covered silver serving dishes. The tiny columns of steam rising from the edges of the handled lids warmed her soul and revived her dissipating hunger. As the lids were removed, she noticed in one container crisp slices of breast of duck, and in the next, a very thick creamed spinach casserole. It was at this time that Lily conceived a new strategy for indulging her obsession.

When passed to her, Lily took a polite serving of the duck, and then a more generous helping of spinach. As the various platters made their way around the table, Lily reached down to her purse which she had parked on the floor by her side, and cupped the loose bud she had brought in her right hand. Using just her fingers, she managed to split the bud in two. She then very subtly brought one of the halves to her plate and quickly comingled the piece with her spinach. She gave the pot some time to soften somewhat in the velvety cream, and then popped a mouthful of the augmented vegetable.

While Sidney was explaining to Evelyn his difficult encounter with the landscaper earlier in the day, Lily chewed her spongy nugget diligently and thoroughly. It was a more difficult task than she had assumed it would be, but she managed to swallow the fat bite before Sidney finished his sidebar with Evelyn.

Lily had only occasionally masticated cannabis into her system, almost always in the form of some sort of baked good. She recalled the pleasant, creeping sensation she would experience as the hallucinogen navigated purposefully along her digestive tract. Tonight's morsel wasn't as scrumptious as some of the cookies and brownies she had previously frolicked with, but she was hopeful the consequences would be comparable.

Fifteen minutes later Lily was not yet feeling the impact of the drug, but she *was* suffering the dull smugness of Evelyn's banter. She wished that Evelyn would be more direct when sharing about Iris and George. Instead, she'd waltz out every adulatory adjective she could muster in praise of the pair. Although Lily was anxious to learn what she could, she was having a hard time sifting through Evelyn's drivel.

Sidney, who had been in the kitchen for the last ten minutes, returned to the dining room with a Lucite tray bearing three ceramic ramekins. He proudly announced that the dark chocolate "volcanoes" were ready to eat, placing the first of them before Lily.

After she and Evelyn had emoted their perfunctory "oohs and aahs", the light bulb in Lily's head, which was starting to grow dimmer, flicked on. She discreetly reached for the half bud she had not yet consumed and hid it in her hand. After allowing the erupting mound of chocolate, which sat on the table like a living lump of dirt, to cool slightly, she dug for the brown "lava" with a spoon and placed it in her mouth. Feigning an overabundance of heat on her tongue, she covered her still full mouth with her other hand, slugging back the rest of her treasured plant. Although the texture wasn't quite appealing, Lily was instantly gratified; the taste of the chocolate complemented the weed much better than the absurd spinach combination she had eaten earlier.

The three adjourned to the living room once everyone had put down their spoons and dabbed at the corners of their mouths with silk napkins. Sidney had offered Lily coffee when dessert was served, and now Evelyn repeated the offer. She smilingly declined both times, confessing her affinity for the aroma but dislike of the taste.

Scanning the room, Lily noticed a beautiful, serpentine shaped, wooden piece of furniture by the far wall, which, for all appearances, looked to be a bar. She was curious as to why she had never been offered anything stiffer than coffee to drink. She assumed it was due to Evelyn's self-righteous personality. The bar was probably nothing more than a conversation piece anyway, holding no liquor at all. If there was some booze cloaked behind its latched doors, where did it come from? Lily couldn't envision Evelyn parked in a checkout line at the liquor store, bottle of Smirnoff in hand.

While Lily was contemplating this image, Evelyn began telling a story about Iris. She started gesticulating wildly while attempting to illustrate yet another of Iris's virtues. Lily's focus gravitated toward Evelyn's exceptionally white teeth—shining, faultless Chiclets of porcelain veneer tucked behind unspoiled, painted red lips—that wouldn't stop chattering.

Out of the blue, Lily started laughing uncontrollably; her cackles pierced the otherwise subdued atmosphere. Sidney smiled at this, thinking there must have been something he missed that Evelyn had said. Evelyn stopped altogether and just stared at Lily, watching the girl lose her equanimity while slipping off the sofa, inch by inch. Sidney and Evelyn remained composed, but unsure of what to do.

In Lily's mind, she had not seen anything funnier in her life. The sight of Evelyn's arms flailing about—her expressive face reminding Lily of some cartoon character she couldn't place—was just too much. Lily was laughing so hard as she rolled on the floor, that she thought she may have peed her pants. She reached for her crotch with her right hand to check the status, feeling around for a moment. Sidney saw this and immediately excused himself from the room, silently damning Evelyn's presence. Evelyn was only steps behind her husband, thinking the girl was overwhelmed and needed some time to herself.

When they were safely out of earshot, Evelyn cornered Sidney, desperate to confer with him. She wore an expression reminiscent of the night Alicia tumbled backwards onto their friends.

"Sidney, what should we be doing for the poor thing?"

"Well dear, she's apparently really enjoying herself. I don't think we're supposed to do anything."

"I don't understand!" Evelyn continued. "I was telling the story of how her mother would donate her Coach bags after every season to the St. James Orphanage, and she just lost her mind!"

"I'm sorry Evelyn, but I can't go back in there," Sidney said.

"It looked like she needed to be alone."

"Maybe it's best she spend the night, Sidney. I wouldn't *want* her to be alone like this."

"That's an excellent idea dear. You go ask her if she wouldn't mind, and I'll make sure there are fresh towels in the guest bath."

When Evelyn returned to the living room, she found Lily still sitting on the floor, but propped up with her back against the sofa. Her arms were spread and resting on the seat cushions behind her. She wore an even wider grin than usual, but her guffaws had turned to whimpers.

"Are you okay?" Evelyn asked meekly.

"Oh, I'm wonderful," Lily replied. "I'm so sorry Evelyn. I didn't mean to lose control like I did. Please forgive me?"

"Of course, dear," Evelyn responded. "I have never in my life seen anyone act anything like that, that's all. Sidney and I are just very concerned for your welfare…speaking of our concern, we insist that you spend the night. We have a fully made up guest room, and we won't take no for an answer."

Lily was way too stoned and way too tired to argue, and so she agreed to Evelyn's offer.

Chapter Eight

Lily awoke the next morning feeling slightly confused, but otherwise great. As she relaxed in the Banks' king sized guest bed—a thick, white, down comforter tucked neatly under her chin—she reflected on how she had landed in this feathery nest of ostentation. It surely had something to do with the spectacular level of inebriation she had achieved after swallowing some of her parents' pot, along with her inability to preserve control as she became engulfed by its potency. Somehow though, she could recall most of what Evelyn and Sidney had shared about her parents.

Lily determined that the glorious ganja she'd been exploiting had indeed belonged to Iris and George. They were too meticulous to have an unaccounted-for, wayward box anywhere in their home, even in the far reaches of a remote closet. Plus, the stash itself was too organized; it fit right in with the ordered tidiness of the rest of their lives.

What confused Lily though was the peculiar way the Banks' had treated her when she was stoned. If they were in fact close friends of her pot-smoking parents, then they'd certainly had at least some exposure to the buzzed condition. But Lily was pretty sure Evelyn and Sidney had no idea she was wasted when they insisted she spend the night. She even recalled Evelyn saying something to Sidney about "all the stress she must be suffering, poor thing—it's really taking a toll."

Lily pondered the possibilities. According to the Banks, the Hanovers were a step from sainthood, incapable of deviant behavior; they must have been clueless to the fact that their close friends possessed a well-used frequent flier card. It was also possible that Iris and George had chosen to remain straight whenever they were scheduled to see the Banks. Their apparently well-honed organizational skills may have allowed for this. If true, then Lily believed Iris and George were much more hip than the Banks were giving them credit for. It made sense then that Evelyn and Sidney didn't really know their friends as well as they thought they did.

While pushing the fat, marshmallow-soft blanket from its tightly fixed position below her chin, something caught Lily's eye. She lifted her head to find a nicely wrapped gift box nudging her leg. The elaborately cloaked container begged attention, like a cat pleading for breakfast. Looking closer, she spotted a label at one of the corners, which read: "To Lily—From Evelyn". She tore the bright paper and fancy bow away from the package, her curiosity pinning any self-restraint she possessed to the mat. Under sheets of pink tissue paper, she found a light grey, long sleeve Calvin Klein knit top with coordinating casual slacks, store tags still attached, prices removed. Although not exactly Lily's taste, the pieces were her size.

Lily's gaze fell to a small, carriage-style clock that was perched like a sentry on the nightstand; it was barely after nine a.m. She wondered how Evelyn had found the time to purchase this somewhat timely, strangely relevant gift. She couldn't fathom why the woman would want to give her anything at all. Lily had a notion that Evelyn was trying to be motherly and was simply doing what her dear friend would have done if the situation had been reversed.

As she lifted the box to move it aside, her eyes caught a splash of something white trapped beneath the sheets of pink paper. It was a neatly folded pair of new Calvin Klein panties; they were unlike anything Lily would wear, if she were wearing any. They were a size larger than she needed, and they were a full brief style—more like Evelyn's size and Evelyn's taste, Lily thought. Evidently, Evelyn was making some sort of statement. Lily just wasn't sure what it was.

As Lily contemplated her peculiar situation, Evelyn tapped on the bedroom door and asked if she could come in. Lily gathered the comforter around her naked body and invited her to enter.

Evelyn took a seat on the boldly striped, thickly cushioned divan facing the large bed, delighted to see that Lily had opened her gift.

"I hope you like the clothing, dear." Evelyn announced. "It's just sheer coincidence that you're in need of it today!"

"Thank you so much, Evelyn. I don't understand why you would give me such a lovely gift, but you are absolutely right. I suppose I could really use a change of clothes. You are so thoughtful!"

"Nonsense dear, nonsense—now, how are we feeling today? You know, Sidney and I were a bit worried about you last night. In fact, Sidney thought maybe it was something you ate, but the two of us managed to survive the meal intact, and we did eat the same things. I think the past week is just catching up to you, dear. I'm sure you just need some rest."

"I think you're right, Evelyn. I just need some rest. I'm between shoots right now. I should take a month and get away from it all."

The conversation was going just the way Evelyn had hoped. Since the funeral, she had been searching her mind for the most appropriate way to honor her good friends. She knew these situations typically called for a donation to the research organization that battled whatever malady the deceased had suffered from. She had tried to think of what institute or league existed that supported those injured or killed by collapsing portly people, and even asked Sidney for his help with this. His only response was that if such an organization existed, any donation would certainly not be tax deductible. Then, after last night, Evelyn realized the greatest tribute she could pay her dear friends would be to keep an eye on their daughter for them, at least until she was stable. Iris and George would have certainly appreciated this—despite having kept the girl's existence private.

"Lily…I wanted to ask you something, dear. I was hoping to get to know you better, and would truly love to spend some more time with you. You don't have to answer right away, but…what would you say to spending the next month here as our guest? This would be your room, and you'd have free reign over the whole house! It could be very relaxing for you, Lily. Have you seen our pool?"

The offer caught Lily off guard, but her initial reaction wasn't at all negative. As much as she loathed Evelyn's behavior, she appeared to be a very sincere and good person. Sidney just seemed lost, as any man would after years spent with the likes of his wife. Maybe this would be an opportunity, Lily thought—an opportunity and a challenge. If she spent a month with this woman, maybe she could fashion her into a more real person—someone who would tolerate her friends as they were instead of who she wanted them to be.

"Evelyn, you are too sweet," Lily replied. "I would enjoy being away from the grind for a while, and your home is so lovely…but I couldn't possibly impose."

Evelyn's face brightened quickly with Lily's response. She would have a month with the cheerful young lady to get to know her better and determine once and for all if she could ever serve as a replacement for her cherished lost friend, Iris.

"Believe me darling, it would not be an imposition whatsoever! You have such an aura of joy around you—that smile never seems to leave your beautiful face. You would be doing *us* a favor if you were to accept my invitation."

"Well then, Evelyn—if you're certain I wouldn't be a bother, I graciously accept."

"Wonderful, dear—wonderful!" Evelyn exclaimed, her eyes lighting up like holiday sparklers. "If you have no other plans, perhaps we could go shopping this afternoon and buy you a small wardrobe for your stay!"

"Oh Evelyn, that does sound like fun; but why don't I finish my business with Mark Dean tomorrow, and then I can fly home and put some things together. I'll return on Saturday. Does that sound okay?"

Evelyn of course thought it sounded lovely and insisted on giving her new friend a lift to the airport. Lily booked a flight for the next evening, and Evelyn dropped her at the curbside valet with plenty of time to spare. Evelyn explained to Lily that one could never get to the airport in Phoenix too early, as there was no telling what delays would occur in that dreadful security line. Lily envisioned Evelyn being pulled aside for a thorough frisking, daring the security agent to even think about fingering through her precious Judith Leiber jeweled handbag.

When they arrived at the airport, Lily asked Evelyn if she wouldn't mind keeping one thing at the house for her until she returned. Of course, Evelyn was more than happy to perform this small favor. Lily walked to the back of the SUV, opened the hatch, and removed her suitcase along with one other item. She returned to the passenger door and positioned a round box with a colorful striped cover and twisted rope handle on the empty seat. Then, carefully avoiding the darting and scuttling traffic, she trotted back to the driver's side window, leaned in to give Evelyn a hug and proclaimed she couldn't wait till Saturday.

Chapter Nine

Saturday afternoon, Sidney and Evelyn collected the young Hanover and her baggage from the airport and drove straight to the house. Sidney had volunteered that morning to make the pick-up, and Evelyn was happy to let him—just not alone.

Lily smiled appreciatively toward Sidney while he toted her assorted, mismatched bags to the guest room. As he was showing her about the space, she spotted the colorful, striped hatbox she had left with Evelyn. It had been placed squarely in the center of the precisely made-up bed, as if it were a welcome back gift. Lily was absolutely certain that Evelyn had not peeked inside the box; the transgression would not only have been an act of impudence, but a major breach of the etiquette bible that guided the woman's daily life. Besides, Lily had placed an innocuous piece of tape on the edge of the lid that would have tipped her off to any shenanigans. She wouldn't have minded so much if Evelyn had taken a look. She just wanted a little notice before the inevitable flood of circuitous, uncomfortable questioning commenced.

Evelyn entered Lily's room moments later, wanting to make sure that the young lady had everything she needed. She made several remarks regarding the wonderful, unique fragrance that emanated from the box on the bed. She couldn't wait for Lily to divulge the secrets of this exotic potpourri. Lily couldn't wait either.

The two women smiled and embraced each other, their excitement swelling to a rush of giggles as they anticipated the fun weeks ahead.

Evelyn promised Lily a simple dinner at home as she was sure that they would all be exhausted after such a hectic day. She asked Lily to settle in, relax, and then join them in the dining room about seven o'clock.

As soon as the guestroom door had snapped shut behind her hostess with a crisp click, Lily began to empty her suitcases, placing her belongings in the generously dimensioned walk-in closet. At the center of the closet was a waist high, square shaped wooden counter that doubled as a chest of drawers. Lily thought the closet was a bit too spacious for one guest, or four guests for that matter, but then considered it might serve her well as a personal fort should things get exceedingly weird during her stay.

At seven o'clock, Lily made her way to the dining room. Evelyn had just finished situating the Italian food, which moments earlier had been delivered by Lena's catering, on the table. Evelyn had created a decidedly more casual feel for this meal, replacing the fine table linens with wicker placemats and red and white checked cloth napkins. The silver serving pieces had been exchanged for pale blue, unassuming china. Lily figured there probably wasn't a dramatic difference in the cost of the set-up, but it did convey a more unbuttoned feel.

On each of the placemats two plates nested hand in glove, a firm reminder to eat first things first, and not first things with second things. The top plate supported a classic Caesar salad that had been embellished with fat, salty anchovies, and glistened from a glaze of creamy dressing. Lily quickly surveyed the rest of the setup, taking note of the place settings and glassware. She could all but confirm that no alcohol of any sort was on the menu.

"I hope you had enough time to settle in a bit," Evelyn said to Lily. "And I hope you enjoy veal cannelloni!"

"It smells great, Evelyn. I can't wait to dig in!" Lily hesitated before continuing, "I don't mean to be presumptuous, but doesn't this meal just scream for a glass of Chianti?"

Sidney, who had been behaving perfectly per Evelyn's firm instructions, shot a quick look at his wife to catch her reaction to the question. She returned a glancing glare, which was Sidney's cue to handle the situation. Of course it called for a glass of wine, he thought. Tonight he assumed would qualify as a social gathering, which was the only time Evelyn would condone, or at least suffer, the repulsive ritual. But Lily would be staying with them for weeks, and Sidney wasn't sure how this affected things. If he were allowed to open a bottle this evening, would prohibition then be lifted for an entire month? This was something he could not envision. There were few opportunities like this in Sidney's life however, and he would risk a night sleeping on the sofa for the chance to throw back a couple swallows of intoxicant.

"Of course it does, Lily. Where have my manners gone?" Sidney replied, sneaking a peek at his wife who maintained her steely grin. "Chianti might not be possible however. If you'll excuse me, I will see what I can come up with."

Sidney had not inventoried his bar in the living room since the night of the Alicia incident and doubted even a single bottle remained on the polished wood shelves. He did remember an unopened case of something red that had been given to him as a gift months earlier. He hoped Evelyn hadn't donated it to some orphanage.

Sidney narrowed his eyes to mitigate any horror he might encounter, then squatted behind the serpentine shaped bar. His face fell when he realized his prized collection of scotch was gone. Disheartened, he pictured Evelyn's smug visage as she ordered the maid to remove all liquor bottles from the bar and dispose of them. He could picture the housekeeper's family enjoying the thousand dollar bottles of quality juice he had slowly amassed, thinking it was the really good fifty-dollar stuff.

Apparently, neither his wife nor his maid had noticed the unopened white box sitting at one end of the bottom shelf. Either that or they had assumed it was filled with glassware or innocuous mixers. But this was the box Sidney had hoped to find.

Sidney slid the box from the shelf, cut through the sealing tape with a house key that had been poking at him all night through his trouser pocket and exposed the twelve bottles to the light of the room. Feeling optimistic, he plucked two of the bottles from the case, tracked down a corkscrew in one of the drawers, and returned to the dining room.

"I have good news, I believe," Sidney announced as he entered. "I found some bottles of red wine. However, Lily, my apologies, but we seem to be out of Chianti."

"My goodness Sidney," Lily responded, examining one of the bottles, "this is even better! Look Evelyn, it's a ten year old Barolo!"

Evelyn feigned interest, at which she was very proficient, and started picking at her Caesar. Sidney uncorked one of the bottles, and then pulled two Riedel crystal wine glasses from the hutch situated behind the dining room table.

"Only two glasses Sidney?" Lily asked.

"Yes Lily, it will be just you and me tasting what I hope is a satisfactory vintage."

"But, I thought I would offer a toast to my most gracious hosts," Lily pouted. "Evelyn, it won't be quite the same if you don't have at least a sip!" Lily conjured the perfect amalgam of dismay and pathos. The Banks were oblivious to the fact that Lily had honed this skill from the countless seduction scenes in which she had starred.

"Of course I'll join you in a toast," Evelyn declared. "You are such a charming young lady—how could I resist!"

Sidney looked over at Evelyn just to be sure she wasn't trying to send him some sort of secret signal, as in "grab the grape juice from the refrigerator for me," then drew one more glass from the hutch.

After the wine was poured, Lily delivered a quite eloquent and flattering toast, which, she supposed, may have crossed the threshold from sweet to exceedingly sticky. Evelyn had several tears mounting at the corners of her eyes.

The three clinked glasses and then drank the warming liquid. Lily swallowed about two-thirds of her wine, Sidney finished his, and Evelyn surprised them both by consuming about half of what Sidney had poured for her. Sidney did not want to waste the opportunity, and announced that he too would like to toast the occasion. After topping off the girls' glasses and refilling his, he countered Lily with a slightly less syrupy, but equally engaging toast of his own.

This time Lily kept pace with Sidney as he tossed back his Barolo, joining his surprising, inelegant race to the bottom of the tumbler. Evelyn astonishingly drank more than she had from her first glass, leaving only a modest amount remaining. Sidney was certain she would be vomiting soon.

Seconds after Sidney had completed his toast, Evelyn announced that she wanted to make a toast as well. She followed by declaring, “I insisted that I am making this.” Sidney couldn’t ever recall seeing his wife drunk and became fascinated at the prospect. He immediately refilled the glasses and uncorked the second bottle.

Evelyn talked on and on, depleting her pocketbook of inflated adulations and charging Lily’s and Sidney’s faces with crescent smiles. When she had run out of things to say, glasses knocked together once more and mouthfuls of wine were swallowed. Evelyn proclaimed her drink to be very delightful. As she was contemplating the remains in her glass, Sidney poured more wine all around. He then announced his hunger to the table and reached to unveil the cannelloni. When he removed the lids from the two sauces—one red, one white—a steamy breath of warm, garlicky sinfulness swelled from the small, matching crocks, while a glazed stupor quieted the room. Sidney passed the crusty, buttery Italian bread to Lily, excused himself, and then scurried furtively to the living room for another bottle of bliss.

Everyone was enjoying the food and the smooth, easy-to-drink wine, which had become even easier to drink as the tally of sips grew. Evelyn was beyond thinking about wine as a utensil of the depraved, and was now drinking it as her dinner beverage. Sidney cracked open the third bottle of the evening.

“This food is so delicious!” Lily announced. “Did you say this is veal cannelloni?”

“Yes dear, veal cannelloni.” Evelyn responded. “Just like the fat opera star we met, right Sidney? Wasn’t her name Veal Cannelloni?” Evelyn started laughing out loud at what she considered a very funny play on words, and what in reality may have been her first attempt at humor—ever.

Sidney wasn’t too drunk to notice that Evelyn may have committed her biggest faux pas of all time, but he was afraid to say anything. Evelyn’s buzz was coming along nicely, and with the evening still relatively young, why ruin it? He did, however, sneak a look at Lily to make sure she wasn’t devastated by the bold reference. Lily was well aware that Alicia Cavaloni, not veal cannelloni, had fallen on her parents and killed them. The black humor did not seem to faze her at all. In fact, she smiled and nodded somewhat vaguely, as if to say, "touché".

"Yes darling," Sidney replied. "I believe her name was Cannelloni. Now, who wants more wine!" Sidney was proud of his ability to create such a quality diversion, and promptly reached for the bottle. Lily made a point of pushing her glass toward Sidney, so he wouldn't feel compelled to walk around the table. As she leaned in and tilted her glass his way, he couldn't help but grab an eyeful of her ample breasts, which strained against her restrictive blouse like tethered dirigibles. He quickly shifted his attention to Evelyn's drained goblet, hoping Lily hadn't noticed his unseemly churlishness. He didn't peek at Lily again until after he had made several comments regarding the quality of the evening's feast. When he finally did make eye contact, she was looking straight at him, still smiling.

"Who wants to hear a story *I* can share about my parents?" Lily asked, as dinner wound down. "It's a good one!"

"By all means, dear!" Evelyn exclaimed. "Any story about Iris is a friend of mine!"

Sidney was pretty sure he'd be carrying his wife from the table if she so much as sniffed any more wine.

"Well," Lily started, "I found something quite interesting while exploring their house." Lily paused, evaluating the level of interest on the Banks' faces. Evelyn's eyes were canyon wide; with one hand propped under her chin, she braced her unstable head. Sidney was staring at his empty glass, contemplating another. "Maybe it's best that I don't say. I don't mean to be impolite. I must be a little tipsy."

"Come, come now dear," Evelyn reacted. "They were our best friends. I'm sure you wouldn't surprise them, I mean us, and it wouldn't be disrespectful whatever it is, I'm sure of it. Sidney maybe I'll have just a little more sip please in my glass."

Sidney smiled and poured a small amount for his wife, then filled his glass.

"Okay," Lily started. "Evelyn, you know that potpourri you were curious about? Well, I found it in a closet at my parent's house. And you know what? It's not potpourri! Do you know what it is?" Lily now had the Banks' undivided attention and was milking the moment.

"Tell us, tell us!" Evelyn begged.

Sidney swallowed a copious amount of wine with one gulp, hoping this was going to be good.

"Inside that box, which, I want to remind you, belonged to Iris and George, is a giant stash of weed!"

"Oh dear, oh dear," Evelyn muttered. "Iris and George saved weeds? That *is* absurd! Sidney, you don't collect such things, tell me you don't." With that, Evelyn started laughing, as she found the whole concept ridiculous.

"Sweetheart," Sidney interrupted, "I don't believe Lily's referring to the sort of weeds that you have in your mind—right, Lily?" Sidney was laughing too, because he did understand what Lily said, and he found this tidbit quite delicious.

"You're funny Evelyn!" Lily chirped. "You knew what I meant—you have quite the sense of humor!"

"Actually Lily, she has no idea what you meant," Sidney said, continuing to chortle. "I think you need to be a bit more specific!"

"Oh my goodness," Lily announced, "Evelyn, you know I'm talking about marijuana, right? You know—pot?"

"Of course I do dear," Evelyn replied, still laughing. "Everybody knows that!"

"She still has no idea what you're talking about, Lily," Sidney said, directing his comment to the young lady.

Lily thought this was damn funny and left the table to fetch the Hanover's hatbox. When she returned, she opened the box and set it in front of Evelyn. Sidney informed Lily that the display was irrelevant, as Evelyn had no idea what she was looking at. Sidney however asked if he could take a look, as he was finding this whole revelation about his friends to be quite entertaining.

"Pretty nice, huh?" Lily asked Sidney as he pawed through the greenery.

"Yes, of course!" Sidney answered, not really having any idea if he was touching high-end marijuana, or lawn clippings. He remembered from his college days something called Acapulco Gold. He had never smoked pot, but this was a term he frequently heard in reference to a quality buzz. The tight green buds he now examined shimmered with a dusting of gold, and he thought maybe this was the stuff deified by his university brethren so many years earlier.

"Evelyn dear, this is marijuana. It's a hallucinogen, and it belonged to Iris and George." Even though Sidney was pretty toasted himself, he felt like he was explaining a fork to a two year old. "Apparently, our good friends used to get high on occasion." Sidney looked over at Lily, in part to confirm that he was on the right track himself. She smiled back at him, and he assumed he had nailed it.

Evelyn's epiphany arrived about a minute later. She was as relaxed as she had ever been, and was still a little giggly.

"Well, I can completely understand why they'd need to do that marijuana," Evelyn slurred. "You know Sidney, this girl's okay. This girl's okay."

"Thanks Evelyn," Lily responded. "And you know, I understand it too. I don't think there's anything wrong with it at all. In fact, I'm glad my parents let go every now and then and had a little fun. I think everyone needs to do that on occasion."

"I couldn't agree more," Sidney said as he raised his glass. "Now, I think we should move this party into the living room!"

As Sidney was talking, Evelyn slumped over in her chair, the room filling with her abrupt, brash snores.

"On second thought Lily," Sidney added, "it looks like we have to call it a night. Do you mind?"

"Not at all Sidney; I could use some rest myself. Let me help you with Evelyn first though."

Sidney and Lily managed to haul the limp noodle to her bed, and then tucked her under the covers. Lily gave Sidney a big hug, and thanked him for a memorable evening. Sidney told Lily that he was the one to be doing the thanking, as it was one of the best nights of his life. Lily shot Sidney a wink and sauntered off to her room.

Chapter Ten

Lily slept very well. She also slept very late, at least per the Banks' routine. At about ten a.m., she navigated her way toward the kitchen. She passed by the dining room, which had been a semi-disaster of dirty plates and sticky glasses when she had left it the night before, but noticed it was now spotless and completely sanitized. There was, however, one object of note that had not been moved: the hatbox remained positioned just as it was. Lily turned into the room, picked up the box, and returned it to its proper hiding space.

Evelyn was perched at the kitchen table cuddling a mug of hot tea between folded hands when Lily entered. Lily expected her to look a wreck, but she appeared as coiffed and neatly arranged as always.

"Well, good morning sleepy head!" Evelyn chirped. "My goodness, is that what you slept in last night?"

Lily was still attired in her sleepwear, a slightly oversized pink t-shirt with the large letters MP screen-printed across the chest.

"Yep—it's very comfy," Lily replied. "I'm sorry I haven't dressed yet. I thought I'd grab a glass of juice if that's okay and then jump in the shower."

"Of course, dear—please make yourself at home. Are you wearing anything under that shirt by the way?"

Lily was hardly jolted by the question, having heard it many times. "It wouldn't be as comfy if I did, Evelyn! I usually sleep without anything on when I'm at home. But, I realize I'm not the only one in this house, and I thought I'd cover up a little."

"Thank you dear," Evelyn responded. "Say, what if you and I were to go on a little shopping expedition today? I could really use some new sportswear, and I would so appreciate a charming young girl's advice...and you know, they have some adorable sleepwear at Nordstrom. I think we should make a day of it!"

"Are you feeling okay Evelyn? I mean, we did have quite the night, didn't we? Maybe we should just take it a little easy today."

"Nonsense," Evelyn replied. "I did get a bit carried away I suppose. It was your 'welcome to our home' party, and it was cause for celebration. Now, aside from this bothersome headache that is dissipating by the minute, I am fine. And what could make a girl feel better than a day at the mall!"

"Alright Evelyn, a day at the mall it is. This should be fun!"

"So, are you going to tell me what MP stands for, dear?" Evelyn asked, nodding toward Lily's chest.

"Oh, it's from a studio I worked with once," Lily replied. "It stands for Mountin' Pictures."

"Mountain Pictures," Evelyn mused, "You have such an exciting life, Lily—you are just like your mother!"

•••

"Mr. Banks, I…I finished the research you asked for sir," Ruth Knapp announced, fidgeting with the papers in her hands. Ruth was Sidney Banks' elderly secretary, as he referred to her, or executive assistant, as she referred to herself.

"Thank you Ruth," Sidney replied. "Do they look like a solid company that we would want to do business with?"

"I sent you a link to their website, sir. You may want to take a look for yourself."

"I'm a very busy man as you know, Ruth. Do you think you could perhaps take one extra step for me today? Could you just give me an overview please?"

"Well sir. I don't believe they're really the studio we want producing the training video for our new tax services division." Ruth backed away from Sidney's desk as he tried to make sense of her simple statement.

"Please, Ruth. Can you help me out here?"

"Okay…you see sir, Quick Release Studios—well, they seem to produce only pornography."

"Are you sure, Ruth?" Sidney asked.

"Like I said sir, I sent you a link to their site. I'm not going back for another look, but you are certainly welcome to check it out."

Ruth left Sidney's office, closing the door till it latched

behind her. Her boss tended to keep the volume turned high on his computer, and there were clients in some of the adjacent offices.

Sidney clicked on the link Ruth had sent him. Within seconds, he was reaching for the piece of paper he had scribbled the name on: Quick Release Studios. He was sure when he wrote it down that this was the name Lily had given him, and although the name that currently flashed on his computer screen matched, he knew there had been a mistake. He immediately assumed it was his error; after all, it was hours after Lily had offered him the name before he remembered to write it down. He thought of trying alternate versions of the same name, like Fast Release Studios, or Quick Relief Studios, but feared the results could be worse. He imagined calling up one of these sites, only to have his company's computers infected by some ravenous worm. A soft smile crossed his face as he pictured the worm—comically long and thick, pounding away at his software.

He looked back to the shadowy stream of unclothed humans reaching for and touching each other's' silhouettes, the implication of sex just around the corner—or in this case, just after clicking the "enter site" button. Sidney stared at the images, contemplating his next move. He was already at the website's door so to speak. If a virus were to contaminate the office from his reckless inspection of this trashy, infectious site, it was too late—the home page had already been prancing about his screen, taunting him, calling to him. Besides, Ruth was the one that had sent him this link. There would be no inquest as to why he had jeopardized the company's mainframe security, or why he possessed such an exceedingly active libido.

After over-contemplating his options, Sidney decided he could peek just a little deeper. He punched the About Us button at the top of the screen and was instantly bombarded with a listing of the studio's curiously titled offerings, elucidated by crowning moment thumbnails. Crisp, lurid images of fornicating couples braided together, hand in glove, sailed through Sidney's field of vision. He wished to understand the mechanics of these twisted visuals, and he wanted desperately to retain them all. As his mind flittered off to some unrecognizable planet's surface, he became lost in a rush of sex and pleasure. A ringing phone smacked him back to consciousness, and he quickly closed the site.

•••

"Evelyn, you must try on this BCBG top. It would look so cute on you!" Lily had her arms filled with trendy separates that all the fashionable L.A. girls were wearing to the clubs.

"I don't think so dear," Evelyn responded. "But I have an adorable Lagerfeld jacket here that just screams your name!"

"It's gray Evelyn," Lily replied. "I'm not sure that it's screaming anything. Do you see what's happening here? We're shopping for ourselves and not each other."

"I suppose that's true, Lily. If you weren't charmed by the jacket, I was planning on taking it myself."

"Okay then, let's do this," Lily announced. "I will absolutely purchase at least one item you pick out for me, but you must buy something I select for you—deal?"

"I suppose. But nothing too newfangled for me dear; those clothes make me look imprudent."

"Don't worry Evelyn. I'll find you something just a little flirty, but not too seductive."

The girls wrapped up their four-hour visit to the mall after amassing an almost unmanageable quantity of shopping bags. They dragged their treasures into the house, promising each other a fashion show after brief naps. They separated for seemingly the first time all day, each off to their respective bedrooms, each toting their respective hauls.

After lying in her bed about fifteen minutes, Evelyn realized she wasn't going to fall asleep. She took naps quite often, usually once every afternoon. Typically, she was down for about an hour, or until she was refreshed and ready for the rest of her meaningful day. Today though, she was hyped-up over her new clothes and was having difficulty relaxing.

Evelyn had concealed from Lily that she had already been contemplating a small revamp of her wardrobe, perhaps adding a splash more color to her overcast, inoffensive closet. Although she had agreed to purchase just one piece on Lily's advice, the girl's constant nudging finally penetrated her resolute sense of conformity. Every outfit that Evelyn acquired on their excursion smacked of Lily's taste. She was excited to try on her new clothes once more, just to make sure she hadn't gone overboard with her acquisitions.

Evelyn popped out of bed like a bouncy teenage girl. She snatched a pair of Diesel jeans and a white frilly blouse from one of her shopping bags and stepped quickly into them, like a runway model between sets. Posing in front of a full-length mirror, which spanned half the interior of her den-sized, walk-in closet, she startled herself. She wasn't displeased—actually, quite the opposite. The jeans were far more figure hugging than any slacks she owned, and she took delight in how they added a measure of firmness to her legs and rear. The blouse exposed way more bosom than Evelyn ever shared—even more than any piece in her lingerie collection. Evelyn twirled to and fro, hands on hips and a smile across her face. She felt much younger than she had just a day earlier. In her mind, she looked darn good for a woman just a smidge over sixty.

Although Evelyn was anxious to pair the other outfits and give them a try, she was too excited to keep this one to herself; she just had to give Lily an early peek. Evelyn considered that the young lady was likely to be mid-nap about now, but as the architect of record, she'd certainly be anxious to see her work so exquisitely displayed. This would be a pleasant disturbance, if there were such a thing.

As she approached Lily's room, she thought she heard sounds coming from behind the closed door. She assumed that the young lady was either watching television or chatting with a friend on the phone. Either way, Evelyn was somewhat relieved that she would not be intruding on a sleeping guest. She knocked gently three times, and waited for a response. The muffled sounds were gaining in volume, but Evelyn was able to decipher Lily's plea to "come in."

Evelyn pushed open the door and proceeded to model strut her way toward Lily's bed. As she looked down to gather in the young Hanover's reaction to her new outfit, her eyes filled with a sight she at first could not comprehend. Within seconds however it became quite obvious what was going on, and in short order she grew tellingly embarrassed. Evelyn transformed into a frozen reflection of herself, barely able to move—though her hands found their way to her mouth, covering it in horror.

Lily, on the other hand, was moving about quite well. Her naked body was writhing face-up on the bed, as if she were performing some sort of perversion-laced aerobic routine. With a chokehold on a zucchini-sized, gelatinous pink rod (that Evelyn guessed to be an overstated caricature of a penis) she stabbed playfully at her bald mound.

"Coming! Coming!" Lily screamed, as the phallus entered her repeatedly. As she edged toward her nirvana, her right hand jerked the rubber organ at a quickened pace, in and out of her slippery slot. Her left hand was busy kneading her firm, full breasts, while her fingers tugged gently but deliberately at her hardened nipples. The dildo sparkled from Lily's surging juices, appearing then quickly disappearing through the petals of her fully blossomed floret. As her orgasm subsided, her body fell flat against the mattress, her legs separated and relaxed. Her arms lay weary at her side, a fat, glistening pole still clutched in one hand.

"Evelyn, you have to wear a thong when you wear those pants," Lily stated matter-of-factly to the paralyzed woman standing by the bed. "I can see your panty line."

Evelyn, who had so desperately wanted to turn and run much earlier, but for some reason couldn't, was at a loss for words. Her mind was like a large ice cube: viable, but needing a good thaw to start flowing.

"However," Lily continued, "I think you look fabulous! Those clothes make you look so young, so stylish!"

Evelyn's bright teeth shined through her petrified smile. With all the strength she could muster she forced herself to turn from the girl, and then she walked slowly from the room.

Chapter Eleven

Sidney was on his way home from work after a slight detour through the aisles of his favorite liquor store. He needed to stock up; all he had in the house was the balance of Barolo from Lily's welcome dinner.

The disappointment that punched at his chest when he came across the barren shelves of his serpentine shaped mahogany bar had been devastating. All that sorrow had evaporated like alcohol on hot cement though when his wife swallowed her first glass of wine. If she would drink one night, she would drink on another night as well, per Sidney's new rationale. And if he could ply her with just enough wine... Sidney's voyage to the Quick Release Studios website had jerked his libido from stand-by status to ready-to-launch. He had never wanted to be intimate with his wife more than he did now. If he could entice Evelyn to loosen up again by having a glass or two, his chances of liberating his stockpiled seed would increase dramatically.

Sidney wasn't certain that Evelyn would be open to expanding her tastes beyond red wine, and he didn't want to push it. However, alongside the bottles of Pinot Noir and Merlot placed carefully in the trunk of his car, were bottles of Chardonnay, Hypnotiq liqueur, Amaretto, Kahlua, and Hangar One Raspberry vodka—all favorites of the ladies, at least according to the very helpful manager that assisted Sidney. Of course, he couldn't leave without purchasing at least one bottle of Scotch as tribute to his lost cache—and so he purchased three very old, very special, very expensive bottles.

The house seemed exceptionally quiet when Sidney entered. He was sure Evelyn was home, as her Lexus was parked in the garage. But she wasn't flittering about, as she usually was when he arrived. This wasn't necessarily a bad thing, as Sidney had several boxes of liquor he needed to transport from his trunk to the living room, and he was certain Evelyn would consider this an obscene display of immoral activity.

Surprisingly, he was able to maneuver all the bottles to their proper place inside his bar, without disturbing anyone. Now he gave more thought to where his wife may be. He guessed that she had overextended her afternoon nap, so he ventured into the bedroom to check.

When he entered he found her wide awake, sitting up on the bed, fully clothed. The television was off, and she seemed to be staring at its dark screen.

"Are you okay, Evelyn?" Sidney queried.

"What? Oh, Sidney darling, when did you come home?" Evelyn asked, breaking free of her stupor.

"I just walked in dear…what is that you have on?"

"Oh, this?" Evelyn replied grasping at her blouse. "Lily and I did some shopping today dear. I'm afraid I went overboard with my purchases."

"Let me see for myself," Sidney said as he drew nearer to his wife. "Are these clothes to wear outside the house as well?"

"Yes?" Evelyn wasn't sure her husband would approve, and she was having second thoughts herself.

"I love it! Stand up and let me take a good look at you!"

Evelyn stood and did a model's spin for her husband. He wasn't sure if it was due to his exceptionally lustful state, but his wife looked spectacular. He couldn't recall her wearing denim before, ever, and he was sad she had waited so long. Her legs looked tight and sensual behind the dark blue cloth, and her rear was firm and well defined. If not for the unsightly lines of her underwear bulging through the fabric, the package was perfect.

Sidney looked up to draw in the rest of the outfit. Evelyn had worn soft lacy fabrics before, but there was something about the gauzy material of this blouse that made it quite stirring to him. Perhaps, he thought, her unmasked breasts had something to do with it. Sidney wasn't a mathematician, but he quickly calculated that three-quarters of her boobs were exposed to the air.

Taking advantage of Evelyn's proximity, as well as her apparent new leaning toward a more relaxed standard, Sidney wrapped his arms tightly around her in an emotional embrace. Evelyn seemed responsive to her husband's sudden outpouring of love, resting her head on his shoulder.

Realizing he may not need to use alcohol to further his case with his wife, Sidney lowered his hands and started stroking his wife's behind as amorously as his expertise would allow. He tried to dance Evelyn toward the bed, but met with resistance when she realized their destination.

Evelyn released her arms, explaining to her husband that she had too much on her mind to continue where they were headed. She also reminded Sidney that they had a guest just down the hall, and that it wouldn't be an appropriate time for that sort of activity.

As soon as those words left her mouth, her mind became tangled in a rush of confusion. Lily was not an excuse to avoid relations with her husband—not after what had just occurred. Evelyn needed a while to digest the whole matter, but, in the meantime, she was in no mood to jump into the sea of debauchery that was engulfing her home.

Sidney was disappointed that his intuition had failed him, and that his wife wasn't quite ready to bend the rules that steered her existence. He was not terribly surprised however, having been married to Evelyn for thirty years. Something seemed to be weighing heavily on his wife's mind. He didn't think it was his awkward advance that had put her in a mood. She seemed to be a little off when he first walked into the room. Perhaps, he considered, she was still reeling from her performance in the dining room the previous night. Sidney remembered the first time he consumed more than one alcoholic beverage. As he recalled, it wasn't pretty.

"What seems to be bothering you?" Sidney asked.

"It's nothing really, Sidney. I just had a long and tiresome day, that's all."

"Well, I love what you bought on your little outing, dear. I hope there's more like this in the closet!" Sidney gently touched Evelyn's sleeve. "Say, where is our young guest anyway? Did you wear her out as well?"

"No—I mean, yes!" Evelyn hurriedly corrected herself. "She is sound asleep I'm certain. Please don't bother her, dear."

"Of course I won't," Sidney responded. "So, what sort of plans do we have for dinner this evening?"

"I'm not sure. What do you think of the girl anyway, Sidney?"

"I'm sorry, what are you talking about?" Sidney's hopeful mind had already shifted to slabs of prime rib and shots of scotch.

"Lily, dear. What do you think of her? I know she's only been with us for a short time, but the young girl confuses me."

"I'm not sure what sort of response you're after Evelyn, but she seems quite the sharp tool to me," Sidney replied. "The more I see of her, the more of Iris and George I see *in* her. She's a bit spunkier I guess than her parents, but I'm wondering how well we really knew those two after all."

"You mean the drugs, Sidney?"

"Yes, I mean the drugs. I must say, Iris and George were the last two people I would have ever considered to be marijuana users. I'm not sure how I missed it, but I did. I can't imagine why they weren't more up-front with us Evelyn. They were our dear friends, were they not?"

"Of course they were."

"Then Evelyn, maybe their daughter is a blessing, sent to us by her parents as some sort of emissary to help us better understand who they were." Sidney had never been a very spiritual person and felt odd talking like this, but he liked having the girl around and didn't want to say anything negative.

"Maybe you're right Sidney. Maybe there's a deeper meaning to her visit that I hadn't considered until now."

"Sure Evelyn; there's a deeper meaning. So, what did you say our dinner plans were?"

Evelyn hadn't given any thought to their evening meal, and she was ashamed she didn't have a ready response to her husband's question. She was still too shaken to feel like an evening out, and she was certain that Lily would need to take a shower before doing anything. It was getting late, and her only thought was to order in.

"I had planned to order Chinese food to be delivered, Sidney—any special requests?"

"No, but Chinese food does sound delightful. Just make sure you order some of those seafood dishes—you know, shrimp something and lobster something. And don't forget some of those crab roll appetizers they do so well, and maybe an order of their imperial fried rice or whatever they call it. Just order whatever you want, dear."

With her new focus on dinner, and with her husband's calming advice regarding their guest, Evelyn's shoulders fell to a relaxed state, her mind having found a new thread to follow. She could not discuss what she had seen in Lily's room with Sidney. Even if she wanted to, the words to accurately describe the incident did not exist in her expansive vocabulary. But, more importantly, Evelyn thought her husband would find Lily's behavior dreadfully inappropriate, possibly leading to her early eviction. Evelyn was convinced that, as raw as the girl seemed, she was fated to be spending this time with her and Sidney, and that there was a purpose to her actions.

While Evelyn was busy putting together the dinner order, Sidney was formulating his thoughts on beverages for the evening. As much as he had hoped to break the seal on a bottle of Scotch, Chinese food was on the way, and he wasn't sure he could stomach that combination. Plus, he was more excited about the prospect of Evelyn enjoying herself with a sip or two of something, and he knew she would be more likely to indulge if everyone were having the same thing. Sidney scurried to place three bottles of velvety Chardonnay in the freezer for a quick chill.

Before dinner arrived, Evelyn set the table in the kitchen. She had no thought of transferring the delivered food from their ubiquitous white cardboard containers to serving dishes, and the kitchen was more casual and more suitable for out-of-the-box cuisine. The round, black granite table was generously proportioned, easily able to seat eight. In the middle of the table was a substantially dimensioned lazy Susan, a horseless merry-go-round capable of cradling and displaying the entire oriental feast. As she finished preparing for the food's arrival, Sidney placed a Chardonnay appropriate glass by each of the three place settings. Evelyn was busy straightening placemats and took note of her husband's actions. Sidney paused a moment, waiting for a reaction from his wife. While he lingered, the doorbell rang, trumpeting the arrival of dinner.

•••

Lily had been relaxing in her room when she heard someone at the front door. It was still early in the evening, at least to the young Hanover, but she imagined it was well past the Banks' suppertime. She considered it odd that Evelyn hadn't at least discussed the evening's meal with her. Lily didn't mind, but Evelyn always made such a fuss over every meal that she thought something might be wrong. She silently wondered if she had upset Evelyn earlier. She had never returned to show off any more of her new outfits.

Perhaps the Banks had invited company over, Lily thought, and that's who was at the door. Lily smiled at the prospect of Evelyn and Sidney having friends that would drop by during the week. She had been somewhat concerned that her parents, now gone, were their only close acquaintances.

Lily had been pleasantly surprised at how much she had enjoyed her visit to this point, and was actually looking forward to the next few weeks. The Banks had been nothing but cordial to her, bending over backwards, albeit clumsily, to make sure she was comfortable and happy. In fact, her stay had been much less drama-filled than she had anticipated. Even Evelyn appeared to be winding down somewhat from her perch. Lily's ambition of converting the supercilious woman to a more companionable human was going well, she thought. She even felt a little guilty about encouraging such hurried alterations to someone who had probably sustained the same personality her whole life.

It was sad to Lily that Evelyn had such a thin veneer of superficiality and pretentiousness, that it could so easily be peeled away and replaced. If Lily didn't think the whole world found Evelyn's sort abrasive and generally useless, she would have left the woman to her own shell of a life. In fact, it bothered her to interfere in other people's lives. It was Evelyn's lack of tolerance that had disturbed Lily when they met, and now she was disregarding her own broadminded philosophy on tolerance, only to prove something to herself about her own parents.

As Lily sat pondering her circumstances, she heard a soft tapping on the bedroom door. She announced in a loud enough voice for whomever it was to "come in." A moment later, she heard another tap. Realizing the tapper wasn't going to open the door, Lily reached for it herself. Evelyn was standing in the hall, peering at the ceiling. Lily looked up too, thinking there may be a bug crawling her way.

"Lily, dear," Evelyn said as she took a fleeting look at the young Hanover out of the corner of her eye, "dinner is ready. I hope you like Chinese!"

"That sounds great, Evelyn," Lily responded, continuing to search for a bug that must have flown away.

By this time, Evelyn had captured enough of Lily's form to see that she was fully clothed and so could now look directly at her. "We'll be eating in the kitchen tonight, darling. Please come along!"

Evelyn led Lily down halls and through rooms until they reached the kitchen. Sidney had already been sitting at the table, but stood when the two girls entered the room. Although the atmosphere was very casual, at least per the Banks' prescribed scale, the table was set precisely. By each place setting were four pairs of chopsticks, every pair a different color. Lily appeared quite confused, as she had never seen such an arrangement.

Before Sidney could sit down, Lily embraced him with a genuine, firm hug; he mirrored her actions in response. Evelyn, who witnessed the friendly greeting, reached for the filled glass of white wine that was resting at the far edge of her bamboo placemat and took a sip.

"Oh look, white wine for everyone!" Lily cheered as they all sat. "Yum, this is delicious—Chardonnay?"

"Very good, Lily—you do know your wines!" Sidney responded.

"Yes, this is quite appealing, Sidney—very fruity!" Evelyn chimed in. "Now, everyone help themselves to the food while it's still warm!"

Although Lily possessed better than average dexterity when it came to using chopsticks, there were four pairs before her, and this threw her off course. Sidney noticed the confusion on her face, finding her puzzlement adorable. He would help her in a little while, but first he wanted to bask in the warmth of the moment. Within the last several seconds Sidney had received an honest hug from a beautiful young woman and watched his wife voluntarily raise a glass of wine and proclaim its quality. He was feeling good.

"Lily, we only use the outer pair of chopsticks," Sidney murmured. "If you'd like to use any of those other colored pairs you can—I'm sure they're clean. Evelyn went a bit overboard on our last trip to China and must have purchased fifty sets; she likes to use them as décor."

Evelyn smiled as she stole another sip of wine.

"That's so cute, Evelyn," Lily said. "This all looks yummy. I am so hungry!"

The three diners foraged their way through the boxes of oriental delicacies, but after almost an hour of chewing and chatting, the containers still appeared to be full. Two wine bottles had, however, been emptied.

"Evelyn and Sidney, I want to thank you for this wonderful meal," Lily announced. "The food was amazing, and the wine matched perfectly!"

"You are quite welcome, little Lily!" Evelyn replied, meshing her words somewhat. "But Sidney, he's the one that picked this wine. He did very good."

"Thank you dear," Sidney responded. "It's a bit light for my taste, but I too enjoyed the fruit forward flavor."

"Ha!" Evelyn screamed. "Say that five times fast! Fruit forward favor, fruit foryard flavor, fuit forward flavor…"

"Evelyn, dear," Sidney interrupted, "what sort of fruit did *you* taste in the wine?"

"I tasted wine fruit!" Evelyn was feeling witty again and started to laugh at her own humor.

"I detected some bright grapefruit notes, Sidney," the smiling young Hanover announced, her sunny voice a disruption to the swelling condescension in the room. "Spicy grapefruit."

"Excellent Lily," Sidney replied. "And I think there was more than a whiff of pear, as well."

"I think I tasted grapes, because that's what the wine was made from," Evelyn said, stony-faced. "My father told me once that if I had to drink wine, to make sure it was the grape kind, and not the cheap stuff. Did you buy us the cheap stuff Sidney? Huh?"

"Yes, dear—they were having a sale on grapefruit and pear wine, and I just couldn't pass up the bargain." Sidney turned toward Lily and rolled his eyes somewhat, just to make sure she knew he was being sarcastic. "I'm sorry, Evelyn—I will go back to the wine store tomorrow and stock up on only quality wines."

"Evelyn, how about that fashion show we promised each other!" Lily interrupted, hoping to keep the party going.

"That sounds like great fun, Lily!" Evelyn replied.

Chapter Twelve

Evelyn had indeed been feeling the effects of the wine as dinner was wrapping up. She managed to stay within herself however, even though her speech had become somewhat stained with bad grammar and slurry pronunciations.

She meant what she had said about her father. There were lots of things Carl Seymour had told her when she was very young that she would never forget, including never to buy wine that wasn't made from grapes. He was quite serious about this, as he was about the other pearls of wisdom he would impose upon her. One after another, her father would preach to her from his catalog of "never dos". "Never do this," he would say, followed by a set of circumstances that if handled incorrectly would inevitably lead to some level of crisis. "Never buy wine that's not made of grapes," was one of the mantras he had ingrained in the young Evelyn.

These life lessons would have never left her father's lips if she hadn't entered the fifth grade—Evelyn was certain of this. Her life had been pretty simple before that time. She had her little girl friends and played with her little toys. She was a good student too, which kind of set her apart from most of the goofy boys who were in her class. In fact, all of Evelyn Seymour's friends were girls. It's not that she didn't want to like boys, or that she thought they were below her in any way, but the girls only played with other girls and the boys only played with other boys.

When Evelyn was in the fifth grade, a very popular toy made its debut. All the girls made their parents buy them a Hula Hoop, and all the girls became very adept at using them.

A few weeks into the school year the Principal decided that during one of the monthly school assemblies, it would be fun to hold a Hula Hoop contest. All the young ladies were very excited about this, including Evelyn. She practiced diligently every day after school and sometimes even before breakfast. She really wanted to win the contest, which meant she'd have to spin the Hula Hoop around her waist longer than any of the girls. If she could be one of the five best "hoopers," she would qualify for the finals. During the finals, each girl would have two minutes on the stage of the school's auditorium by themselves to show off their extraordinary talent with the hoop. A round of applause from the students in the audience would determine the winner.

Evelyn was very confident that she could make the finals. She sometimes practiced with her friends after school and always seemed to be the last girl spinning. There were some other girls in her class who were pretty good though, and she thought it might be hard to win the whole thing. She decided that she needed a strategy that would separate her from the rest of the contenders.

Instead of just standing on stage, wiggling her hips and trying to wow the crowd without doing anything special, Evelyn practiced hula hooping while twirling her body around like the ballet dancers she had seen on television. After hours spent in the basement of her home perfecting this skill, she became quite accomplished; she could hoop and twirl with the best of them. She didn't stop there though. Evelyn wanted to do more than just hoop and twirl. She decided to write a poem that she could recite while she was performing. This would most definitely separate her from the pack. She was feeling pretty good about her chances.

On the day of the competition, Evelyn woke up extra early to make sure she looked just right. She had laid out her new pink jumper the night before, along with a crisp, white, short-sleeved blouse to wear under it. The skirt of the jumper was hemmed just above her knees, which scratched at the school dress code for length. A fresh pair of white bobby socks and pink and white saddle shoes completed her ensemble.

Evelyn walked to school that morning, silently reciting the poem she had written for the finals competition, trying very hard to commit it to memory. She was also very careful not to mess up her pretty outfit.

When the first ever Cloverdale Elementary School Hula Hoop contest was ready to begin, forty-two girls entered the school's all-purpose room, hoops in hand. They lined up in rows, but spread out enough to not interfere with one another. One of the teachers, Mrs. Lucas, quieted all the children and then told them to pick up their hoops for the start of the contest. She counted backwards from ten, and after she reached the number one, her shrill voice initiated the competition with the word "go."

Within a few seconds a number of hoops descended sluggishly to the floor, eliminating a scattering of participants from the contest. Ten minutes later, the five finalists had been determined. Evelyn was one of them.

That afternoon, all students from grades one through six filed into the school's large, prosaic auditorium and took their seats. The principal applauded the children for accomplishing this exercise in such a quiet and organized manner, and then delivered his usual mind-numbing announcements.

The last item on the agenda was what everyone had been looking forward to—especially Evelyn.

Three girls preceded Evelyn on stage. None of them did anything out of the ordinary; they just spun their hoops above their waists and smiled brightly. After each of these three performances, the kids from the school released their hoots and hollers, even though they had been told that the actual voting wouldn't occur until all five contestants had finished.

It was now Evelyn's turn, and she took her mark center stage. The school's singular spotlight flooded her silhouette with bright light, leaving a distorted pool of a shadow on the floor behind her. She picked up her hoop and started swinging it around her waist until it had achieved the momentum she was striving for. This was her big moment, when she would start reciting her poem. She was confident that this added extra would differentiate her from all the other girls. She beamed as she began her poem:

"Hi my name is Evelyn; I hope you'll clap for me,
I'm here to spin my hoop for you, as fast as it can be,
And now I'll twirl around and around, while all of you just sit,
I hope I make you happy, even for a little bit."

With that, Evelyn began pirouetting while simultaneously maintaining the proper spin on her Hula Hoop. All the children in the auditorium started cheering wildly, as this was quite an unexpected twist to the competition. Evelyn had never been to this place in her soul before, where she felt so warm and so good. She didn't want the moment to end, and so she repeated her poem in an even louder voice while doubling the velocity of her twirls. The children became quiet when she started reciting her poem again:

"Hi my name is Evelyn; I hope you'll clap for me,
I'm here to spin my hoop for you, as fast as it can be,
And now I'll twirl around and around, while all of you just shit,
I hope I make you happy, even for a little bit."

Evelyn was spinning so fast now and was so focused on keeping her hoop rotating above her hips that she didn't even realize that she had said a bad word. Unfortunately for her, all the kids had heard it and started laughing hysterically, especially the boys.

That's not all they were guffawing over. Evelyn's spinning momentum had lifted the skirt of her pink jumper to an almost horizontal level. She was so focused on keeping herself and her hoop spinning while shouting out her poem, that she wasn't aware of this situation. What made matters worse is that she was performing at the front of the stage, perched high above the kids in the audience. Evelyn's clean white panties, which were now riding tightly up her anatomy, were clearly on display for the whole school to scrutinize.

The kids were roaring now, and Evelyn could sense the difference between this resonance and the cheers she had heard a few seconds earlier. When she finished her performance and walked off stage, she could still hear the audience's ceaseless laughter. The cackling continued even as the last contestant started her routine.

The Principal eventually had to step in, silencing the children with threats of detentions and calls to parents.

The other finalists who had already finished their routines greeted Evelyn off stage with giggles and snorts as she walked toward them. Evelyn still wasn't certain what had happened, but broke down in tears from the humiliation.

When the last of the contestants, Joyce Farmington, walked off the stage, she saw the state Evelyn was in, and did her best to comfort her.

"Evelyn, you did really really good hooping today," Joyce said. "I'm sorry all those *stupid* boys had to ruin it for you."

"Everyone was laughing at me, Joyce, and I still don't know why!" Evelyn moaned between tears. "What did I do?"

"Don't you know, Evelyn?" Joyce answered. "Didn't you hear yourself say the dirty word?"

"That's not all she did!" Cheryl McCarley, one of the other contestants shouted. "She showed her underwear to all the school!"

Evelyn demanded her friends share with her the bad word she spoke, as well as explain to her how the entire school saw her underwear. Joyce eventually whispered the word "shit" in Evelyn's ear after giving up trying to rhyme it with other words and hoping she could make the connection. Evelyn honestly couldn't recall spewing out the profanity, although she knew this was a bad word. She wasn't sure what it meant, but she knew it was bad.

Cheryl slowly detailed for Evelyn how everyone got to see her underwear, and even named a couple of the boys' who were sitting in the front row.

Evelyn stood, her head bowed, her arms hanging heavy at her sides. She never wanted to look at anyone again. After the assembly she left the auditorium via the stage door, which emptied to one of the school's hallways. Mrs. Lucas, the teacher who was responsible for the contest, was standing in the hall by the door when she saw Evelyn. She approached the fifth grader with a big smile and a big ribbon, congratulating her on winning the competition.

Evelyn was shocked and surprised that she had won, and for a few seconds was actually feeling pretty good about things. Just then, a gaggle of sixth grade boys came walking by. The leader shouted: "Evelyn Seymour! We got to see more than we wanted to!" Even though Mrs. Lucas squeezed the young man's ear with her bony hands and led him away to detention, the ridicule was only beginning.

Making her way to her classroom so she could pick up her books and walk home, Evelyn was bombarded by mockery and pointing fingers. Some comments the kids made were just stupid, like: "Evelyn, it's a good thing you didn't have sit in your underwear, cause we would have all seen it!" to the more personal, such as: "Hey Evelyn, wait till your parents hear what you said!"

Evelyn did tell her parents of the incident that evening at the dinner table. She was terribly distraught and had nobody else to turn to. Plus, since she had won the contest, she needed to share the victory with someone who would respect her efforts.

Her parents were incensed that their young daughter had been tormented, and so they made a big deal over her victory with visits to the neighborhood ice cream parlor on five consecutive nights. Her father even created a huge "Evelyn Is The Champion Hula Hooper" banner that he suspended across the wall of her bedroom.

The taunting continued for months, withering slowly to sporadic disparagements as the school year came to a close. Even in the years that followed, gossipy classmates chatting in the hallway would invariably rehash the incident as Evelyn passed by.

Evelyn remained so troubled over the situation that her father took to consoling her on a regular basis. At least once a day he would remind his daughter to "be more careful from now on." This evolved into the never-ending succession of warnings and "never-dos" that he would issue to her until his eventual passing many years later.

Evelyn came to loathe all the kids that were too immature to move past this small mistake in her life. Over time she began to despise all children, even the ones who had nothing but nice things to say to her. Though Evelyn was still a child herself, she couldn't wait to leave this condition and become an adult as quickly as possible. She knew that once she was grown up, she would never again be taunted by other kids.

The Hula Hoop was just another toy to most children of the fifties, but for Evelyn, it was her last toy.

Chapter Thirteen

Lily's first week with the Banks seemed to fly by, at least according to Sidney who disclosed these feelings to his wife and the young Hanover while unwinding in the den.

Evelyn and Lily grew a little closer each day, as they spent most of their waking hours talking, shopping, and eating with one another. Sidney would join them for dinner, listening to their adventures for the most part, opening his mouth only when he had something fitting to add. When they'd all dine together, they'd share lively conversations, which became even livelier as bottles of wine emptied. Much of the banter tossed back and forth at the dinner table and beyond involved Lily's parents. Between the three of them they would try to sort out and understand who Iris and George really were. Evelyn and Sidney obviously knew them best, and, in their own direct, yet tactful, way reminded Lily of this whenever they were discussed.

The Hanovers weren't hard people to figure out—unless their closeted box of marijuana was thrown into the equation. This most curious deviation to the couple's otherwise straightforward behavior always seemed to be the elephant in the room. Lily thought it was time to reintroduce the topic, as both Sidney and Evelyn were currently sober.

"Do you think my parents got high a lot?" Lily asked the lazing Banks.

"Are you talking about drinking or doing that marijuana?" Evelyn replied.

"Marijuana," Lily responded. "That box of pot just doesn't mesh with the people you've described to me."

"Evelyn and I have given this some thought," Sidney said. "At first when you showed us the box you found in their home, we couldn't deny the possibility that it was theirs, thinking that they did enjoy a puff on occasion. But, I have to say I just can't picture it. Iris and George were as pure and good as people could be. I think we both have our doubts that they were tangled up with such an immoral, not to mention illegal, substance."

"I know plenty of upstanding people who smoke pot,

Sidney," Lily responded. "I don't think we can dismiss the possibility just because they were so special."

"Do you know of any of our acquaintances that use marijuana, Sidney?" Evelyn asked.

"I can't say that I do, dear. Frankly, I can't imagine any of our friends or neighbors using any sort of drugs."

"What about Mrs. Anders from across the street?" Evelyn inquired, her husband's comment having kindled the notion. "I've seen her fetch the morning paper—in her underwear!"

"We're not talking about prescription drugs, darling," Sidney replied, as he admired his wife in a snug pair of white cotton capris, hemmed at the calf and notched very seductively up the sides. Her pale blue pullover blouse was loose enough and delicate enough to make things interesting when she moved. He kept his eyes on alert.

"Listen," Lily interrupted, "I'm pretty sure Iris and George smoked pot. I just wonder if they smoked it often."

"That would be so sad, Lily," Evelyn commented, "if this were a regular routine of theirs, and they could never confide in their good friends. Do you think Sidney and I are so unapproachable and so out of touch, that they were afraid to tell us about this habit of theirs?"

"Maybe they had a medical issue," Sidney said. "I've read about people who use marijuana for therapeutic purposes. I could see George not wanting to burden us with his personal problems."

"You know," Lily said. "It's actually kind of fun to get high."

Sidney and Evelyn snapped a quick look at each other, then at Lily, who was sitting cross-legged on the leather side chair by the couch, her ever-present grin beaming brilliantly back at them.

"Um," Sidney stumbled, gathering his thoughts, "of course it is."

Evelyn wasn't pleased with her husband's reply, as it intimated his familiarity with the illegal substance. She stared at him harshly, waiting for his clarification.

"I mean," Sidney continued, "Iris and George were smart people. Unless they were using this drug for therapeutic purposes, I'm sure they must have at least been having fun with it."

This answer didn't sit well with Evelyn either, as she just peered out the window and shook her head.

"Haven't you guys ever tried pot before?" Lily asked the question just to keep the conversation moving, not because she really needed the answer.

"We certainly were exposed to it when we were at the university," Sidney responded. "Of course, it wasn't quite as popular back then."

"I've got a great idea," Lily said. "I think as homage to Iris and George, we should smoke a bowl of their weed. What do you think?"

"I think not, Lily," Evelyn answered at a gallop. "Iris and George may have had their reasons for using marijuana, and I'm sure somehow they were rational, mature reasons, but Sidney and I have no intention of traveling down that road."

There was an uncomfortable lull as Evelyn waited for Sidney's corroboration of her answer. Lily smiled at Sidney, trying to read his mind.

"Maybe that's what we should do, dear; we should try some of Iris and George's marijuana." Sidney fluttered his hands as he spoke. "Maybe that's part of the reason Lily's with us—remember? Don't you want to learn more about our friends? Hmm? Perhaps if we put ourselves into their shoes, we might uncover some of their secrets—secrets they had wanted to share if only given the chance."

Evelyn's face exhibited an incongruous combination of wonder and dismay as she settled back on the couch. Using marijuana was not something she would have ever considered. It was an act relished by immature lawbreakers whose objective was to avoid the realities and substance of life—not by a woman of stature. Evelyn's decision would have been simple and straightforward, if not for her dear friends the Hanovers. Instead, they had made things complicated and foggy.

There was not one aspect of Iris's life that Evelyn didn't aspire to emulate. Her friend was no longer available to her, but she was still her mentor and always would be. Now Iris's unimaginable legacy was confronting her, and she wasn't sure what to do.

"I just can't do it," Evelyn announced. "I've never smoked anything in my life, and I'm not prepared to start now. I'm sorry Lily, I appreciated your mother's reasoning regarding all aspects of life, but I can't seem to wrap my brain around this one."

"We don't have to smoke it, Evelyn." Lily lobbed the words into the conversation and allowed them to simmer for a moment.

"If you think I'm melting it down to some sort of lethal liquid and injecting it in my body, you can think again young lady," Evelyn snorted loudly.

"Dear, you *have* experienced plenty of needles in your face. Surely this can't be worse," Sidney pleaded.

"Um, I'm not sure, but I don't think injecting weed is even a possibility," Lily reasoned. "I was talking about eating it."

"Lily, I've had my share of atrocious food over the years, but I would certainly gag chewing a nasty weed!" Evelyn said. "I believe we've gone beyond reason here—I'm sure Iris and George had many rapturous moments with their narcotics, and I'll just leave it at that."

"Evelyn," Lily responded, "I would never think about chewing a weed either—at least as you're imagining it—here, take a look." With that, Lily produced a large, clear plastic vial from her purse and handed it to Evelyn.

"I'm not sure I understand," Evelyn said, examining the powdered contents. Sidney leaned in to have a look for himself.

"It's from my parent's stash of pot!" Lily explained. "I just took a few buds and chopped them finely."

"And this tastes better?" Evelyn asked. "It looks like bad oregano." After making this comment, she passed the vial to her very annoying husband who had been flitting about her face trying to get a better glimpse.

"Exactly, Evelyn," Lily replied. "It looks like bad oregano; but it's not. It's more like fun oregano!"

"What are you proposing, Lily?" Sidney asked, rotating the vial slowly in his hands.

"I'd like to make dinner tonight, Sidney," Lily replied. "You haven't tried my famous capellini with mushroom sauce—and my garlic bread is to die for!"

"Ah, but instead of garlic, you'll use the marijuana!" Sidney was proud of his deduction.

"No silly," Lily giggled. "The powder will simmer in the sauce! You really won't even notice it—at least for a half-hour or so."

Sidney looked up at his wife, who was tightly wound on the couch, her arms and legs all folded together. She appeared to be desperately searching for another excuse to not partake of the Hanover's unlawful hallucinogens.

"It's illegal, Lily," Evelyn blurted out. "I must say, I'm uncomfortable just having that stuff in my house—Sidney?"

"Yes dear. But remember where this illegal substance came from, and don't forget how we promised to understand this side of George and Iris—the side we were never privy to."

Evelyn could remember bits of this promise, but didn't recall the part about jeopardizing her freedom and risking incarceration so she could better understand her deceased friends. She sat silently on the couch, trying to avoid eye contact with Lily and Sidney.

"I just don't know," was all she could muster.

"Tell you what—I would like to fix dinner anyway, if you don't mind. And also, if you don't mind, I'd like to make capellini with my yummy mushroom marinara. You don't need to know anything else, okay?"

"That sounds wonderful, Lily!" Sidney exclaimed. "Take my car to the market, if you like."

Sidney jumped up to grab his keys for Lily, like a cat that had just spied a mouse scampering by. He wasn't about to give his wife the opportunity to shut down what looked to be a promising evening of new adventures.

•••

Lily spread a meal's worth of assorted colorful ingredients across the expansive granite countertop in the Banks' kitchen. She didn't have to look hard for the cookware. It was suspended above the center island, directly over the Viking gas burners.

For a couple who possibly had never cooked a meal at home, they had quite the set-up. The orderly strand of Mauviel pots that hung from the copper fixture above the range appeared to have never heated a crumb of anything. They seemed more like pristine, shiny works of art, than cooking utensils. Lily had a hunch they were part of the kitchen's décor, meticulously masterminded by Evelyn. After searching the cupboards and not discovering any lesser cookware, she reached high and retrieved the pieces she needed.

It wasn't a difficult or lengthy meal for Lily to prepare. It took just a little over an hour for her to have it in proper serving dishes and on the dining room table.

While Lily was busy cooking, Sidney carefully arranged plates, silverware, and napkins on the table. This wasn't something he would normally do, but Evelyn was in the bedroom trying very hard to relax, and he didn't want to disturb her current state of amenability by asking her to do this work.

The house filled with aromas reminiscent of an Italian trattoria, and Sidney breathed deeply, wondering if he could detect a hint of Columbian cantina as well. When he saw Lily transfer the completed meal to the dining room, he informed his wife that it was time for dinner.

Evelyn, Sidney, and Lily sat with dubious anticipation, their chairs tucked smartly to the table—close enough to caress the warm vapors rising from the crowded platters. Lily had found fresh asparagus at the market that she prepared with a drizzle of olive oil and a quick run through the oven. The narrow, spring-green spears shimmered atop an oval-shaped, deep blue china platter. Positioned next to the vegetable was a much larger platter weighed down with nests of freshly buttered, steamy capellini. By its side a silver wire tray, lined with a heavy cloth napkin, offered up crispy, golden chunks of garlicky Italian bread. And then there was the covered tureen, an ominous, unsettling grenade, planted amid the otherwise soothing spread.

The savory delights were passed around the table, everyone taking what they wanted. Evelyn was cautious with the sauce, barely ladling a spoonful over her pasta. Sidney was prudent with the asparagus, selecting just two spears for his plate. Evelyn was hoping to minimize the sauce's impact on her poise, and Sidney was hoping to minimize the asparagus' impact on his pee.

"Evelyn," Lily said, "please tell me you'll be having more of my sauce—you barely took any! Trust me, it's delicious!"

"It looks wonderful, darling," Evelyn replied, "but I just don't seem to have much appetite this evening."

"Evelyn, dear," Sidney chimed in, "It really is marvelous. You can't even taste anything unusual about it…I'm sorry Lily, I didn't mean to say that it's unusual in any way—it's fantastic, really!"

"I'm just fine, thank you," Evelyn responded, as she prepared to take her first bite.

Sidney and Lily watched Evelyn reach for her pasta spoon with her left hand and her fork with her right. The two utensils hovered over her plate, as if she weren't certain where to start. Sidney noticed this frustration and instructed his wife just to twirl a little pasta on the fork and use the spoon as support. Evelyn gave him a stern look, indicating that she'd performed this task many times, and to please mind his own business. She looked back at her plate, again positioning her fork and spoon over the food. As she pushed down into the tangle of pasta, her hands started to shake and her spoon fell, clanking hard on the china.

"My goodness, what was I thinking!" Sidney exclaimed loudly. "I forgot to serve wine!" Sidney stood at once and scurried off to the living room. He hurriedly pulled several bottles of red from his bar, and then rushed back to join the others. "I'm so sorry everyone," he apologized as he filled three glasses.

Evelyn lifted her glass as soon as it was placed before her, taking several sips before setting it down. She then successfully managed to jam a coil of capellini onto her fork. The bite wasn't heavily burdened with sauce, but there was enough for her to taste.

"This is quite delightful, Lily," Evelyn announced. I do so appreciate your going to the trouble of preparing this exquisite meal!"

"Oh, it's my pleasure, Evelyn," Lily replied. "Sidney, are you happy with the food as well?"

As Sidney rambled in response about the wonderful cuisine,

Lily took the opportunity to spoon a bit more sauce on everyone's plate, including Evelyn's. Evelyn stole three more swallows of her wine.

The wine flowed warm, though not warm enough to blanket Evelyn's fragmented nerves. She clawed at a piece of garlic bread from her plate and scooped it toward her mouth. While chewing on the crispy slab, crumbs shot with volcanic spirit from her lips, scattering haphazardly. Evelyn looked about for the wayward scraps, her eyes darting like a skittish squirrel. When she discovered flecks of green had settled randomly across her hand she twitched dramatically, as if a deadly fungus were commencing its assault.

"That's oregano," Lily said between bites.

"Evelyn dear," Sidney said, "you must calm down. We're not playing a game of food roulette here. All of this is safe to eat—I assure you."

"He's absolutely right, Evelyn," Lily chimed in. "If I had prepared sushi for dinner, then you might want to be nervous."

Evelyn started to relax somewhere into her second glass of wine. The conversation at the table loosened up somewhat as well. Sidney made more comments about his wife's new clothes and how happy he was to see her updating her look. This started an extended exchange about the world of fashion—where it had been—where it was headed. Evelyn wore a demure smile as Lily explained to Sidney that he'd be next in line for a fashion makeover. Sidney quickly changed the topic to Lily's parents, an interminable and habitual source for conversation.

Everyone finished their meal then slouched deep into their chairs, hands interlocked across their laps, expressions of satiation dragging across their faces. All three dinner plates had been emptied but for a few scattered crumbs.

Lily lifted the lid off the tureen and confirmed that there was no sauce left. She had dutifully ladled it out to everyone as they ate, carefully balancing the distribution as well as the pace at which it was consumed. When asked by Evelyn why everyone couldn't just take their own, Lily replied that it needed to be finished as it wouldn't keep, not even for a day—and that she wanted to make sure it would not go to waste.

Lily promised to clean off the table and do the dishes, then shooed Evelyn and Sidney out of the room. She had planned a surprise dessert, which she thought would be more fun to eat in either the den or the living room—Evelyn's choice.

Evelyn convinced Lily that she was far too full to attempt even a bite of anything else, and that they should all relax in the living room. She thought perhaps after their food had settled, Sidney and her would share a small plate of whatever Lily had conjured up. Lily acquiesced and said she would join them after she had cleared a few dishes. Evelyn argued that she would have the mess cleaned in the morning, but Lily persisted, eventually winning the battle. She kept an eye on Evelyn and Sidney as they paraded to the living room.

Uncoiling with her husband on the sofa, Evelyn shared that she had indeed been stressed at first about the marijuana that was in Lily's sauce, but was perfectly fine with it now. In fact, she mentioned to Sidney, "It feels as if I just had a few glasses of wine, nothing more."

"You did have a few glasses of wine, dear," he reminded her. "And as far as we know, Lily didn't alter any of our food with the Hanover's tonic."

"No, I'm sure you are wrong my big man," Evelyn countered. I think we are maybe just too strong, or maybe just too old to succumb to such nonsense as that marijuana."

"Darling, that's hogwash, and you know it," Sidney replied, relishing his wife's use of the words, "big man". "Now, why don't you slide on down the sofa and I'll give you a nice kiss to prove it."

"Sidney!" Evelyn exclaimed. "How would a kiss prove anything? I think maybe *you* had some of that marijuana."

"Come on, Evelyn," Sidney pleaded, "don't you remember the summer of love, and hippies, and Woodstock, and all those things? Those happened because of marijuana—remember? Now, if I'm not mistaken, the marijuana makes you want to do things, like kiss—and even more, I bet. I guess if you won't move closer to me, I'll just have to move closer to you!"

"Sidney Banks!" Evelyn shouted.

Lily heard a great clamor springing from the living room and went to see what was going on. When she entered the room, she spied Sidney standing in front of the sofa, arms spread wide, jockeying side to side. His wife was scooting from one cushion to the next like a distressed fly attempting to escape the swatter. When Evelyn noticed Lily standing in the doorway, she stopped moving and made a guttural ahem toward Sidney to gather his attention.

"I'm so sorry to have disturbed you two!" Lily exclaimed, smiling brightly. "I thought I heard shouting, and I wanted to make sure it had nothing to do with my food!"

"Oh gracious no," Evelyn replied, dismissing the thought with a flick of her wrist. "Your dinner was absolutely marvelous, darling. Sidney and I were just discussing what sort of new sofa we'd like to purchase."

"Well," Lily said, "If you didn't find the dinner objectionable, maybe you could stomach a little dessert now?"

"I had much too much dinner, dear," Evelyn answered. "I don't think I could."

"What is it, anyway?" Sidney asked.

"Let's see, Sidney," Lily replied. "I found some wonderful, fresh from the oven lady fingers at that cute little bakery next to the grocery. I've never seen pastries so puffy and delicately crisp."

"I believe I'll have one of those, young lady," Sidney announced without hesitation.

"Wait Sidney, there's more!" Lily announced. "After I warm them in the oven, I thought I'd scoop some dark chocolate, raspberry ribbon ice cream on top."

"Raspberry ribbon?" Sidney asked.

"Oh yes," Lily answered. "I always keep a pint in my freezer at home. It's like a highway of pure raspberry jam, tunneling through the richest, darkest chocolate ice cream…anyway, I toasted some fresh pecans earlier, and I thought I'd drop a few above the caramel sauce that I'll be spooning over the ice cream. It's warming in a saucepan on the stove right now."

"Let's do it!" Sidney shouted.

"Sidney darling!" Evelyn interrupted. "This is not one of your business meetings! Please behave yourself! We'll each take one, Lily dear—and don't skimp on the caramel!

"If you've got just a little patience," Lily added, "I thought I'd whip up some fresh cream topping so, you know, it will taste just perfect—okay?"

Evelyn and Sidney turned toward each other, their jaws unhinged, their tongues piercing the gaping space. They lapped at their lips like synchronized Olympic performers. They wanted to respond to Lily, but found it very difficult. Their mouths felt heavy, and then everything felt heavy, and they weren't sure if they would ever find the strength to stand. The image of a dollop of fresh whipping cream blanketing the treasure Lily had just described dominated their fuzzy brains, and they wanted it, no, needed it, desperately.

"How much time?" Evelyn wanted to know.

"I'll be back before you realize I'm gone. Why don't you put on some music while I'm getting the dessert together?" she said, walking toward the door.

Sidney and Evelyn sat side by side on the couch, staring at the dormant fireplace across the room. Neither could speak, not like they could think of anything to say. Something shook Evelyn from her hypnotic state, and she reminded Sidney that he was supposed to be putting on some music. It took a few minutes, but Sidney eventually gathered some energy, rolled off the cushions, and ambled to the master bedroom, where the built-in equipment was located.

Evelyn worried that she was under a spell and was trying very hard to determine who would have cast such a thing over her, when she heard her husband's call for help. She approached the bedroom taking tiny steps, hoping to avoid tripping on the carpet. She leaned into the room and spied Sidney, all crumpled shoulders and downy eyes, scrutinizing the tall stack of electronics. He wore a puzzled look on his face, as if he were trying to understand the mechanics of a particle accelerator.

"Did you call for me, dear?" Evelyn asked.

"Yes," Sidney replied. "I forget how this works."

The couple stood in silence, facing the black-matte tower of buttons and gauges, waiting for an epiphany that was not obliging. They had seen the patterns of electric blue lights erupt across the equipment before and were aware they had something to do with the many speakers flush mounted into their home's walls and ceilings. But the configurations of switches and knobs they stared at now were too overwhelming to comprehend.

"I've never used this before," Evelyn admitted to her husband. "Don't you know where the on button is?"

"I've only used it a couple times myself," Sidney replied.

The pair remained motionless, contemplating their next move, eyes fixed on the equipment. Sidney was starting to feel as if he had been trying for hours to find a way to make the stereo work. Evelyn wasn't sure what she was looking at, but found it fascinating nevertheless.

Enveloped by their trance, Evelyn and Sidney were jolted by the sound of Lily's voice calling to them from the other side of the house. Like kids being summoned from recess, the couple lumbered—though it seemed to them as if they were sprinting—toward the living room.

Lily had become the old witch from Hansel and Gretel, luring ravenous and innocent children with massive bowls of warm, gooey deliciousness. She trusted *this* tale would not be laced with disaster though, and was certain all the players would survive to become better, stronger individuals.

Sidney and Evelyn attacked the load of sugary excess as if they hadn't eaten for days. Lily was pretty aggressive with her spoon as well, but unlike Sidney, managed to keep the softening treat inside her mouth.

Nobody spoke a word until the bowls in front of them were drained of their sticky contents and an entire pitcher of iced water had been consumed.

"I like your taste in music," Lily said to no one in particular, analyzing the remains in her bowl.

"Thank you, Lily," Evelyn answered with a smile.

"She was being sarcastic dear," Sidney commented. "There is no music playing."

"Oh…oh, that's right," Evelyn said. "Sidney, your face is a mess! You look like a one year old who's just eaten his first ice cream cone."

"And it looks like you have your appetite back," Sidney

replied smartly, motioning toward her spotless bowl.

There was a hushed atmosphere after Sidney's comment, and for about thirty seconds the room was reminiscent of a scene from Madame Tussaud's wax museum—three characters quietly frozen in their seats, staring into space.

As had happened before in this very room, Lily was suddenly unable to rein in her emotions and broke out in uncontrollable laughter. This time however, she was joined by both Evelyn and Sidney, who tried desperately to maintain respectable giggles, but instead guffawed riotously as they rolled about the sofa.

"To George and Iris!" Sidney exclaimed between snorts, raising a fictitious cup.

"To Iris and George!" Evelyn countered, mirroring her husband's toast.

"To Evelyn and Sidney!" Lily added, witnessing two obscured souls bursting from tightly sealed kernels.

Chapter Fourteen

"Were you being serious last night when you spoke of Sidney's wardrobe?" Evelyn faced Lily as they sat at the kitchen table, both tearing apart warm cinnamon buns with their fingers.

The two girls had begun their morning like sluggish sloths, unwrapping themselves from their very comfortable beds at a much later hour than usual. As had been the routine, they found their way to the kitchen when they woke, had some form of breakfast, and formulated their itinerary for the day.

Evelyn was always at the table first—a goal of hers which was not hard to meet—so she could assure the kitchen, and the rest of the house for that matter, was perfectly ready for her guest. Today, however, she and Lily managed to amble into the room at the same time, two sets of feet shuffling toward their daily rendezvous.

"Do you mean, when I threatened to give him a fashion makeover?" Lily answered, wiping the stickiness from her hands with a cloth napkin.

"Yes, dear. I've been selecting the man's clothes for over thirty years—I'm ready to let someone else have a shot."

"I was sort of joking with him Evelyn. Anyway, aside from being a little sleepy, I'm feeling great today—how about you?"

"I must say, I feel surprisingly well. I was certain that I'd be paying a price this morning for my wayward behavior last evening—but if anything, I feel refreshed. Now, about Sidney…"

"What about me?" Sidney asked, steering his way into the kitchen and toward a freshly squeezed glass of orange juice. "Lily, in case my manners escaped me last evening, I want to let you know that was some kind of dinner you prepared for us—just fantastic!"

"You mentioned that several times, Sidney," Lily replied, "but thank you again."

"Lily just revealed to me how dearly she would like to visit the mall today," Evelyn said to her husband. "And she wishes you'd come with us so we could all spend our Sunday together. I think we'll have lunch at Cowboy Ciao—I've been dying to try their Stetson chopped salad. And you can have that chicken-fried trout you enjoy so much, Sidney. Oh, this will be a fun afternoon!"

"I don't think so, Evelyn," Sidney responded. "You know I'm not much of a shopper. Why don't you and Lily go and have some fun. I'll be fine here."

"Lily, please tell Sidney how much you'd enjoy his company at the mall," Evelyn said, widening her eyes at the young Hanover.

"Well Evelyn," Lily answered, "I suppose it *could* just be the two of us. I need to shop for a swimsuit, because I can't wait to use your pool. I'll want your opinion on what looks good on me, of course. And you know we do need to spend some time in the lingerie department. Sidney would just be bored to tears!"

Sidney wasn't stupid and knew he was being played on this one. Going to the mall was nothing but aggravation for him, and he did not want to go. Every one of these trips was the same: Evelyn would find a store or a department in a store that piqued her interest, place Sidney in an institutional style chair somewhere near the fitting room, and then be off for the next hour or so, dragging one outfit after another into the room to try on. Occasionally, she would step outside the curtain for Sidney's approval, which he had learned over time was best given. Of course, these were always the least expensive items for which she sought his advice. She wouldn't trust his flip-a-coin attitude on the finer pieces. Just thinking about an afternoon at the mall made Sidney feel exhausted and aggravated.

"You are absolutely right, Lily," Sidney said. "I would be bored to tears."

"Sidney," Evelyn chimed in, "You really could use some new outfits, and it would be so much easier for me if you came along. Besides, with two extra arms to carry bags, I might even find an item or three for myself!"

"Evelyn," Lily said, "I don't believe Sidney is interested in going with us. Let's not be pushy; it's his day off, remember?"

Lily let her words fall to the ground like a small child who was told she could not buy a toy. Appearing forlorn, she stood to clear her dish and napkin, and then began walking from the table. Sidney could not help but notice the slightly oversized pink t-shirt she was wearing, with the large letters MP screen-printed across the chest. He wanted to ask her what the letters represented, but before he had a chance the napkin fell from her hand and she bent to retrieve it. Sidney's eyes naturally followed this sequence of events, and he was instantly rewarded with an unambiguous view of Lily's fully exposed, perfectly shaped cheeks, and the sensuous, vertical crevice between. It was the creamiest, firmest ass he had ever seen. As her right hand stretched to grasp the fallen napkin, he could see bunched up in the space between her flexing legs, everything he had imagined. The small, bare frontier of creases and folds, affixed neatly like a ripe peach tight to its bough, brought a sudden, virile energy to the man.

"We could buy her some underwear," Evelyn whispered softly to her husband.

Sidney quickly agreed that a day of shopping for bathing suits and so forth was not a bad idea. He hadn't been to the mall in some time, plus he thought the girls might require a man's opinion on some of their selections. He didn't want some other poor fellow's day interrupted by a couple of bothersome hens.

After showers and dressing, they drove to Scottsdale Fashion Square, Evelyn's home away from home.

The girls thought it best to shop for Sidney's clothes first, while he was still attentive and receptive to the idea. Lily and Evelyn worked their way through the men's department at Nordstrom like efficient, undaunted termites gnawing from one end of a log to the other. After culling through armloads of options, they presented Sidney with a season's worth of sport shirts, assorted slacks, and shorts. He gathered the bundle from the girls, took a deep breath, and was whisked off to a pleasant, spacious fitting room by a very accommodating sales associate.

As he tried each outfit, Sidney would appease his wife and Lily by modeling the clothes for them. They made the decisions on keeps and discards based on fit, color, and of course, style.

At one point, Sidney was reluctant to leave the dressing room. The outfit he glared at in the mirror seemed quite over-the-top, and he was concerned the girls would insist it looked phenomenal. He knew though that if he failed to model the shirt and shorts now, he'd just have to try them on again. His wife had a keen memory for such things. He slumped out of the room, hands in pockets, eyes facing the floor, trying very hard to project his lack of enthusiasm.

"Sidney, straighten up immediately!" Evelyn barked at her husband. "Let's have a look at you."

"That outfit looks like shit," Lily remarked, as she gave Sidney the once-over.

Sidney straightened up, not because of his wife's command, but from the shock of Lily's unexpected outburst of impropriety. He didn't mind—in fact, he found it quite refreshing.

Lily's startling frankness had quite a different affect on Evelyn. She appeared as if she were becoming nauseous, noticeably gulping the rapidly accumulating fluids in her mouth as her face flushed red.

"Did you mean to say that word, darling?" Evelyn struggled to ask.

"You mean shit?" Lily responded. "Yes I did—the shorts make him look like he's trying to be a teenage punk, and the color of the shirt totally washes out his complexion. I'm sorry Evelyn—I know you picked this out for him—but for me, it just doesn't work."

Evelyn looked around searching for a place to sit, but couldn't find one.

"Are you okay, Evelyn?" Lily asked. "Can I get you anything?"

"She'll be fine, Lily," Sidney responded. "This happens to her sometimes…when she hears certain language."

Sidney walked over to Lily and whispered in her ear: "She has quite adverse reactions to hearing any sort of profanity—especially the word 'shit'. She'll be okay in a minute."

"I'm so sorry, Evelyn," Lily said in a very consoling voice. "Believe me, I didn't intend to offend either of you. I guess it was a natural verbal reaction to my feelings, that's all."

"Thank you, Lily," Evelyn replied. "I'll be okay."

"Evelyn," Lily started, "I don't mean to make a big deal

about this, but don't you hear rough language all the time? I can barely watch five minutes of TV without being exposed to a slew of profanities. I don't know how you make it through your day!"

"We don't have cable," Sidney answered.

"Well Evelyn," Lily shrugged, "I'm very sorry. I'll try to be more careful. I wish there was something I could do to help you through this situation."

"She's been like this since she was a young girl, Lily," Sidney remarked. "I've tried to get her to seek professional help, but she just won't hear of it."

"Evelyn," Lily announced, "There's only one thing to do then. Let's let Sidney sort through his options, while we go do some damage of our own!"

"That sounds wonderful, Lily," Evelyn replied. "Sidney, we'll be somewhere in the store. Come find us when you've checked out."

The girls summoned their shopping legs and padded at full tilt to the lingerie department. When they reached their destination, Lily insisted that Evelyn select a dozen pairs of thong underwear—her treat. Since Evelyn had never worn anything of the sort, it took some convincing by Lily, along with the threat of a graphic fashion show, before she assented.

Lily also encouraged Evelyn to consider "cropping the front lawn" a bit, before attempting the new style. Evelyn pondered this advice for a moment, and then turned a shade of crimson once the metaphor became apparent.

After her natural color returned, Evelyn asked Lily to pick out some undergarments for herself—whatever sort she found comfortable and fun. If she promised to wear them, Evelyn would buy her as many pairs as she liked. Lily found this very humorous, assuring Evelyn she already owned more panties than she could ever wear. Evelyn surmised she must own one pair.

Her scheme having failed, Evelyn was resigned to the fact that she'd be enduring the young lady's naked behind every morning at breakfast. She decided it was time to move their hunt forward, and so she led Lily to the designer sportswear department.

Sidney found the girls about thirty minutes later, toting what

Evelyn considered a disappointingly small shopping bag. He had apparently wandered through several other departments, including ladies swimwear, searching for them. Evelyn informed him that she and Lily had avoided that area. They had too much dessert the night before and were fearful of trying on anything so deficient of fabric, and so form fitting.

Evelyn had been giving thought to the consequences of her actions regarding the Hanover's marijuana. She was concerned, beyond the legal and moral implications of the drug, that if she continued to ingest it she would quickly ascend to a larger, more matronly appearance. She wondered aloud how Iris was able to maintain her graceful figure.

Sidney revealed to his wife that continued marijuana use increased one's metabolism, and that it was all a wash in the end. This was a fabrication he pulled from nowhere, but was spoken so convincingly it sounded legitimate as it rolled off his tongue. He thoroughly enjoyed the mellow state of consciousness he had achieved as the drug progressed through his body, and he hoped to be able to repeat the experience again—all the more likely if Evelyn was on his side.

Evelyn wasn't quite sure how to respond to her husband's assertion, but her expression indicated she was taking it under advisement. She knew Iris would have never used marijuana if it wreaked havoc with her perpetually slender profile. She also knew her friend was very smart and would only have been involved with the drug if there were something redeeming about it. Because of Lily's persistence, Evelyn now understood.

An hour later the girls declared they had done enough damage and went to collect Sidney, who was planted on a large divan by the escalator.

The ride home from the mall was almost void of conversation, as three minds were busy pondering important life issues: Evelyn was questioning her desire to want more of the vices she knew should not be part of her life; Lily was contemplating how to help someone who suffered unhealthy physical reactions from hearing simple profanities; and Sidney wondered if wearing his new clothes might just put his wife in an amorous mood.

Chapter Fifteen

Lily and Evelyn strutted in their new outfits, snaking their way along a crowded sidewalk and into The Greene House restaurant Monday afternoon. It was tough finding a convenient parking space at the upscale "Main Street" patterned shopping center where the restaurant was located, but that didn't seem to be a problem for the pair. They were both feeling good about the way they looked and were happy to show off their recent acquisitions to the well-heeled sophisticates they passed on their brief walk.

Evelyn flaunted her new off the shoulder, black and white Max Azria silk top and clingy knit pants. A chunky Donna Karan statement necklace –all bolts and screws up close, but a silvery proclamation from a further distance, was wrapped loosely around her neck.

Lily's pale pink denim pants rode low on the waist, her unyielding abs faintly exposed to anyone squinting for a peek. On top, a white linen Trina Turk halter, although a relaxed fit, did nothing to un-define her covetable form.

They lucked into one of the see-and-be-seen tables on the patio, modestly separated from the passing shoppers by a low iron fence. The day was warming quickly, but the misting system anchored above the diners assured all would be comfortable. Evelyn and Lily were looking over the extensive menu when their server, Molly, approached for their drink orders. Evelyn ordered iced green tea; Lily mulled her options briefly before asking for a "flirtini". Molly commended the ladies on their choices and was back in short order placing the filled-to-the-brim glasses on the table.

Lily flashed her perpetual smile, delighting in the pinkish cocktail set before her. Evelyn's eyes fixed on Lily's oversized martini glass, her face contorting slightly as she analyzed the mysterious concoction, trying to discern its contents. She had diminishing interest in the tall, ice-filled, lemon-garnished glass of tea she had ordered, and Lily could sense this.

"Like to try a sip?" Lily asked. "It's really very delicious."

"That's quite alright, dear," Evelyn replied. "I don't think I could stomach a martini. It's such an interesting color though."

"Have a sip," Lily insisted. "It tastes nothing like a traditional martini. It's fruity!"

Evelyn continued to gawk at the potion as if it were a cute, fluffy puppy that she yearned to pet, but wasn't sure if it would bite. Just then, Molly returned for their food order.

"I'd like the salmon salad with caper-mustard vinaigrette please," Lily requested.

"And I'll have the sea scallops with caramelized cauliflower and snap peas," Evelyn added. "And one of those too please," she said nodding toward Lily's drink. "Could you tell me what's in it, Molly?"

"Of course," the server replied. "It's a combination of raspberry vodka, lime juice, and pineapple juice. What makes it really special though is the splash of champagne our bartender adds. Would you still like one?"

"I don't suppose it would hurt," Evelyn replied.

Molly hesitated for a moment, not sure if her customer was asking a question, or agreeing to the order. Lily could sense the confusion and asked Molly to please bring another one of the drinks.

Halfway through their meal, Lily looked across the table and realized she was glimpsing a much different Evelyn than the one she had known just days earlier. This one seemed to be grasping for pieces of her soul that had been buried under the weight of the moon her whole life. Lily could tell it was a struggle for her, but that she was trying—dipping one toe at a time into the cold water.

"I hope you're enjoying your lunch," Evelyn said.

"It's excellent, thank you," Lily responded. "You haven't mentioned if you like the flirtini."

"It tastes like spicy punch," Evelyn replied. "I'm afraid I'm enjoying it. By the way, what would you say to a nice manicure this afternoon?

"I can always use a manicure, Evelyn. But don't we need an appointment?"

"We have one, actually. I scheduled us with Jen at three

o'clock. I'm sorry—I don't know where my head's gone lately. I should have informed you of this long ago, but I'm so glad you're up for it!"

Their plates were ladylike-level empty when Molly stopped by the table to run down the dessert specials and offer refills on drinks. Lily politely declined for both of them, aware that they didn't have much time before their salon appointment, and knowing full well that one of them would have to be able to drive. Evelyn seemed slightly disappointed, as if she were unjustly abandoning the sticky-sweet martini glass parked on the table.

The girls paraded back to their car with perhaps even more swagger than they had exhibited earlier, thanks in part to the modest dose of vodka and champagne enjoyed at lunch.

They arrived a little early for their manicures and were rewarded for their promptness by Jen, who informed Evelyn that due to a last minute cancellation, she now had the time to offer mini pedicures as well. This sat very nicely with Evelyn, who'd gone a week and a half since her last appointment, and simply adored Jen's talent with toes.

Jen, who was close in age to Lily, was a very friendly and inquisitive type, and seemed anxious to get to know her new client. Lily attempted to fill her in on the particulars of her life while Jen shaped and polished her nails. Evelyn, who was seated at the unoccupied pedicure station next to Lily, eagerly added what she knew about the young Hanover, as if she were her press agent. She had most of the details wrong of course, but it made Lily feel warm that Evelyn cared enough about her to want to boast of their relationship. She guessed this was how mothers talked of their daughters when they were showing them off. It was a different type of compassion than Lily was used to, or had ever experienced.

After her manicure, Lily watched Jen deftly polish Evelyn's toes. She had seen plenty of fancifully coated toes before, especially amongst the girls she worked with, but nothing as cleverly crafted as the miniature works of art Jen was fashioning across Evelyn's feet. All ten of her nails were treated to a thick, glossy, blushing pink base, carefully applied to avoid contact with any adjacent skin. The big nails were indulged as if they were tiny canvases, each a peerless creation of faultless white polka dots dancing amid a backdrop of miniature silvery rhinestones. Lily admired the work, praising Jen even before she had finished.

When it was Lily's turn for her pedicure, Jen asked if there was any special design she had in mind. Since Lily hadn't anticipated this opportunity, she asked if there was a menu of sorts from which to make her selection. Evelyn giggled politely in the background. She, of course, was very familiar with Jen's imaginative and resourceful abilities, and knew there was no purpose for any such chart. Jen promised Lily she would attempt any pattern or motif, as long as it could fit on a toenail.

Lily gave it a moment's thought and then asked if she could have tulips. As Jen created truthful representations of the flowers on Lily's toes, she asked if they had any special meaning. Lily considered the question while gazing at the soft-hued flowers taking form, and then compliantly and meekly nodded. She told Jen that they were something she had back in California, and that she was starting to miss them.

Evelyn leaned over for a first peek at Lily's toes as soon as Jen had finished. She was very impressed and considered aloud that she may want the same design on one of her future visits.

The girls thanked Jen once again for her artistic efforts and then tottered to the car, careful not to damage their newly minted adornments.

•••

Minutes after they arrived home, Evelyn begged Lily to follow her into the living room. She led the young Hanover to the mahogany, serpentine shaped bar and asked her, in a somewhat earnest voice, if she could recall the ingredients of the cocktail they drank earlier in the day.

"Ah, the flirtini," Lily said. "I think I remember, Evelyn. I'm pretty sure it's made with lime juice, pineapple juice, raspberry vodka, and champagne."

"I see," Evelyn responded, twisted lines of befuddlement

stretched across her brow. Bent at the waist, she glared at the modestly stocked shelves of the bar.

"Would you like *me* to check?" Lily asked.

"I'm pretty sure we can't make a flirtini," Evelyn replied. "Most of these bottles seem to be Sidney's Scotch. Look at this, Lily—I bet he can't even pronounce the names on these labels. They probably dream up these awful sounding brands just to keep us women away. I wouldn't touch any of this—would you?"

Lily leaned in to see bottles of Bruichladdich, Auchentoshan, and Ardbeg Uiqeadail, among others.

"Look Evelyn," Lily said, reaching deeper into the bar, "you do have raspberry vodka—and there's a bottle of Hypnotiq as well!"

Lily was explaining the tropical fruit yumminess of this turquoise potion to Evelyn, when Sidney entered the room.

"And how was your day, ladies?" he shouted.

Evelyn was a little jarred that her husband chose this moment to arrive home from work, quickly stepping away from the bar.

"We've had a wonderful day, Sidney," Lily responded. "Look!" she continued, stretching her uncovered feet toward him until his eyes rested on her toes.

Evelyn made the same gesture with her feet, and Sidney reacted as if it were the first time he had seen her with freshly polished nails.

"Those are spectacular!" he exclaimed to both Evelyn and Lily. "So, it looks like we're about to have a little drink! I believe I'll have a sliver of Scotch."

As Sidney reached for a bottle, Lily filled two tumblers with ice, pouring a generous dose of Hypnotiq for Evelyn, and filling her own glass with raspberry vodka and soda water.

Everyone crowded into the den, beverages in hand. Evelyn poked Lily, and then asked Sidney what type of Scotch he was drinking. He responded without hesitation: "Highland Park—thirty years old." Evelyn shrugged, disappointed that Sidney hadn't selected the Ardbeg Uiqeadail.

Everyone had become quite relaxed as the glasses and the

conversation lightened. Lily was particularly happy and comfortable, which was not an unusual condition for her.

•••

The girl with the perpetual smile never seemed to be having a down time. But to those who were familiar with her life story, it was difficult to believe that her persistent happiness was real. Analyzed from a distance, her years appeared to be pocked with woe, her prospects for a contented life, meager.

Lily wasn't quite an orphan, nor had she been abandoned, at least not technically. She was dislodged as an infant, sent by her parents to live in another place, in a different state. They provided money and as much emotional support as could be expected from a remote ATM, but wanted nothing to do with her. They disassociated themselves as much as they could from their own creation—their own blood. This would have been enough of a blow to affect a permanent mark on most any child's psyche.

Beyond that trauma, the young girl lost her great aunt Rose, her stand-in parent figure, when she was only thirteen. She lost her home as well with her aunt's passing and was forced to spend her critical teenage years in a boarding school, alone but for the schoolmates she counted as family. Lily led a life on the run without ever going anywhere, a life that never aligned with any of her classmates or acquaintances—a life void of many things.

After school, Lily chose a career in a field popularly considered demeaning and desperate. But for Lily, it was fun, rewarding, and made her happy—very happy. She was happy that she could do and say and feel what she wanted. She was happy to be on her own, even though she always had been. Nobody was going to try and guide her life, tell her what to do or what not to do. She breathed the essence of liberty when she removed her clothes and lived and loved. She had an appreciation for this freedom that she was certain others could never understand, and she did not care if they ever did.

But Lily never really loved. There were lovers, and there

were loved ones—but never anyone she could call her own. It was the only thing missing, yet she did not seem to care. She was happy, and as far as she could tell, she always would be.

•••

The sun was low on the horizon and Evelyn, Sidney, and Lily wrestled against the booze-fueled languor filling the room. The alcohol had taken them to a good place, but they weren't ready to call it a day.

Lily reached for the antique glass serving dish and grabbed a handful of roasted cashews, hoping the carbs and protein might give her a lift. She had sat back on the couch, her fingers gritty from the salt and oily from the nuts, when a swirl of fading colors swaying outside the den window caught her eye.

"Sidney," Lily said, "I know I'm a bit drunk, but I'm pretty sure there's something moving in the back yard."

"You're right," Sidney replied, peering out the window while draining his glass. "It looks like giant marbles rolling about the yard."

It was difficult for Evelyn to lift herself from the couch, but with a little effort she managed to wind her way to her husband, latch on to his right arm, and peer through the open wooden shutters. "They're not marbles, Sidney. They're beach balls, floating in our pool."

"Oh, I can see that now," Lily said, standing behind the Banks and stretching for a look. "I don't remember those being there before."

"Our pool service must have been here today," Evelyn said, trying to remember what day of the week it was. "I ordered those balls three weeks ago from their shop. I thought they were so pretty when I saw them. They promised to blow them up for me."

"Well, you certainly weren't shortchanged darling," Sidney responded. "There must be twenty balls floating out there."

"Let's go swimming!" Lily exclaimed, suddenly energized.

"It's dark out there Lily," Evelyn commented. And Lena's is dropping off dinner in half an hour…at least I think I ordered it—ha!"

"Perfect!" the young Hanover shouted. "I just want to get wet—let's go!"

"You go have a good time, dear," Evelyn responded. "Sidney and I will be right here."

Lily frowned and then skipped to her room to change. Sidney spent the next five minutes sulking, trying to convince his wife that it would be a fun time to swim. As he pleaded his case, the muffled sounds of Lily chirping wildly and splashing about rang bright in the background.

Sidney continued acting like a child whose parents forbid him from ever having any fun. Evelyn knew they would both be miserable until he got his way, and so encouraged him to join their guest. She announced that she would stay in the house awaiting the arrival of dinner, and that perhaps she'd enjoy just one more cocktail in the meantime. This clumsy attempt at luring her husband back to the couch was, however, unsuccessful. He quickly flittered out of the room.

Sidney rushed to put on his swim trunks, and in short order was standing at one end of his large rectangular pool, privately assessing the landscaped acreage he so infrequently enjoyed. He absorbed all he could in the darkness, through the faint shadows that danced atop the forty by twenty foot span of shimmering water. The arrow-straight line of the pool ran parallel to the house, mere feet from the covered back patio. Alongside, a quartet of thickly cushioned lounge chairs sat stoically atop ample amounts of richly marbled travertine decking. At the far edge of the deck, orchestrated lines of mature Queen Palm trees hovered like soldiers on duty and skirted deep into the yard.

Somewhere amongst the sea of colorfully striped, surprisingly elegant spheres drifting across the choppy water, Lily was splashing about, making playful sounds. Sidney had a hard time distinguishing anything as he scoured the bouncing waves. He looked eagerly for telltale signs of the girl. Lily watched this struggle from the far end of the pool and chirped out his name coyly, beckoning him to join her.

After a self-conscious jump into the obligingly warm water, Sidney fought through the drifting armada of beach balls until he finally reached her. She was facing away from him, holding on to the edge of the deck with her fingertips, her feet barely grazing the floor of the pool as she attempted to gain a foothold.

Sidney approached from behind, contemplating a playful gesture to initiate their exchange. He first thought of bouncing one of the inflated balls off the back of Lily's head and grabbing her attention with the surprise blow, but then realized he was not drunk enough to pull off such an immature stunt. He *was,* however, intoxicated enough to do something only slightly more responsible, and so he stealthily advanced from behind and looped his arms low around her waist. He hoped to catch her off guard and perhaps elicit a modest squeal from the unexpected surprise.

Sidney had considered grabbing Lily slightly higher, but understood the perils of this move. He was well aware of the general span of her breasts, and so consciously grabbed lower to avoid even glancing contact with the ample globes. He didn't want to do anything improper; he just wanted to have some fun.

Somehow, Sidney managed to avoid Lily's bobbing assets as he gave her a start, and he relished his puerile achievement for a fleeting moment. His glee unexpectedly gave way to mortification however, when he realized he was fondling the unclothed body of his best friend's daughter.

Sidney thought he had carefully weighed the risks associated with his mildly mischievous approach, but this was one snag he had never considered. This was something that happened to James Bond, not Sidney Banks. Sidney had never even seen Evelyn in the pool without a suit, positive the idea had never crossed her mind.

It was a very awkward moment for Sidney. He hadn't just tapped the girl's hips, which would have been the most innocent of moves. Instead, he had wrapped his arms around her torso from behind, and as she squirmed from the surprise, his hands pressed hard into her flesh, far below her navel. He had briefly rubbed across her opening, the telltale feel of her slit spread beneath his blind fingers. This was not what Sidney had in mind. He had yet to try this move with his wife of thirty years. He hadn't even *thought* of trying this with his wife. His mind was numb, unprepared, and unable to react.

Trapped by the gathering cluster of beach balls behind him,

Sidney attempted to stand, his feet unstable on the plaster beneath the deep water. He squeaked out an apology to Lily, who had turned to face him.

"I never found a suit at the mall, remember?" Lily replied, in a half giggle voice.

Although Sidney could not clearly distinguish her form below the dark and undulating water, it didn't stop his mind from evaluating the vague shapes flickering before him. He tried very hard to disregard the images and found himself looking up at the evening sky.

"What a fantastic evening for a dip," he announced, his words clipped as if he were enveloped by ice water.

Wanting to put a little more space between them, Sidney pushed away with his feet and slowly started drifting backward into the huddle of beach balls. Lily floated toward him, her naked ass breaking the water's surface.

"Please don't feel bad, Sidney," Lily said softly. "I kind of liked what you did. It felt good."

"I didn't mean to…you know," Sidney replied, staring at her approaching face. "I just wanted to grab your, um…"

"My what, Sidney?" Lily asked, her smile widening.

"I was just going to grab you around the waist—that's all."

"Like this?" Lily reached for Sidney's midsection and pulled herself on top of him. "Sidney, you have a pretty nice body. It's very hard."

"Yes, well, Evelyn likes it that way," he responded, not even sure what he was saying.

"I bet she does," Lily snickered as she pushed away, rubbing the front of Sidney's trunks as she escaped.

Sidney wasn't certain what to think, or how to properly respond. His mind wasn't able to react, but his body could. The stirrings of arousal charged his groin when he grasped at Lily's skin. Now his erection pressed angrily against the nylon material of his suit, seeking freedom.

His eyes fixed on the girl as she swam back to the edge of the pool nearest the house. Her silhouette was much more defined when she was this close to the surface, and it was difficult for him to look away. He chose to remain in place though, hoping the distance and the darkness would shield his condition.

There was a sudden explosion of light when the bright bulbs fixed in the walls at each end of the pool lurched on. The body of water suddenly became a luminous island in the otherwise dark yard. Lily showed no reaction to this abrupt transformation, but Sidney became the proverbial deer caught in the headlights. He assumed Evelyn had used the remote light switch mounted in the kitchen by the patio door, and that she would be poolside shortly.

With the lights brightening the water, it was easy for Sidney to see much more than Lily's shadowy silhouette. He hated these moments, though they existed rarely in his shielded life, where he had to choose quickly between the right thing and the pleasurable thing to do. He compromised, lowering himself deep below the surface for an innocent look at Lily from behind. She was facing away from him, holding on to the deck with her hands, kicking her legs slowly back and forth.

Sidney snapped as many mental photographs as he could before his lungs let him down and he needed to breathe. He damned himself for releasing his personal trainer a year earlier. The man had insisted that Sidney commit to more aerobic exercise, and Sidney dismissed the concept as unmanly. He promised himself he would re-enlist the man's services first thing in the morning.

When he surfaced for air, he watched his wife take a seat on the edge of one of the cushiony lounge chairs, close to the water. Sidney was concerned that she had changed her mind and now was ready for a swim. She apparently wasn't wearing a bathing suit, but he feared the pair of shorts and scooped-neck tee she had slipped on was serving as a cover-up for swimwear lurking beneath. If she jumped in the pool now, he was pretty sure his life would never be the same.

From his perspective, Sidney was confident Evelyn couldn't observe Lily's lack of attire. The girl was flush against the wall of the pool, close to where Evelyn was sitting. Sidney, who was bobbing up and down in no-man's-land, wrapped his arms around a passing beach ball to conceal his state of arousal.

"How's the water?" Evelyn yelled, as if they were at a rock concert.

"It's great, Evelyn!" Lily responded. "Why don't you join us?"

"She's not wearing a bathing suit!" Sidney quickly rejoined. He then realized Evelyn may have thought he was talking to her instead of Lily, and he added, "Evelyn's not wearing a bathing suit!"

Both Lily and Evelyn shot him a curious look.

"Someone's has to listen for the door—Lena's catering is on their way," Evelyn slurred, lying back onto the chaise.

"Evelyn, did you have an extra drink while we've been out here, you naughty girl?" Lily asked slyly.

"Maybe I did!" Evelyn answered as she stared at the cloudless sky. "That's the bell! Sidney, go answer please—I don't wanna move."

Lily turned toward Sidney, her bright smile and bouncing breasts both daring him to leave the sanctuary of the pool. Evelyn was spread out on the chair, not attempting to move, and Sidney could hear the faint rapping growing stronger at the front door. He knew the caterer would stand there all night if he had to. With all the business he had given Lena's over the years, he thought they might be considerate enough just once to set the food by the door and send him a bill. But their delivery man had the patience of an hour glass; after all, a tip was forthcoming.

Sidney closed his eyes and tried desperately to focus on anything but the naked beauty five feet away. If he were to attempt to leave the water, he would need to rapidly shrink his robust baton, or deal with the unexplainable awkwardness of his inflated state. Even if he managed to conceal his waxing trunks and escape the scrutiny of the female onlookers, he still had to answer the door and face the jolly caterer. He was sure his situation would induce a pleased look on the man's face.

Sidney's mind twirled about, seeking images of sports stadiums and dirty restrooms. For some reason, he started contemplating soap. He wondered how people could tell if soap were clean or dirty. When a person rubbed a bar of soap across their rear end, could they safely use that bar for something less superficial, like their face? How could you clean soap? And how would you be sure it was clean? Should he ever use soap again?

This conundrum perplexed Sidney to the extent that he

quickly lost his rigidness and was able to exit the pool and answer the door in a dignified manner.

After a few minutes, Evelyn went in the house to check on Sidney. Lily used the disruption to towel herself dry and dress quickly.

Following a dinner of spit roasted chicken, carrot soufflé, and a garden salad (Evelyn was still too concerned about her weight to have requested potatoes, or a dessert), Lily announced that she would be showering and going to bed. Evelyn claimed she was tired as well and left Sidney to himself in the den.

Chapter Sixteen

Sidney fixed himself an after-dinner Scotch with the hope of unclenching his knotted gut. He had unintentionally wandered through the gates of the cruelest of amusement parks and was now on some sort of sadistic, sexual roller coaster. The crest of the hill was always in sight, but the release of the train would never come.

Evelyn had been gone about twenty minutes, but Sidney was confident that she had yet to fall asleep. Although it wasn't his birthday or any other such milestone day in his life, Sidney was desperate, and decided to make a move on his wife. She had loosened up in so many ways; having more sex had to be somewhere down the list.

Ever since Lily had arrived, Evelyn was more open to almost everything. She was still a traditional woman at heart though, and Sidney, Scotch in hand and several more in his belly, realized she was probably just waiting for him to ask. He wasn't sure why he hadn't thought of this before. He had danced around the subject enough—he just hadn't been direct enough.

Tossing the balance of his drink and remaining withered, glassy ice cubes down his throat—to keep the flavor and his nerve going—Sidney made his way to the bedroom. He opened the door, expecting to find his wife flossing her teeth or removing makeup. Instead, he found her sitting in the large marble bathtub at one end of the sprawling suite, her head bowed toward her chest.

Evelyn didn't react to Sidney's approach as she was facing away from him, somewhat deafened by the noisy trickle of water splashing into the tub. The drain was not closed, and so the water's accumulation wasn't much more than a shallow puddle. Sidney hurried toward his wife, thinking something might be wrong.

When he reached her, she was sitting with her back against the end of the tub, her legs extended and slightly spread. She was holding a small pair of scissors in her right hand and appeared to be quite focused on some sort of task.

Sidney looked down at his naked wife, unable to determine what she was up to. Evelyn didn't appear terribly surprised at the presence of her husband, but she flinched a little when she first noticed him hovering by the tub.

"What are you doing?" Sidney asked, even though he now had a pretty good idea.

"I'm mowing the lawn, or something like that," Evelyn responded, continuing to labor on her tufted mound.

Since he wasn't shooed away, Sidney watched, mesmerized, as his wife carefully trimmed close to the skin. When she was finally done with the scissors, she reached for the multi-bladed razor she had used at one time on her legs but had abandoned when she had the annoying hair permanently removed via laser treatments.

Lathering her private vestibule with a modest amount of soap and water, she continued the grooming process, narrowing what had been a wide expanse of brown curls, into a thin ribbon of fuzz.

Evelyn stood when she was finished, leaving a jungle of ringlets to rinse slowly down the drain. She stepped out of the tub, and, using a face towel, leisurely dried and organized her re-fashioned front yard.

Sidney hadn't moved more than a foot since he had approached his wife. He had also remained silent, not wanting to disrupt the seductive theater he had been thoroughly enjoying. He wanted to take his wife right there, on the floor by the tub.

He remembered what he had considered earlier while nursing his drink, about being more direct with his wife regarding sex. Even though Evelyn had been shamelessly luring him into her web with provocative behavior for the last fifteen minutes, Sidney did not want to take any chances. He reminded himself that he needed to be more direct.

"Evelyn darling, you impress me more and more every day."

"Well Sidney," Evelyn replied, "I have all this new underwear that Lily insisted I purchase. There's so little fabric, I had to do something."

"I think it's wonderful!" Sidney exclaimed. "I have always found you incredibly attractive, my dear. You have just one-upped yourself!"

Sidney was lost in his wife's enhanced beauty, his words, and the Scotch. He clumsily removed all his clothes, presenting Evelyn with an obvious offer.

"Sidney!" Evelyn shouted. "I'm not sure what did this to you, but I think you should put that away right now."

Sidney couldn't remember if he had formally asked his wife to have sex, which was his original intention. He assumed he had not; therefore, the barefaced snub.

"My dear," he started, "I would very much like to make love to you right now…what do you think?"

"I think I just had my nails done, Sidney," Evelyn replied. "I'm not sure they're quite dry."

Sidney tried to establish, to no avail, how many hours it had been since his wife's manicure. He had listened to this excuse many years earlier and had written it off at the time as a standard female defense against male predators.

"That was this afternoon, darling," Sidney pleaded. "You've already done so much since then that could have ruined your nails. I promise you won't have to use your hands."

"Sidney, don't be silly. It's not just my hands—it's my toes too! Didn't I show you? Now, I promise sometime soon we'll make arrangements. Be sweet, okay?"

There wasn't much Sidney could do to plead his case further. His wife wasn't in a negotiating mood as usual, but she did offer a glimmer of hope for a future rendezvous. He hated to endanger this possibility by starting to badger her now.

Standing naked in the room, Sidney watched his wife slip on a pair of her new panties and pose at all angles in front of the full-length mirror. He noticed that the small piece of striped fabric fronting the kerchief-sized lingerie covered only her essentials, while the thread running up the back had seemingly vanished, devoured by her pleasantly shaped cheeks.

Evelyn didn't seem to be paying any attention to Sidney, or his thoroughly engorged appendage, as he soaked in her new degree of sensuality. He had been jolted by so much sexual energy recently, and he wasn't sure how much more he could absorb. He was very close to wrapping his fist around himself and taking care of his own release. It would have been the first time in a long time, but he just couldn't do it. No matter how much he needed this, he would just have to wait.

•••

Sidney Banks was not a spoiled child, even though he was raised in an affluent neighborhood in Towson, Maryland by two loving and doting parents. His father owned a medium sized company that brokered food purchases for the federal government. His mother was a devoted volunteer, spending much of her time raising money for various charitable organizations.

Sidney's parents could have easily afforded to send him to private school, but chose instead to send their only offspring to a close-by public school. They wanted him to have as normal a life as possible.

His life *was* pretty normal. He had lots of friends he could count on for a spontaneous game of catch or an afternoon at the movies. He loved flying balsa-wood planes in the summer and having snowball fights in the winter. He was a pretty good student, and he generally made his parents proud.

When Sidney was about thirteen, he started noticing girls. He had always had friends who were girls, most of whom lived in his neighborhood. They would play tag and run around the block together. He even became proficient at jacks, having been taught and encouraged by one of his girlfriends. The girls that he knew always seemed to like him. He liked them too—but never thought of them as anything more than silly girls.

As he entered his teen years however, he started to appreciate them as more than something silly. He thought of girls all the time when he was at school—the way they'd cross their legs under their desks, or the way they'd stroll up to the blackboard to chalk in an arithmetic answer, their full, round behinds shifting back and forth with each step.

His buddies would always speak of girls as if they had personal knowledge. Of course, none of them did, but their graphic misrepresentations only served to advance Sidney's interest.

Sidney would lie awake in bed, thinking of the neighborhood girls who he had once been able to call for a quick game of four square, but who now avoided him as much as he feared them. These girls, as well as the girls at school, constantly bounded about his head, wreaking havoc with his mind and his clean pajamas.

On Sidney's fourteenth birthday, his father surprised him by taking him on an adventure—just the two of them. This wouldn't have been anything extraordinary, but Saturdays were usually reserved for activities that had been planned well ahead, usually by Sidney's mom.

His dad had been acting squirrelly all that morning, and right after lunch asked Sidney if he'd run an errand with him. He drove his son to the local sporting goods shop, where he presented him with his first surprise of the day—a shiny new Ebonite bowling ball. He hadn't brought the gift home earlier, as the store manager had promised to custom fit the ball for Sidney and drill the three finger holes while he waited.

After leaving the store, his father took Sidney straight to the alleys to test out his new gift. Sidney could sense the difference immediately between his new ball and the worn lane balls he normally used. He rolled a strike in his very first practice frame in fact, and went on to beat his usual score by twenty pins in the first game.

His father had started to write their names on the score sheet for game two, when Sidney noticed the lane next to theirs awakening abruptly—the dark cave at the end of the alley filling with a dazzling spark of light.

Three people arrived shortly after the lane was illuminated, sat bluntly on the bench behind the scorer's table, and began lacing up their bowling shoes. To Sidney, they appeared to be a husband and wife about the same age as his parents. The girl with them, he guessed, was their high school age daughter. His dad didn't seem to know the couple, since he only greeted them with a mechanical "hello there."

Sidney completed his first frame of the new game and then traded places with his father at the scorer's seat. He looked over toward the next lane and watched as the high school girl prepared for her first practice roll. Before she snatched her ball from the return, she casually removed the thin white cardigan she had been wearing. It was then that Sidney really took notice of her.

What caught his eye first was that she was wearing shorts. This wasn't something that Sidney was prepared for. The only girls he ever knew to wear shorts were the little kids in his neighborhood. The girls in his school were forbidden to wear them, and beyond that, they just weren't very popular—at least among the older girls.

The shorts this girl flaunted were spellbinding to Sidney. They were black and made from some sort of stretchy material. The dark color was striking against the girl's milky skin and the fabric hugged her pert figure perfectly, almost giving everything away.

It was a long while before Sidney's eyes made their way up her body to soak in the splendor of her full pointy breasts, toothy smile, and shimmery blond hair—done up in a bob and perfectly framing her scrubbed face.

Sidney wasn't able to garble one word to the girl, as she was far more advanced and sophisticated than him, a lowly eighth grader. Distressingly, his confidence with all girls had left him once he realized how special they were. He didn't do anything to improve his odds with this one either, feigning total disinterest anytime she shot a look his way. His father, who also seemed to be aware that the girl was something special, kept signaling Sidney with raised eyebrow winks whenever the girl would step onto the lane. Sidney just acted annoyed and played it off with a shrug.

In spite of his casualness, Sidney was smitten and memorized every inch of her from head to toe.

After Sidney and his dad had finished with their games, they sat on the bench and changed back into their street shoes. The girl and her parents were still bowling, and Sidney looked up to grab one last stare at the magical shorts.

On the ride home from the lanes, Sidney's father tried to make small talk about the girl, but Sidney dismissed her significance and changed the subject to baseball. He didn't want his precious image of her to be tarnished by any goofy comments or advice his dad was about to provide.

Sidney's mom greeted her husband and son when they arrived at the house. She wished Sidney a happy birthday for about the fifteenth time, asked about the bowling, and then reminded him that today he was welcome to have his cake before dinner. It had been a long-standing Banks' tradition to allow the birthday celebrant to have an early slice of cake, and she knew this was one of Sidney's favorite things.

His mother explained that the cake wasn't quite ready however, and asked if Sidney could occupy himself in his room for about an hour. She promised to call for him when it was iced. She went on to say that he was not allowed to hang out in the kitchen—it was going to be a special cake, and she didn't want Sidney to see or smell it until it was ready.

Sidney didn't have a problem with this, certain that if he were spending time with his parents, his dad would surely bring up the cute girl from the bowling alley and his mom would start asking all sorts of embarrassing questions. He trotted up the stairs taking them two at a time and then paced to his room at the end of the hall.

Grabbing a handful of comic books from the top of his dresser, Sidney dove onto his bed and spread them out to see what he had. He chose one of his favorites: a dog-eared copy of an old Superman issue. Although he'd read most of his comics dozens of times, he enjoyed flipping through them, looking for favorite parts or neat action drawings.

He skimmed through the book, stopping on a page that featured Superman's alter ego, Clark Kent. In several of the panels, Clark was having a lively conversation with one of his female co-workers, Lois Lane. Sidney knew that Clark really liked Lois, but because he could never reveal his true identity to her, their relationship always seemed to sputter and never quite got off the ground.

Sidney understood Clark's frustration better than anyone. Getting close to a girl seemed like an insurmountable task to him, as it was for Clark. This reflection lifted Sidney's mind away from the page and soon he was back at the bowling alley, watching the pretty blonde hoist her ball and saunter slowly down the alley.

Dropping the comic book to his side, Sidney leaned back on his bed, closed his eyes, and conjured every image he had in his head of the high school beauty. He focused intently on the girl as she slowly peeled her black shorts down and away from her creamy thighs. Then, flashing a coy, sideways look, she lifted her blouse over her head, mussed her hair slightly, and exposed her hard, white bra with its complicated straps.

She picked up her bowling ball again, held it tight under her chin with both hands, and turned toward the white pins at the end of the lane. But this time, she wore only her yielding white underwear and stiff bra. In slow motion, she moved toward the pins while extending her right arm back, the ball grasped firmly by her fingers. Approaching the line, she stretched her muscular legs and dipped low, the back of her left leg snug against her soft behind.

Sidney opened his eyes and checked the door to his room, making certain it was closed. He slid his pants below his knees, and his underwear followed. He had learned by now to remove his shirt as well, which he tossed to the floor by his bed. His erection pointed at his chest, and he was ready to resume his mental defiling of the girl.

For the past several months, this had become almost a daily ritual for Sidney. After school, before school, weekends—it didn't matter. This was his own personal fun time, a time to invoke all the fantasies that plugged his head. There was never a downside to the adventure. His only regret was that he hadn't discovered this pleasure sooner.

He started slowly, his thumb and forefinger working their way up and down, over and over. He pictured the girl removing her bra now, her pointy breasts jiggling in response to their freedom. She walked toward him, her thumbs at her hips making their way inside the stretchy edges of her underwear, tugging them down unhurriedly.

Sidney used more fingers and more pressure. His pace quickened with the imminent revelation of her secret patch of softness. She stood bare in front of him, beckoning him to pleasure her. He was not going to deny her this pleasure. His hands reached for her chest, and she moved in close with her lips spread and eyes closed. She started tapping loudly on his chest, begging for him to enter her. She tapped again and again, asking if it was okay. He shouted "yes!" as he neared his climax.

The door to Sidney's room opened with a swift force, rousing him abruptly from his purposeful daydream. His friends and his parents had been gathering in the hallway outside his room, and now all of them struggled for a peek at the birthday boy. Jamming hurriedly into his room, they shouted in unison: "Surprise!"

Marcy Corman, Sidney's old playmate from down the block, was the first one to scream. There were two other girls who had squeezed into the room who instantly reversed course, pushing others out of their way in order to leave the site as quickly as possible.

Five of the six boys that surrounded Sidney's bed stood dumbfounded and red-faced, eager to reveal their incredulousness that someone could be doing such a thing. The other one just stared curiously. If Sidney's parents hadn't been standing next to them, they would have certainly shared a different, more vocal response.

As soon as Sidney's mother and father could gather their thoughts, they ushered the remaining boys from the room, following close behind.

Sidney was still undressed and still reclining in his bed. His once proud member had shriveled considerably, and as he looked at its bashful profile, he cursed its power and his own pitiful lack of restraint.

His guests had all left the house by the time Sidney had himself together enough to leave his room. He was sure his parents had quietly encouraged them out the door, imparting to each a word of advice about joining the inevitable gossip mill.

The backlash wasn't as severe as Sidney had anticipated. There were the expected ribbings from his friends, most of whom seemed almost as embarrassed over the incident as Sidney was. The girls went back to ignoring him, but eventually found his daring background and risky personality fascinating as college approached. His parents treated the episode as if it had never happened.

If anything, Sidney gained strength from the experience. His resolve never to be caught in that situation again was only the beginning, and he was determined from that point forward to focus only on the important matters in his life. Frivolity and self-indulgence would have to wait.

Chapter Seventeen

"Lily dear," Evelyn called across the table, "I wonder if I could ask a special favor of you. I hate to impose—I really do."

Lily watched Evelyn stab at a piece of yellowfin and drag it around her plate trying to absorb the last of the balsamic vinaigrette. She couldn't recall having seafood for lunch four days in a row and was thoroughly enjoying the run.

"Anything for you, Evelyn!" Lily chirped after swallowing a forkful of calamari salad.

"Would you be open to preparing dinner for tonight?" Evelyn asked meekly.

"Of course!" Lily replied. "I'd be happy to make something. What did you have in mind?"

"Well, I'm thinking maybe another of your special Italian dishes. You know—with the distinctive sauce."

Lily leaned in and whispered, "Do you want some more pot?"

"I really enjoyed it," Evelyn murmured back. "It reminds me of your mother."

"Oh, I see," Lily said. "It reminds me of her too."

"I hate for you to bother, Lily. It's just that I'm afraid I don't know how to prepare it properly."

"I'm happy to make dinner tonight, Evelyn. You do know though that we don't have to eat it."

"Of course we need to eat it dear," Evelyn responded. "Sidney would just die if we didn't have dinner."

"I wasn't referring to dinner," Lily said in a hushed voice. "I was talking about the marijuana. Let me make dinner tonight—but I'll fix whatever you'd like. We don't have to have Italian."

The girls drove straight to the market after lunch, where they made an adventure out of piecing together their evening meal. Lily scanned the aisles carefully, making sure to select something yummy and sweet for dessert.

When they got home, Evelyn started assembling the chicken and steak kabobs, while Lily went to work on the side dish: couscous with apples, cranberries, and herbs.

They joined forces on dessert, mixing and baking up a seductive storm of fist-sized, sugary sensations. Even before the chocolate ganache cupcakes were pulled from the oven, a warm cocoa aroma had begun to drift ponderously through the house, like a Ghirardelli fog.

Sidney arrived home empty-handed, disappointing Evelyn who had hoped he would walk through the door carting an armful of wine bottles. She was concerned that they were running low on the “flavors” she liked, but Sidney promptly assured her that he would find something in the bar that would work.

Dinner was served a little earlier than usual. Once Sidney had gulped the intoxicating scents of grilling meats and freshly baked cake, he instantly pleaded starvation. Evelyn and Lily hurried through the rest of their preparations, while Sidney tracked down two bottles of Seghesio old vine Zinfandel from the living room.

The three diners retired to the den after their meal, relaxed and full. Sidney commented that the home-cooked dinner was so wonderful he could finally justify the fifty thousand dollars he had spent on kitchen appliances. He looked over at Evelyn, who was oblivious.

While Sidney tried to explain to Evelyn in more direct terms how much he appreciated her cooking, Lily reached in her handbag, pulled out her parents black stone pipe, and loaded it with a pinch of their stash.

Evelyn and Sidney stopped their high-pitched blathering when they heard the spark of a lighter and caught a wave of butane spanking their nostrils. They turned to see Lily toking hard on a small black piece of stone, sucking a cloud of smoke deep into her rising chest. They gawked at the girl, waiting for her to release the white haze back into the room. When she did, she looked over at Evelyn and Sidney with moist, glassy eyes, and handed the pipe their way.

Sidney reached for it, brought it toward his mouth, and attempted to replicate what he had just witnessed. He sucked deep and held his breath as if he were Houdini, shackled inside a vertical coffin of water.

Lily giggled as she watched Sidney struggle to retain the non-existent smoke.

"You might want to light it first," she said, her laugh dying short. "Here." She hefted Iris and George's gold lighter, passed it, and studied Sidney as he sucked the flame down into the pipe.

This time, he managed to swallow a chest full of smoke, but could only hold it in for a second.

"Wow!" was all Sidney could say. His hands were on his knees and he was sitting up, a damp shroud of queasiness worming up his face.

"Are you okay, Sidney?" Lily asked, moving closer to him.

"Um…I'm great! I think I'm great!"

"Okay then, its Evelyn's turn," Lily said, shifting direction. "Wait—let me put a little more in the bowl."

Evelyn slithered back into the corner of the couch when she saw Lily turn to grab another bud. In her mind, Lily was suddenly an unnerving doctor clutching a giant hypodermic.

"I'm not sure how to do this." Evelyn swallowed hard, as Lily handed her the pipe.

"Let me start it for you," Lily offered.

Lily ignited the weed and then passed the warm, black pipe to Evelyn, who feigned a modest inhale. It was pretty obvious to Lily and Sidney, who had been staring at the wisp of smoke hovering over the bowl, that the pot wasn't being pushed or pulled anywhere.

Lily asked Evelyn to hand her the pipe. She then instructed her to breathe out all the way, and hold it. Lily quickly fired up the grass and stuck the slab of black stone back into Evelyn's mouth. The trick worked, and Evelyn was soon overwhelmed by the concentration of thick smoke inhabiting her lungs. She exhaled swiftly, shooting an opaque cloud of elixir deep into the room—along with a burning ember of weed from the pipe.

Sidney jumped from his seat, searching for the fiery missile that his wife had launched. He found it glowing atop the thick carpet by one of the end tables and quietly snuffed it out using a heavy, brushed silver candy dish that was close by.

Once the panicked group had settled, they resumed the rotation of smoking and passing the pipe. When it came back around to Evelyn, she passed, claiming her throat was too parched from her first puff. She picked herself up from the couch and announced that she was heading to the kitchen for a glass of water. She instantly realized that she had failed to offer beverages to Lily and Sidney and apologized for her absent-mindedness.

Sidney contemplated an after-dinner drink, and Lily asked if any wine were left from dinner.

"I think there might be one glass in the bottle," Sidney announced, jerked from his dream state.

"Wine sounds like a much better idea than water," Evelyn chimed in. "Good choice, Lily."

"Evelyn, I want you to have the wine. I don't need it—really."

"Nonsense, dear," Evelyn replied. "Sidney, please open another bottle of wine for us, would you?"

Sidney nodded, and then was seemingly gone forever. He eventually shuffled back into the den carrying three glasses and one bottle.

"We have Bordeaux," he announced, working the sharply pointed, coiled opener into the cork. "Chateau Branaire-Ducru."

"What are our other choices?" Evelyn pouted. "I'm thirsty, and I don't feel like sipping something. You always give me that look when I take big swallows of the fancy stuff."

"You're welcome to chug this wine, darling; we have nothing else to choose from. Don't worry though. We've got more of the same in the bar, and I promise to stop by the store tomorrow to get you a few bottles of whatever you want."

The Bordeaux seemed to lubricate Evelyn's stale throat well enough to overcome at least her physical resistance to more marijuana. She waved off the pipe, however, as it was coming her way for the fourth time. She was feeling very good about *almost* everything.

"I don't understand why you only buy a little bit of wine at a time, Sidney," Evelyn garbled. "A little baby bit—that's all you buy."

Sidney was surprised to hear his wife talking like this, but he assumed she was as stoned as he was, and that she didn't really know what she was saying.

"Wine needs to be stored properly, Evelyn," Sidney responded in a heavy voice. "If I were to buy cases of it, it would become tinted…I mean tainted, before it was drunk."

"Well then," Evelyn replied after a minute of silence, "you should get a storage unit. The Winkelman's down the block keep one in their back yard."

"They're remodeling their house, dear. They don't keep wine in that giant metal container."

"Then we should remodel our house too!" Evelyn exclaimed. "I think we need a bigger selection all the time, don't you Lily?"

"I think you should have what you want, Evelyn," Lily replied, hitting the pipe for the umpteenth time.

"Then it's settled," Evelyn said, literally putting her foot down. "Sidney, tomorrow I want you to get us a storage unit, or a container or whatever you want to call it."

"It's not like that," Sidney said in an admonishing tone. "People that keep a lot of wine in their homes have wine cellars. I guess technically it's a storage unit, but…"

"A wine cellar!" Evelyn said gleefully. "That sounds beautiful, doesn't it Lily? A wine cellar—I want you to buy us one of those tomorrow!"

Sidney spent the next thirty minutes explaining, or trying to explain to his wife, that a wine cellar is like a room addition, or a room conversion—not something best purchased at the mall. An intense dialogue ensued while Evelyn danced about the house in pursuit of the best location for her new cellar.

While Evelyn and Sidney were going back and forth regarding the potentially expensive remodel, Lily lumbered to the kitchen and spent twenty minutes arranging a half dozen chocolate ganache cupcakes onto a serving plate. She filled a tall pitcher with ice water, then spent another five minutes maneuvering the plate, the pitcher, and three water glasses back to the den.

"Cupcakes!" Lily screamed to the ceiling, unable to discern the whereabouts of the Banks and their muted squabbling.

Evelyn and Sidney came bounding into the den, like slow-footed dogs called to dinner. The cupcakes were eaten quickly, and the Banks sat back on the couch, heaving the sighs of efforts and yearnings fulfilled. An expression of plucky triumph flushed across Evelyn's face.

"Lily dear," Evelyn started, "guess what? Sidney has agreed to us having a wine cellar!"

"Don't be too excited Evelyn," Sidney murmured. "I'm pretty high. When I realize tomorrow what I've agreed to tonight, I'll probably change my mind. I mean, we're giving up our game room to accommodate your 'storage unit'."

"Sidney, it was never much of a game room," Evelyn countered. "The only game you ever played in there was the 'sneak one extra drink' game. You never even bought one of those pool tables, because the room was too small."

"There was only one time that I had an extra Scotch in that room, Evelyn," Sidney countered defensively. "But now I'll have a proper place to store my rare single malts, and I can have as many as I want—right dear?"

"C'mon everybody," Lily said, exhaling a visible mass of smoke. "Let's be cool. You're both going to get what you want. I think it's a fantastic idea."

"She's right, Evelyn," Sidney admitted. "But I want you to deal with it—and don't make it half wine cellar, half shoe closet. If we're going to do this, it needs to be done right."

•••

Two days later, the first contractor Evelyn had scheduled to bid on the wine cellar arrived. Evelyn wasn't home to deal with him however, having previously scheduled a lip and brow wax. Lily insisted Evelyn not miss her appointment and had volunteered to meet with the estimator, show him the space, and answer any questions she could.

Lily opened the door and found a very tall, young, athletic looking man with dark wavy hair and piercing brown eyes. He wore a white polo shirt embroidered with three interlocking Cs, stitched exactly where a pocket might have been. The letters, taken as such, stood for Creative Custom Cellars, the company's name. In his right hand the man held a brown, wooden clipboard clutching a fresh work form with a vice-like grip. His left hand rested on the handle of a small, rolling black case, similar to a weekender bag that would fit in an airplane's overhead compartment. Lily assumed the case contained tape measures, calculators, and whatever else was necessary for the appealing man to produce a bid.

The man shifted the clipboard to his left hand and extended his right toward Lily, introducing himself as Gerald.

Gerald followed Lily as she led him down hallways to the Banks' game room, the clank-clank of his case's small, hard wheels interrupting the otherwise quiet journey. They entered the room, and Lily asked if he had any questions before she excused herself.

Of course, Gerald had plenty of questions. He asked about the number of bottles and cases to be shelved, materials to be used, if display or tasting counters were desired, and on and on. Lily kept deferring the questions to the absent Evelyn, promising that she would be able to respond to Gerald later in the day, perhaps by phone.

Gerald eventually asked Lily a question he was sure she could answer—if she was single. Lily contemplated her answer while she evaluated the estimator's toned physique and intriguing eyes one more time.

"I am," Lily responded, not wasting any words.

"Maybe I could take you out for drinks sometime?" Gerald asked cautiously.

"We'll see," Lily said. "Maybe you should just take measurements, or whatever it is you're supposed to do."

"I would *like* to take some measurements," Gerald remarked, his eyes scanning Lily's seductive form.

Lily enjoyed these games and hadn't gotten to play in a while. She had no intention of having drinks with this guy she didn't know, but she considered maybe doing something else. She would play along for now, just to see how good he was.

"Do you think you have the right tool?" Lily asked, coyly wrapping her arms around herself.

Gerald didn't approach Lily, like she thought he would. Instead, he took a step back, demonstrating a sudden case of nerves. He couldn't respond quickly, and he became fidgety. At this point, Lily lost whatever interest she previously had in the man and started to leave the room.

"Wait!" Gerald called out, eyeballing Lily's seductive posterior as she scurried away. "Please come back!"

Lily was pretty certain that he didn't want to discuss the wine cellar, but she did promise to help Evelyn, so she stopped just outside the room and turned around.

"Yes?" Lily said from a distance.

"We do excellent work," Gerald said, trying to get the conversation back on track.

"That's great," Lily replied. "Do what you need to, and I'll have Mrs. Banks call you later."

"I'd like to show you some of our brochures…if that's okay."

"Sure," Lily said, approaching Gerald.

He produced several colorful booklets and handed them to Lily. She started to skim the materials, intrigued by the multitude of shelving options available. While she spun through the pages, Gerald placed his right hand on her left arm. She didn't react.

"You know," Gerald started, "I could probably get you a great price on our product. In fact, I know I could get you a better than great price."

"That's wonderful," Lily reacted, still browsing the brochures. "I'll give these to Mrs. Banks—I'm sure she'll be interested."

"I'd like to start over," Gerald said—"with you, I mean."

"Okay," Lily replied.

Gerald started to rub his hand up and down Lily's arm. He looked into her eyes, hoping to make contact. She continued to stare down at the booklet, scanning vivid pictures of wooden lattice pieces stuffed with rows of wine bottles.

Risking everything, Gerald leaned in and surprised Lily with a kiss on her lips. Lily didn't react dramatically, but sat back and contemplated his action. Slowly, she peeled her striped knit top up and over her head. She had nothing beneath, and her hardened nipples pointed straight at the cellar salesman.

Like a ravenous wolf, Gerald lunged at the alluring display. Lily pushed him away, stepped back, and glanced down at his khakis. Gerald understood the signal, and with unsteady hands yanked his pants and boxers to the floor. His muscular appendage strained against the open air, and Lily relished the sight.

Lily slid her soft shorts to the floor, touched herself soothingly, and brought her moistened fingers to her lips. Her unblemished, naked flesh was ready for his advance. She waited for him to embrace her, but he stood in place, his face flush with confusion.

Seconds passed, yet he remained paralyzed, unable to reconcile the dream he was living. His heart pulsed visibly under the work shirt he hadn't the strength to remove—the three interlocking Cs an animated, illegible mess. Lily's sighs of disappointment were succeeded by a tacit, stunned amusement, as she watched his member lift a notch, throb, and then spurt a forceful stream of milky cream her way. He stood immobile, wanting to grab at something but unable to. More waves coursed from him with lessening force, the game room floor soiled with splashes of his liquid.

Lily reached for her shorts and top and walked out of the room. Gerald dressed quickly. Lily heard the front door of the house latch closed a moment later. She circled back to the game room to see if he had left any information about the cellar. The only thing he had left for her was a stain on the floor.

Using a wet towel followed by a dry one, Lily cleaned the tacky residue thoroughly. She had almost finished, when Evelyn appeared in the doorway.

"What are you doing down there, Lily?" Evelyn asked.

"Hi Evelyn," Lily responded. "I'm just taking care of a little spill—sorry."

"Oh, you could have left the mess the way it was. Louisa would have cleaned it in the morning. So, did our wine cellar man ever come?"

"He sure did, Evelyn," Lily stated with conviction. "In fact, he came early—very early."

"I hope that wasn't a problem for you, dear."

"I can't say it's something I'm used to, but I guess these things happen. Um, I think you'll want to get some more bids though; maybe a company with a little more experience?"

Chapter Eighteen

Evelyn, Sidney, and Lily were finally dressed and ready to leave for dinner. Evelyn had been having a tough time deciding between new outfits, Sidney couldn't seem to locate his cordovan belt that he was certain Evelyn had thrown out or given away, and Lily had just been dawdling—her metabolism finally slowing to a pace more appropriate to the life of leisure she had been living.

The Capital Grille was a short drive from the house. Evelyn had made reservations earlier in the day after Sidney whined about needing a bite of something hot and juicy. She immediately thought of this popular steakhouse, certain that it would fulfill her husband's needs. She also wanted to treat Lily to a nice dinner, in appreciation for her handling of the early arriving wine cellar salesman the day before.

A couple of blocks into their journey, Lily excitedly pointed from the car window to a small group of adorable children playing in a large, grassy yard. Evelyn turned to see five girls who she guessed were about ten years of age, spinning brightly colored hula hoops above their tiny waists.

She watched them giggle at their futile efforts to maintain the hoops aboveground for more than a second. They laughed at themselves and at each other, and they didn't seem to have a care in the world. The bittersweet memory of her childhood victory snappishly burst into her mind, and she was ten again, hoisting a big round hoop and twirling it endlessly around her belly.

The car was more than a block past the children, yet Evelyn was still holding tight to the notion of a squashy plastic ring circling its way around her body.

"I used to be very good at that, you know," Evelyn said, breaking a long silence.

"What's that, Evelyn?" Lily asked.

"Hula hoops—I was a hula hoop champion once. I was about the same age as those little girls. I remember very well."

"Wow, that's pretty impressive!" Lily responded. "I never had a hula hoop for some reason. I tried one once though—it was fun!"

"Yes—yes it was," Evelyn said, her voice trailing off softly.

•••

Sidney handed the car keys to the valet, and then rushed to open the restaurant door for Lily and his wife. The hostess was efficient, seating them promptly at a square table in the middle of the main dining room.

The faint light from the fixtures underscored the relaxed elegance of the room. Crisp white tablecloths, rich leather seating, and paneled oak walls elicited the spirit of a member's only club. Some servers bustled about carrying heavy trays, while others busied themselves juggling menu queries from their inquisitive patrons.

Freshly seated diners occupied the tables and booths surrounding the Banks' party. Many of their napkins still stood at attention, folded precisely to match the others on the table. Evelyn was ashamed that people had never absorbed enough etiquette to place these linens upon their laps immediately after being seated. Still, she was comfortable with her table and its location in the room.

Apparently, a special celebration was taking place at the adjacent table. A couple in their late seventies, and a younger, fiftyish couple, perhaps their children, had just arranged themselves. The elderly couple sported flowers—a boutonniere on his lapel, a corsage on her wrist. A small gift wrapped in glittery gold paper balanced atop the younger woman's purse.

Evelyn, Sidney, and Lily sat with tall menus in their laps, reviewing the savory items from which they would choose. Michael, their waiter, approached and asked for their drink order. Evelyn requested a flirtini, a beverage she did not see on the bar menu. Michael offered to have one custom mixed—however Evelyn would like. This seemed to overwhelm her, and so she allowed Lily to order while she reconsidered. Lily was more curious about wine, as was Sidney, who had stumbled upon an interesting sounding bottle of Bordeaux while scanning the wine list. They unanimously agreed to this inspiration, and Michael left to retrieve it.

When he walked away, Lily whispered to the Banks that she had something special she wanted to share with them. There was a game she would play on occasion with her friends when they were at a nice restaurant, like this one. She hoped that Evelyn and Sidney would be open to trying something fun and different, and promised to tell them more in a little bit.

Michael returned and presented to Sidney a seductive looking bottle of Bordeaux, which he then uncorked and splashed into an appropriate glass. Sidney went through the ritual of sniffing and tasting the plum shaded liquid and then nodded his approval.

Michael asked if anyone cared for an appetizer. Sidney was ready for the question and requested a large order of oysters on the half shell. He had read on numerous occasions that oysters were very much the aphrodisiac; he figured it couldn't hurt. To his dismay, Evelyn ordered the lobster and crab cakes to share with Lily.

Everyone enjoyed a glass of the Bordeaux while the food was being prepared. Sidney distributed the balance of the bottle as glasses emptied and then scanned the room for their server. He caught Michael's eye, who responded with appetizers in hand.

After ordering their entrees and a second bottle of wine, Evelyn, Lily, and Sidney noticed Michael bend toward the grayer of the couples at the adjacent table to offer congratulations on fifty years of marriage.

There was a relaxed silence at the Banks' table as they contemplated their empty glasses. "Alright you guys," Lily said softly, leaning in toward the Banks. "I have a great game for us."

Evelyn and Sidney leaned in as well, closing off the huddle. They wore mischievous little smiles, even though they had no idea what Lily was up to.

"I need you to be a little open-minded for this," she continued. Okay?"

Evelyn's lips pursed and she swallowed hard, belying her rigid smile. Sidney leaned in even further.

"We're going to play a little game called 'Fearless...' I don't know about this. Let's have some more wine."

"What is it Lily?" Sidney asked, sitting back, disappointed. "I want to play 'Fearless'. What do we do?"

"It's not just 'Fearless', Sidney," Lily responded. "There's a little more to it."

"Please tell us," begged Evelyn. "It must be something special if you play with your friends. I want to play 'Fearless' too!"

Lily picked at her lobster and crab cake, mulling over her plan again. She had wanted to help Evelyn and thought this game might do the trick, but now she was reconsidering. She swallowed a small mouthful of wine and shifted her eyes at the Banks, who were anxiously waiting for her to continue.

"Alright," Lily resumed, "the name of the game is 'Fearless Fuck'."

Sidney's smile grew a little broader, and Evelyn sat back somewhat, as if Lily were spreading something contagious. Allowing her words to settle, Lily carefully gauged Evelyn's response, hoping she hadn't said something to trigger a seizure or some other sort of acute reaction.

"I'm not removing any of my clothes," Evelyn stated. "It doesn't matter how much wine I've had."

"You don't have to undress, Evelyn," Lily replied with a chuckle. "It's kind of a word game."

"It sounds great so far," Sidney interjected, "but why would we want to play a game like that in a restaurant?"

"This is exactly the sort of place to play, Sidney," Lily replied. "It's a very simple game, but it just wouldn't be as much fun if we were all sitting around the den at home."

Everyone at the table grew quiet as Michael approached with the second bottle of Bordeaux. He filled the glasses, commented on the imminent arrival of the entrees, and then skillfully excused himself. Almost humorously, Evelyn, Sidney, and Lily lifted their freshly filled glasses at the same time, and, as if on cue, knocked back a slug of wine.

"Okay," Lily continued, "Like I said, it's a very simple game. All you have to do is say 'fuck'."

"I think I can do that," Sidney quickly replied.

"I don't think I can, or will," Evelyn stated defiantly.

"Wait," Lily said. "There's a little bit more. In order to win the game, you have to say 'fuck' the loudest."

"You mean we have to shout the word?" Sidney asked.

"Not necessarily," Lily replied. "But if that's what it takes to win, then yes, you might have to shout it."

"If you two would like to play, you go ahead," Evelyn announced, glass in hand.

"What does the winner get?" Sidney wanted to know.

"I suppose the winner gets to choose whatever sort of prize they want," Lily responded. "Like their choice of restaurant the next time we go out."

"Well then," Sidney said, "I guess I don't give a fuck if we play."

"Very good, Sidney!" Lily exclaimed, applauding like a two year old. "But you might need to say it louder if you want to win the fucking game." Lily said "fucking" a bit more intensely than Sidney's pass at the profanity, purposely putting much more emphasis on the first four letters.

Just then, Michael returned bearing sizzling entrees and steaming sides for the trio. He deftly delivered the filet Oscar to Lily, the veal chop with Roquefort butter to Evelyn, and the dry-aged porterhouse to Sidney. In the center of the table, he arranged large dishes of seasonal mushrooms, Lyonnais potatoes, and corn "off" the cob.

Evelyn was grateful for the interruption and silently hoped the meal would be enough of a diversion to quell the embarrassing contest. Sidney poured more wine, and everyone directed forks and knives at their entrees.

"Evelyn," Lily said between bites, "I do hope you'll play. It's a ridiculous game, I know, but if you joined in you'd see how much fun it is."

"Well, it's dinner time, dear," Evelyn replied. "I think we can put your little game aside for now."

"Evelyn," Sidney interrupted, "Drink some more wine! It's very good, don't you agree?"

Lily could sense that Evelyn didn't want to be the odd man out, but was having a difficult time putting her dignity on the line for a silly competition.

"You can say it really fast if you want, Evelyn," Lily said with a little slur. "You don't have to stand up and shout the word."

"I have a hard time understanding why people intentionally say profanities," Evelyn replied. "I just wouldn't."

"Really?" Lily asked, shooting Sidney a sideways look. "Certainly you've said bad words before. I must say 'shit' at least ten times a day."

Everyone became quiet again as they carved away at their meat. Evelyn held a staring contest with her plate.

"Lily, dear," Sidney said, "Could you please pass me some of those Lyonnaise fuck potatoes?" Sidney's volume level for the vulgarity was higher than before.

"I'm very impressed, Sidney!" Lily commented. "But you can use correct forms of the word; you want to at least sound grammatically accurate. I think you meant to say Lyonnaise *fucking* potatoes."

Evelyn raised her cloth napkin to her face and shifted her eyes to see if anyone had heard what exploded from the wide-eyed beauty's mouth. The surrounding crowd appeared oblivious to the outburst.

"You win," Sidney said calmly to Lily, his elbows on the table and his hands framing his face like a horse wearing blinders. He then dug deep into his supply of corn, placing a spoonful of the crunchy kernels into his mouth.

"Not so *fucking* fast!!" Evelyn bleated at a decibel substantially exceeding any that had thus far been attempted. "Maybe she hasn't won yet!"

Sidney, who was mid-chew, discharged a mouthful of corn beyond his own place setting, choking on what remained. Lily started laughing so loud that some cream from the potatoes she had been working on found its way to the corner of her mouth and headed for her chin.

The anniversary couple at the nearby table turned stiffly to see what sort of trash was in their midst. Their sour faces matched the look of disgust worn by their dining companions.

Some random chortles could be heard in the background—from groups far enough from the explosion to find it humorous.

"You're right dear, you're right," Sidney murmured, half-proud, half-ashamed of his wife's behavior. "You win."

Lily thought she possibly could have topped Evelyn's explosive shriek just to keep the game going, but didn't want to take away her deserved victory. Besides, she considered that she might have fallen short in her attempt. Evelyn's "fucking" was so clear and so loud; it would have taken a passing train to totally muffle the howled expletive.

Evelyn, Sidney, and Lily were wired from the contest and the wine. They resumed eating, but with more passion and enthusiasm than before. A younger couple who had been dining close by smiled at the group as they passed. A gathering of servers clustered against the far wall, grinning as they shared the humorous diversion with each other. Evelyn, Sidney, and Lily noticed these things.

What they hadn't noticed, was that the younger man sitting with the anniversary couple had left his table. He had been gone several minutes, but returned looking visibly smug as he took his seat.

Moments later the restaurant manager appeared at the Banks' table, smiling as he bent close to their faces.

"I hope you've been enjoying your meals this evening," the manager politely remarked.

Everyone nodded as they continued to chew. Sidney was silently calculating what amount of currency he should slip into the man's hand to get him to walk away. Lily was trying to keep her mouth occupied with food, for fear of breaking out in laughter.

Evelyn wasn't acting like the perpetrator of all the commotion—she was absent the panic and anxiety she had exhibited minutes earlier.

"I'd like to do something special for the table this evening," the manager continued. "I've had the kitchen prepare our special key lime pie, chocolate hazelnut cake, and cheesecake with fresh berries—all for you, and with our compliments. Michael is packaging it now, so you may enjoy it when you arrive home. Please keep in mind that the key lime and cheesecake will require refrigeration if not consumed shortly. Again, thank you for dining with us."

Sidney was torn between making a scene and just sucking it up. Then he realized that he had already made a scene of sorts, and thought it best to just drop a few bills on the table and leave.

As they maneuvered by the adjacent table, Sidney bowed to the golden anniversary celebrants, wishing them the best. He then put his hand on the shoulder of the younger man at the table and said softly to him: “I hope your parents had a fucking great time tonight.”

Lily and Evelyn carried the “to go” desserts in large shopping bags out the door of the restaurant, while Sidney asked the valet to retrieve the car. The young man wondered aloud if Sidney would prefer he call a cab. Apparently, interesting stories spread quickly at this establishment, filtering beyond the brick and mortar with ease. Sidney pointed toward Lily, who seemed to be comparatively sober, and told the valet that she would be doing the driving. He almost said “fucking driving,” but remembered that the game had ended, and that it was time to move on.

The mood was euphoric on the drive home. Sidney spread out across the back seat—a perspective and position to which he was not accustomed. Evelyn sat in the front passenger seat, still soaring from her adrenaline rush. She knew she had been naughty, but somehow didn’t see herself as the horrible, ill-mannered person others in the restaurant surely had deemed her to be. She was content with her actions after all. But more than that, she was proud to come away the victor.

Chapter Nineteen

"I'm pretty sure I won't be able to eat anything for a week," Lily said, polishing off the last bite of chocolate hazelnut cake. Sidney and the girls had been spending the afternoon lounging around the house reading books and magazines, when Evelyn remembered the uneaten desserts parked in the refrigerator.

"I hate to say this," Sidney added, "but I may have to skip dinner this evening. I'm really not hungry."

"That's alright with me as well," Evelyn sighed. "Maybe I'll heat up some hors d'oeuvre later, in lieu of a meal. In the meantime, I think you two have forgotten something that we need to discuss—like perhaps the reward for winning last night's contest? As I recall, I get to choose whatever prize I want—right?"

"That's right, Evelyn!" Lily exclaimed. "It sounds like you've given it some thought!"

"Well, I have dear. I would like to spend some time thinking of Iris and George."

"That's very sweet of you Evelyn," Lily responded. "I know I think of them daily. Maybe we should all share another favorite Iris and George story."

"No no, not that, dear," Evelyn replied. "I would just like to enjoy some more of their marijuana."

"Sounds good, Evelyn!" Sidney announced, jumping up from the couch. "Lily, why don't you go grab everything, and I'll put on some music."

Sidney trotted to the bedroom to make certain all music related technical undertakings were out of the way before his capacity for performing such tasks had diminished. He loaded the CD player with a disc, started the system, and returned to the den.

He arrived shortly after Lily, who was busy plugging the small, black stone pipe with a dusty, rifle-green bud. The music sparkled through the room at a modest volume, soft enough to not steamroll the relaxed conversation.

"That's quite a sound system you have there," Lily

commented, her thin fingers nimbly positioning the weed. “I had never noticed the speakers until I heard the music.”

“Yes,” Sidney replied with some pride, “They’re hidden in the walls. It makes it much easier to properly decorate a room—right Evelyn?”

Evelyn turned her nose up and away from Sidney, who took the gesture as a signal to be less caustic with his comments moving forward.

“Anyway,” Sidney recovered, “I don’t recall much detail about the speakers, but I do remember they utilize pure titanium tweeters—for whatever that’s worth.”

“That’s great Sidney,” Lily said. “What are we listening to anyway? I know it’s an opera, but I couldn’t tell you which one.”

“It’s *Aida*,” Evelyn said, accepting the unlit pipe from Lily. “Giuseppe Verde,” she further articulated just before sucking the flame from the Hanover’s gold lighter.

“Well…it’s beautiful,” Lily said. She thought it *was* sort of nice listening to the strings and the wildly modulating voices. But she was really craving something a bit harder to go with the pot. “Do you guys have any rock albums?”

Sidney and Evelyn looked at each other and came up empty. They didn’t own any rock albums. They had never owned any rock albums.

“I’m sorry to say whatever rock and roll we had in our collection must have been inadvertently thrown away some time ago, right Evelyn?” Sidney hoped his wife would play along.

“Could I use that lighter one more time please, Lily?” Evelyn asked, ignoring everything else that was going on.

Lily sparked the butane filled device for Evelyn, keeping the flame above the bowl until she was certain the grass was burning. Evelyn’s lungs filled with smoke, then she hurriedly passed the pipe to Lily, hoping to avoid a messy scattering of embers once her inevitable cough occurred. Lily enjoyed a deep hit, handed the pipe to Sidney, and asked again about the music.

“Would you mind if I took a look at your CDs? I promise not to rearrange your collection.”

“You are more than welcome to have a look,” Evelyn said between gasps. “I’m afraid you won’t find much to your liking, however. Sidney, won't you please take Lily to where we keep all of that?"

Sidney walked Lily to the bedroom and showed her the stereo set-up. Next to the equipment was a black lacquered wood cabinet, packed with CDs. She scanned the rows of music and noticed that most of it had never been opened. She pulled one jewel case after another from the shelves, searching in vain for something familiar. The writing on many of the covers was in a foreign language, but Lily could tell that they were mostly operas, mixed with some classical. She thought the local public radio station would love to get their hands on this collection.

"Why don't you listen to any of your CDs, Sidney?" Lily asked. "You've got quite a collection."

"Evelyn bought all this, actually," Sidney replied. "In fact, I believe most of these Evelyn purchased because of your mother. If Iris recommended something, Evelyn would buy it, or watch it, or read it, or wear it. I'm pretty sure Evelyn has no idea what she's got here."

"What about you? What do you like to listen to?"

"I guess I really don't know," Sidney responded, after giving it some thought.

Lily analyzed the stack of electronics, searching for, then finding, the tuner. She switched it on after turning off the CD player. After a few seconds of spinning through static and FM stations, she hit on something that sounded appropriate, at least to her. She turned up the volume a couple notches, but kept the level subtle enough to not interfere with conversation.

"How about this, Sidney?" Lily asked. "Does this sound good to you?"

Lily had stumbled upon the local classic rock station just in time to catch the first bars of Pink Floyd's *Wish You Were Here* echoing through the speakers.

"That sounds very comforting," Sidney replied.

"Good—let's go get high," Lily said, grabbing Sidney's hand and leading him back to the den.

They entered the room, which had developed an ethereal feel from the hazy cloud of smoke circulating about the ceiling. Evelyn appeared to be very relaxed on the couch, her feet tucked comfortably under her legs.

"Lily," Evelyn said, the small stone pipe in her hand, "I think you need to reload this."

"Sure I will," Lily responded, taking the pipe from Evelyn.

"I like the music," Evelyn said softly.

The pipe was packed with a fresh bud, passed around a couple times, and was now in Sidney's possession. He drew hard, but got nothing.

He didn't want to bother Lily again with the lighting process; she seemed nicely unwound on the couch next to his wife. Besides, it wasn't as if he were a child, ignorant to the workings of a lighter. He told Lily that the pipe had gone out and extended his hand toward her. She smiled with her whole face as she handed him the heavy gold lighter.

Sidney held the pipe above his lap and brought the flaming lighter down toward it. He imagined that he could ignite the weed this way, quickly bringing it to his mouth once it was aglow. But the pot wasn't responding to the hovering flame the way Sidney hoped.

Lily noticed Sidney's attempt and decided to give him one more shot at it before intervening. After a minute or so, she could sense Sidney's mounting frustration and suggested that he bring the pipe to his mouth before sparking the lighter.

He did as he was told, holding the pipe between his lips while maneuvering the lit flame closer to the target. Lily watched from the corner of her eye as Sidney passed the lighter back and forth across the bowl, attempting to fire up the payload. She wanted to tell him to hold the lighter steady over the pipe, but was reluctant to make another belittling comment. A minute later, she wished she had said something.

Sidney kept the lighter dancing around the bowl, making quick, jerky passes over the pot. It appeared as though he feared sucking the actual flame into his mouth. On one of the passes with the heavy, blazing implement he strayed too far.

With a disrespectful flash the fire jumped to the buttery pomade coating Sidney's thick head of hair, like a flea to a furry dog. The smell of roasting hair instantly superseded the musky aroma of marijuana that had dominated the room. There was a delay of a second or two, and then Sidney sensed his scalp flaming like a cherries jubilee.

Evelyn's reaction was slower than Sidney's, even though she had witnessed the entire event unfurling from her front row seat. Her mind was numb, and she considered his antics to be humorous at first. Her weakened analytical abilities eventually wove through her blanketing stupor, and she screamed for him to do something.

"To the pool!" Lily shouted, grabbing Sidney's thrashing arm and yanking him toward the patio door.

Within a few seconds Sidney was on his knees at the edge of the pool, dunking his head in the water as if he were an embarrassed ostrich.

When he sat up, some steam rose from the burnt stubs of his remaining hair.

"Ow!" Sidney shrieked, gathering himself on the pool deck. "What the hell!"

"Sidney!" Evelyn screeched, "Are you okay?"

"I'm great, Evelyn," he replied, catching his breath.

"We need to get you to a doctor right away!" Evelyn pleaded. "Lily, can you drive?"

"I'm not going to a doctor or to an emergency room or anything like that," Sidney said. "I'll be okay. Just give me a minute."

"She has a good idea there," Lily said, trying to soothe Sidney by rubbing his back with her left hand.

"How did this happen? That would be the first question they'd ask. 'Well', I'd say, 'I was trying desperately to fire up some marijuana, and I'm so spastic, I managed to fire up my hair instead! Can you maybe prescribe me some marijuana in pill form, so I don't hurt myself again? Oh, and by the way, I know my company handles all of your accounting work, but really—you shouldn't worry.' Yeah, that's just what I want to do."

"Let me take a look," Lily said, pawing through the singed patches of Sidney's remaining locks. "It doesn't seem like your scalp is burned. You're a lucky guy."

"That Daddy Warbucks look is very popular, dear," Evelyn said, her pulse now settled. "We'll take you to the salon on

Monday. Marlaina will give you a fresh start on your hair. Come now—let's get you dried off."

•••

"Wow!" Lily applauded for Sidney as he ambled tentatively into the kitchen the next morning. "You look great!"

"Thank you, Lily," Sidney replied, rubbing his hands over his freshly shaved head. "It's only temporary though. I'm letting it grow back, starting today."

"Aw, I kind of like it," Lily said. "You should give it some thought. So, what does Evelyn think?"

"Evelyn thinks he should have waited one more day and let a professional take care of the trim," she said brusquely as she entered the room. "Did he show you the bandage? Turn around, Sidney."

"Well, I wouldn't be embarrassed or upset if I were you," Lily said to Sidney. "Like I said—I think you look fine."

"I will say," Evelyn added, "I never would have thought you had the sort of head for this, but it's not a bad look at all. Maybe you should smoke a pipe more often—see what else you can come up with."

"I don't believe I'll be smoking that pipe anymore," Sidney replied. "Someone must have given George and Iris lessons. I don't know how they did it."

"Sidney," Lily interrupted, "there are other options. You should use a bong."

"What's a bong, dear?" Evelyn asked.

"That's okay, Lily," Sidney said. "I don't really need the marijuana anyway."

"Nobody needs it Sidney," Evelyn chimed in. "So Lily, tell us some more about this bong idea."

"It's a water pipe of sorts," Lily replied. "It actually makes the smoke less harsh…and even better, the lit bowl is far from the face so that, well, you know."

"Yes, we need one of those," Evelyn stated. "Sidney, go to the store and buy one, would you?"

"Right, dear," Sidney responded. "I believe they're on sale

today at Nordstrom. There was a full-page ad in this morning's paper. Let me get my hat."

"Actually Sidney," Lily said, "I bet we could find one pretty easily. There's a large university nearby, right?"

•••

After an hour of squabbling with Evelyn, Sidney acquiesced and agreed to purchase the bong. He was very reluctant to leave the house however, having no confidence in his recently acquired, blunt appearance. He had hoped for at least a day's time to acclimate to the look before stepping out the door.

Sidney was pretty sure the bong store wouldn't be open on a Sunday and was thinking he'd be able to push that errand to maybe another Saturday. To his chagrin, Evelyn was not opposed to doing the research and had found a store that was not only open all day, but maintained the largest selection of bongs in town. She of course wasn't interested in doing the actual shopping for the utensil, so it was just Lily who rode with Sidney in his black Mercedes sedan to the shop.

It was about a thirty-minute drive to downtown Tempe, where the store was located. Sidney agreed to listen to music on the way, encouraging Lily to scan for the classic rock station they had enjoyed the day before.

Lily's left hand played with the electronic dials, eventually tuning to what sounded like the right station. She listened to a few chords of *The Grand Illusion* by Styx and was satisfied that she had found what she was looking for.

When she had finished manipulating the controls on the dashboard, her hand fell to Sidney's right leg. She gently massaged his thigh while reassuring him that his inadvertent change in appearance had not diminished his handsomeness one bit. Her fingers slid down his leg, kneading his skin and the muscles underneath—then they headed upwards. She asked if there was anything she could do for him.

"No, I'll be fine," Sidney answered.

He should have been prepared for this question, but he wasn't. Lily had not been ashamed to flaunt her seductive powers on several occasions, and in the back of his mind, he assumed it could happen again.

Sidney was actually pleased with himself for not having a prepared plan of action. There was no telling what he may have come up with if he had taken the time to think it through.

An incredibly beautiful young woman was stroking his leg, asking what she could do for him, and he slapped her advance in the face with four words, improvised off the top of his denuded head. Despite his strained, agonizing condition, he decided it was probably the best thing he could have said.

Lily removed her wandering hand from Sidney's leg as they approached PotHolder's on Mill. Sidney wheeled into a space directly in front of the store's large glass doors.

Before he had the car in park, four young, tousled looking, rail-thin men, trotted out of the store. They were closely followed by two more young men, clothed more appropriately for university students, at least in Sidney's mind. They wore brightly colored polo shirts untucked over khaki, pleated shorts.

Although all six patrons stole a glimpse of Sidney in his large black Mercedes, the first group passed by the car quickly, like they were late for class. The two preppy kids stared a little harder through the tinted glass, chuckling at Sidney's hazy silhouette as they passed.

"PotHolder's?" Sidney asked Lily. "Are you sure this isn't a kitchenware store?"

"Trust me," was Lily's response.

Lily and Sidney crossed the store's threshold and into a teeming shock of law taunting merchandise. Patchouli, sandalwood, and lavender scents floated across the room on invisible clouds. Lily suddenly yearned for lazy days and shoeless dances through flowered meadows. Sidney imagined there had been a bad spill of some sort.

Throughout the store, organic clothing flew like kites from the ceiling, wired to the fixtures below. There were more t-shirts than Sidney had ever seen in one place. Most of them sported images of rock icons, both dead and alive. Others just seemed like throwbacks: tie-dyed garments wrapped in pastels, vibrant colors, and explosive patterns.

Fronting one of the side walls of the sales floor was a succession of long, glass display cases. The items inside the cases were alien to Sidney, but familiar to Lily. She grabbed Sidney's hand and led him directly to this area.

On the wall behind the counter, rows of shelves supported additional merchandise—items that looked to Sidney as though they had been dreamed up by Dr. Seuss. In front of this wall and behind the row of display cases stood a round, middle-aged plug of a man with thick, black eyebrows. His scowled expression exposed an underlying irritation that befuddled Sidney, who was accustomed to a more gracious, obliging class of sales clerk.

"What the hell you doin'?" the angry man asked.

"Excuse me?" Sidney replied. "I'm afraid I don't know what you're talking about."

"Pullin' up in that mob car of yours—scarin' away my clientele. That's what I'm talkin' about. You vice or somethin'?"

"You know, you do have a little Kojak thing going on there," Lily whispered toward Sidney.

"I am not a police officer, if that's what you're asking," Sidney snapped. "I *would* like to speak with your manager however."

"Ha!" the man behind the counter shrieked. "You got the owner, pal. What is it you need?"

"Well…for one thing, how do you stay in business with that attitude? It's remarkable, really."

The storeowner huffed a wet, labored breath, then waddled undaunted toward the end of the row of glass cases. Sidney was sure he was heading his way. This was why drugs were so dangerous, he thought. It probably had nothing to do with addiction or the insidiousness of the stuff.

The man came around the corner, approaching Sidney. He stopped an arm's length away and pointed out to the parking lot.

"Don't be drivin' that shit here again—you got it?"

"Believe me," Sidney fumed, "you won't ever see it again."

"We'd like to see a bong, please?" Lily interrupted, wrapping herself around Sidney's arm.

The owner mumbled something incoherent, then journeyed back to the other side of the counter. Lily snagged this opportunity to have a word with Sidney.

"You know, you *could* drive something just a little more hip."

"You too? I drive a very nice, very expensive car, Lily. I think I'm good."

"What can I show you?" the man asked, gasping for breath.

"Let's take a look at that tall one on the end," Lily said, pointing to the back wall.

Lily inspected several of the tubular water pipes, eventually handing one to Sidney, along with her recommendation. Sidney analyzed what he held, wanting to ask Lily questions, but was wary of being considered un-hip twice in one afternoon.

"Excuse me, Mr. store owner," Sidney said while pointing to the bowl, "is this where you put the marijuana?"

"Alright, that's enough—outta here!" the squat man screeched. "We don't sell drug paraphernalia, buddy. Everything you see here is for tobacco use or home décor. You ain't trappin' me!"

"Wait a second," Lily interrupted. "You need to be nice to this man. He wants to buy a bong, and he wants to use it for tobacco. He's not a cop…he's just never been in a place like this before."

"And this will be the last time as well, I can assure you," Sidney added.

"Sidney, please," Lily said, using an unexpectedly stern voice, "let me handle this."

"What about that blue one on the bottom shelf, Lily?" Sidney asked in a contrived, calm voice.

"This is a Molino, chum," the man said, reaching for the azure pigmented, swirled-glass object. "It's hand blown—a little pricey."

"What do you think, Lily? Do you think Evelyn would like it?"

"It's beautiful, Sidney," she replied. "I'm sure Evelyn would love it."

Sidney told the man to wrap it up, and that he'd be paying cash. He then asked Lily to pick out some incense after confirming with the man that the piquant fragrance was perfect for masking the smell of tobacco.

Lily selected boxes of Jasmine Chamomile and Ocean Breeze stick incense and grabbed three Pink Floyd t-shirts from a display she had spotted when they entered the store. She wanted Evelyn and Sidney to add something special to their wardrobes. They had more than earned it.

Chapter Twenty

Sidney handed his car keys to Doug, his longtime service advisor at the Mercedes dealership.

"I'll take a loaner," Sidney muttered.

Sidney's car was due for a routine check-up: oil change, filters, the once over. He would typically drop his car off in the morning, grab a complimentary smaller, more pedestrian version of his own car, and then return it once all repairs or scheduled maintenance had been completed.

"I'm happy to arrange for one," Doug announced, "but business is very light today—even for a Wednesday. If you'd like to wait, I could have all your work done in about an hour—we have pastries and coffee inside!"

Sidney extended his wrist from his shirt cuff and glared at his watch. He wasn't too concerned about missing work. He would regularly write-off missed minutes, hours, or days for that matter, as executive privilege. He was uncomfortable though spending any quantity of time in the customer lounge.

"You say an hour?" Sidney asked.

"No more than that, Mr. Banks. By the way, I love what you did with your hair. I've thought about shaving my head many times, but, you know, I'm afraid to see what I've got hidden under this mess up here."

"Well, sometimes someone has to light a match under you to get you to do something like this," Sidney sighed in response. He looked around for a few seconds and then said: "I guess I'll wait for the car—thank you for taking care of it so efficiently."

Sidney removed his briefcase from the back seat before being abandoned by his car and by Doug. He glanced around looking for a place other than the stuffy lounge to sit. He found a wooden, slatted bench away from the main building, shaded by two willowy acacia trees. He strolled over and sat alone, biding time.

Sprawled before him was a massive, meandering auto mall of which the Mercedes dealership was a part. He scanned the center, trying to identify the various logos on the eclectic assemblage of showrooms. Most of the signs seemed to announce, with some arrogance, the stock of vehicles for sale within: Jaguar, Lexus, Porsche, Audi, and BMW. Another of the signs was more modest in size and was difficult for Sidney to read. After narrowing his eyes to thin slits the letters were still indecipherable, so he edged closer for a better look.

Somewhere between the bench and the mysterious showroom, Sidney was able to make out the name on the sign: "Mini." Satisfied, he returned to his seat to contemplate the beautiful day and life in general.

His thoughts drifted to the unique young lady who had been staying with Evelyn and him. His life had definitely shifted since her arrival.

He had benefitted a great deal from the unencumbered lifestyle that Lily advocated and modeled. She had given him the strength he needed to soak his parched soul in a liberating sea of vice. Now his life was void of so many stale, tedious habits and dull routines, and he was probably healthier for it.

Lily was a great conciliator as well. Sidney assumed this talent had been inherited from her parents, whom he had always known to be considerate and levelheaded. He recalled the explosive situation in the bong store, just three days earlier. If it hadn't been for Lily, he would have found some reason to have the man, and his store, investigated.

Sidney looked across the way again, focusing on the Mini sign. One of his fraternity brothers used to drive around campus in a green one, he recalled. It had seemed like a glorified go-kart to Sidney at the time, but that was a good forty years ago. He wondered what the models looked like these days.

With a quick glance at his watch, he realized that he'd need to waste more time on the hard bench than his aging frame would allow. Gathering his briefcase, he hiked over to the quirky, modern looking dealership.

A half-dozen of Mini's finest dotted the black and white, checkerboard patterned sales floor, like jellybean-colored sprinkles spattered over freshly iced cupcakes. The diminutive cars appeared eerily familiar to Sidney. It struck him that they'd evolved much less than he had in forty years.

Just inside the entrance door, positioned in a very hard to ignore spot, was a large poster, framed in a freestanding, silver sign holder. The poster was an advertisement for a local charity event. The bold lettering and clever design immediately grabbed Sidney's attention—what he read almost knocked him over.

After a cursory scan of the conspicuously placed placard, Sidney shook away any potential cobwebs then re-read the copy starting from the top. He slowly worked down to the bottom, carefully examining each word along the way.

Grabbing a small notepad from the outside pouch of his briefcase and a Mont Blanc pen from his pocket, he jotted down all the information he would need to answer Evelyn's probing questions once he had given her the juice: a benefit show was to be held at the Scottsdale Center for the Performing Arts—its purpose, to raise money for the Scottsdale Fire Department. "Mini" was one of several supporting sponsors. The revue was scheduled for a week from Friday at 7:00 in the evening. Entertainment included a live orchestra, dance performances, and some noted national singing talent. The featured performer, highlighted in large print at the center of the poster, was none other than the famed opera star, Alicia Cavaloni. VIP seating was available.

Sidney was grateful that the poster included no photographs of the entertainers. He wondered though how Alicia dared show her meaty face, or other colossal features, in this town again—let alone so soon.

Absorbed in the emotion of the moment, Sidney was joggled when Jonathan, a beaming, thirtyish, "motoring advisor" tapped his shoulder.

"Good morning sir, my name is Jonathan—welcome to Mini!" the glowing, fresh-pressed young man announced.

"Hello," Sidney replied. "I'm just having my car serviced a couple doors down. I was only having a quick look."

"Well, be my guest!" Jonathan responded. "If you'd like to take one for a spin, just let me know!"

"Thank you Jonathan. I'm pretty sure these cars are intended for a much younger demographic than mine. I'm just taking a little stroll down memory lane—that's all."

"I beg your pardon, sir," Jonathan quickly countered, "but I think you'd be surprised. People of all ages want to have a little fun when they're sporting about town. Besides, everyone wants to be seen in these cars. They're very hip, you know. Anyway, take a look around. I'll leave you to yourself."

"Wait a second, Jonathan," Sidney said, reaching for the young man's arm. "What do you know about this benefit you're advertising?"

"Um, I think it's a fundraiser for the fire department—yeah, that's what it says here. We're one of the sponsors."

"Does your company have anything to do with any of these entertainers?" Sidney asked, pointing to the sign.

"I don't think so? But I'd be happy to check for you…"

"Sidney—Sidney Banks. That's okay, young man. I just wanted to make sure they weren't under contract with your brand. I'd hate to turn on my television in the morning and witness one of them trying to squeeze into one of your cars, touting their quality, for instance."

"I think this is just a local thing, Mr. Banks. I also think you'd be surprised by what could fit inside our cars!"

"Yes, I would be very surprised. Tell you what, Jonathan, let's give one of these a test—how about it."

Sidney hadn't forgotten Lily's comments from the bong store. He had never really digested them either, having written them off at the time as calming blather. But she hadn't been wrong about much in the brief time he'd known her. If Lily thought he should be driving a more hip car, maybe she had a point.

Jonathan pulled a chili-red Cooper S around to the showroom's front door and invited Sidney into the driver's seat. Sidney was immediately impressed with the interior dimensions of the automobile. It was much roomier than he had anticipated.

Jonathan sat in the front passenger seat, taking Sidney on a quick tour of the gauges. Within a minute, they were puttering down a two-lane road close to the dealership. Jonathan encouraged Sidney to open it up a little—not to be afraid.

Sidney obeyed, pushing beyond the posted speed limit in rapid time. Following Jonathan's directions, he cornered hard into several turns and braked hard at several intersections. His Mercedes was solid and responsive, but he was finding this car to be much more fun. Sidney sported a broad grin as they parked at the front door of the showroom.

"This model is available as a convertible as well," Jonathan remarked, eyeing Sidney as he fondled the wheel.

"I'm going to grow my hair back," Sidney replied. "And I won't be using pomade anymore. I'm not sure that I'd want my appearance to be that of a mad scientist once I'd reached my destination."

"For what it's worth, Mr. Banks, I think you've got a great head to pull off that bald look. You might want to think about it—I mean the hair, not the convertible. Usually it's the wives that are opposed to drop tops. All that time at the salon and then pffft."

"Yes," Sidney replied, "I'm certain I wouldn't be able to persuade my wife to ride around town with the top down. I'll take this one—I like the white roof."

"You've got it, Mr. Banks. Come inside and let's work out the details."

Sidney considered whether to trade in his Mercedes. He thought about holding on to it and writing a check for the Mini, but decided if he was going to shake the old image, he wanted to do it right.

After a semi-confusing call to Doug, it wasn't long before his freshly serviced black sedan was parked in front of the Mini dealership. With the trade, Sidney was owed a considerable sum; Jonathan completed and submitted the paperwork.

Sidney's new car was now parked on the delivery drive, ready to go. Jonathan asked to see his insurance card as a formality, before keys were exchanged.

Setting his briefcase on his lap, Sidney unbuckled the latch and raised the lid. He started to look for the slot inside his case where he kept such things as auto insurance cards.

He was thrown a bit by the presence of a thin, white, unfamiliar plastic bag, lying atop the expected, short pile of business folders. He propped it up and slid two slender boxes from it. Sidney could tell right away that he had something in front of him that needed to be kept private. Keeping the boxes hidden behind the raised lid of his briefcase, he bent forward for a better look.

It was pornography. Graphic photographs of unclothed young men and women posing shamelessly for the camera smothered the two clamshell cases that Sidney held in his moistening palms.

His eyes fell straight to the vaguely familiar logo at the top of both cases. "Quick Release Studios Presents," hovered flirtatiously above the titles of the films.

The DVD Sidney clutched in his right hand was titled: *Ball 5*. He could sense a minor league theme of sorts: five naked young women wearing umpire masks hovered behind a reclining young stud—a Louisville Slugger springing from his crotch. Sidney focused on the bat for a second to assure himself that it was indeed real wood, and not some twisted gift from nature.

The second DVD was called: *All Lips on Tulip*—an equally clever name and just as captivatingly illustrated. The photo on the front of the box showed a beautiful young woman lying contentedly on a bed of flowers. An orgy of naked bodies encircled her, contorted in seemingly impossible alignments while casting their open, hungry mouths toward every inch of her delectable flesh.

The young lady being devoured was apparently the star of this film, and the other film as well—one Tulip Sonrod, as promoted in bold letters at the bottom of both cases. She looked so familiar to Sidney.

"Mr. Banks," Jonathan whispered, as if waking someone from a deep sleep, "the insurance card?"

"What? Oh yes—just give me a minute. I know it's in here somewhere."

Sidney pulled a thick stack of cards from a slot inside the lid of his briefcase and shuffled through them. He quickly found the insurance card and tossed it across the desk.

Jonathan excused himself to make a copy, and Sidney rushed to examine the DVD boxes one more time.

It was Lily on the covers; he was sure of it. His once sharp mind had become a blunt, vacuous husk. How could this not have registered until now? She had given him the name of this studio, for God's sake. He was sure she had provided other hints as well, but he hadn't paid attention. He didn't know he had needed to.

He wondered why she wanted him to know now. Why did she feel compelled to let him in on her other life? He never would have unearthed her secret. Evelyn certainly never would have guessed—unless she already knew.

Sidney experienced a moment of panic, wondering if it had all been some sort of set-up. He knew his wife too well, however, and was confident she was oblivious to all this.

"Here you go, Mr. Banks," Jonathan said with a smile. "Congratulations!"

"Thank you very much, Jonathan. I think perhaps… I'm thinking about purchasing another, as well."

"You want two?" Jonathan asked incredulously.

"Maybe," Sidney replied. "I might buy one for my wife. I wonder if she'd appreciate one of these."

"You know I'd be more than happy to help you with that, Mr. Banks, but unless this is a surprise gift or something, why don't you take yours home first—let her decide."

Sidney knew the young man had a good point; there was no need to rush this decision. A trip to the jewelry store would suffice if Sidney's newfound guilt turned out to be enduring.

"You're an impressive young man, Jonathan," Sidney said, his hand extended. "Certainly you must work on commission. You seem to be missing that greed gene so many others in your field possess. I will be sure to send business your way when I can. I may even return shortly myself!"

Sidney pulled away in his new car, eyeing his Mercedes in the rearview mirror until it had completely vanished from sight.

•••

"You won't believe this Evelyn," Sidney bellowed, storming into the den.

"Oh my goodness, Sidney!" Evelyn shrieked. "You've been in an accident! Are you okay?"

"What? No, no Evelyn—something else."

"You're home so early from work! And you pulled up the drive in that sad loaner car they gave you! What happened, Sidney?"

"It's not, it's…whatever. Anyway Evelyn, Alicia Cavaloni is back in town—or she will be next week. She's performing at a benefit for the fire department! Can you believe the gall?"

"How do you know this?" Evelyn asked. "Alicia Cavaloni—I thought I'd never see her again."

"I don't think you ever will, my dear. She's apparently in town just for this show, and then I'm certain the murderous, margarine-coated monster will be on her way once more."

"Nonsense, Sidney," Evelyn pooh-poohed. "I shall buy us tickets to this show. I think it would be beneficial to both of us—closure and all that."

"Closure? Are you serious?" Sidney's voice was escalating. "The woman fell on our best friends and killed them. If I see her again, it will be the opposite of closure!"

"She didn't exactly fall, dear. If I recall, she was pushed somewhat? I suppose she must be mended from her horrible injury. Now, give me all the details, please."

Sidney continued the unwinnable debate with his wife, eventually succumbing to her unbending resolve. He was not looking forward to the benefit, but was determined to make the best of it. He considered bringing a sack of rotted tomatoes to throw at the beast, then realized she probably had noodles hidden in her skirt and would contrive a way to make a quick lasagna.

"By the way, Evelyn," Sidney wanted to change the subject, "that car in the drive is not a loaner. I bought it. What do you think?"

"I think you must have used the bong pipe this morning, dear. When will your car be ready at the shop?"

"That *is* my car now, Evelyn…do you think it makes me look hip?"

"I think it just makes you look poorer," Evelyn replied with a haughty hmmpf. "So, what should we do about Lily?"

"What do you mean?" Sidney replied with a twitch. "She's done nothing wrong, really."

"Of course not, dear. It's a question of whether to purchase a ticket for her to the benefit."

"Oh…why wouldn't she want to watch her parent's killer perform on stage? I would think she'd jump at the chance."

"I'd actually be happy to go," Lily interrupted, sauntering into the room. "I've heard a lot about this woman. I'm kind of curious."

"I don't know that that's a good idea, Lily," Sidney countered. "It's not a pretty sight."

"Sidney," Evelyn said, "if she wants to go, I see nothing wrong with that. Maybe it will offer *her* some closure."

"Do you guys have company by the way?" Lily asked. "I noticed someone parked on the driveway."

"That's Sidney's latest indulgence, dear," Evelyn answered. "His old car evidently wasn't nice enough."

"Good for you, Sidney!" Lily exclaimed, with a wink at the bald man in the room. "That is one cool car—very cool! I can't wait to take a ride."

"Thank you, Lily," Sidney replied. "Thank you for everything."

Chapter Twenty-one

There was little happening at the office, and Sidney's large, competent staff had been handling the routine drudgery well, so he left early. Besides, it was only his second day with the new car, and he was antsy to play with it some more. After a half hour of darting through traffic, cheating through recklessly sharp turns, and taunting the more lethargic behemoths, he headed home.

Sidney called out for Evelyn and Lily, barking their names loudly as he entered the house. He realized they wouldn't be expecting him this time of day and did not want to frighten them. He received no response.

Not wanting to scream for them again, Sidney made himself comfortable at the large round table in the kitchen. He shoveled a scoop of roasted whole cashews into his hand and started nibbling while he waited for one or the other of the girls to happen by. While he was daydreaming, he noticed a piece of Evelyn's stationery neatly positioned on the adjacent counter. He read the scribbled note:

Sidney-

You may be home before us. Lily and I went to lunch and then for manicures and pedicures. We will call you before we leave the salon to see if you would like to meet us for dinner. I'm certain the three of us would have a difficult time squeezing into your new car anyway.

Think of a place we can go.
-Evelyn

It was not quite three p.m., so Sidney assumed he wouldn't be hearing from his wife for at least a couple hours. When she did call, she would ask if he had given any consideration to where they should dine. Evelyn would do this to him from time to time whenever she did not want to think of, or be responsible for, the evening meal. Sidney, of course, would choose Mastro's

Ocean Club. Evelyn, of course, would expect this. For some reason she enjoyed this little game, and for some reason Sidney always played along.

His mouth parched from the salted nuts, Sidney was desperate for something wet. Despite it being the middle of the afternoon, he contemplated raiding his store of fine Scotch. He considered that he wouldn't have had this thought if Evelyn was home, and he laughed to himself. It was no longer necessary for him to wait for his wife to disappear before sneaking a dram or two of his favorite tonic. She was actually supportive of the practice these days.

Having a quiet sip alone was too hard to resist, so Sidney plopped three small cubes of ice into a crystal rocks glass and drowned them with a twenty-five year old Talisker. He promised himself that he would stop at two; he would be enjoying the rush of driving his new car in only a few hours, and he wanted his wits about him.

Sidney lay sprawled across the living room sofa, the ice in his emptying tumbler clinking out a comforting tune. His feet stretched to rest on forbidden ground—up on the sofa's flawless, soft leather arms. When a glassy calmness had loosened his mind, Sidney remembered that he had left his briefcase by the kitchen table. He was always careful to secrete it in his bedroom closet, mostly out of habit, partly for security. He would occasionally carry confidential papers from time to time and preferred to keep them stored in a low visibility area.

But Sidney wasn't too worried about misplacing classified information or sticking to his concealment ritual just now. He would need more motivation than that to budge from his comfortable position. Then he remembered stashing Lily's unusual gift in one of the zippered compartments of his briefcase. That was motivation enough. If Evelyn were to stumble upon something so unexplainable, it would take a lot more of his energy to calm her down, than it would just to hide the damn thing.

After refreshing his glass with a drizzle of Talisker, Sidney returned to the kitchen to rescue his case. He set his drink on the table and performed a perfunctory search for the DVDs, just to assure they were still in place. The white plastic bag that hid the obscene graphics from the otherwise nontoxic contents of his briefcase was, as he had left it, in the zippered compartment. Sidney hesitated, one hand still clutching the bag. He couldn't help but take one more look at the covers. He knew there would be no better time than now.

Laying the two boxes on the kitchen table, he studied the young Hanover closely. Her hair was different, somewhat shorter, but other than that the films could have been shot yesterday. Sidney turned the boxes over to see if he could determine a production date and discovered that both had been copyrighted ten years earlier. The girl was almost ageless.

He wanted to watch the movies, but he was too close to the main attraction. There was not enough distance between her and him. He had his own perception of Lily, and he was sure this would change if he were to watch her perform. Over the last few weeks she had slowly unraveled, exposing little slivers of herself at a time. He preferred it this way.

Too many "what ifs" were involved in Sidney's decision to view or not to view. He was sure Lily wanted him to watch the films—otherwise why would she have thrown them in his face? What if this were just another of her reckless come-ons? Sidney knew he couldn't, or shouldn't, do it. He became uncomfortable just thinking about the DVD player.

He was entranced, however, by the covers. Lily was a beauty, sure, but the other performers were attractive as well and seemingly not shy at all. Everything was so graphic, so sexual. Sidney allowed himself to become engrossed in the tales painted by the photos, the scenes playing out in his head as fully and explicitly as his imagination would allow. Soon he was yearning to be in the middle of the fondling, the touching, and the licking. He envisioned himself as one of them.

He tugged on the zipper and released his hardening erection from the custom fitted dress pants that could no longer contain him. The working part of his mind calculated that he had at least two hours alone. The stressed-out, unraveling part of his mind informed him that he just didn't care anymore.

He balanced astride a precipice, precariously engaged with

fabricated stories he had conjured from the obscene photographs plastered across the DVD covers. With one hand clinging to a ten-year-old picture of Lily and her friends, and the other embracing his scorned, neglected friend, Sidney committed to relieving the ripened snarl-up that influenced his daily behavior. He prayed he wouldn't be regretting his Mercedes trade as soon as he was done.

After a minute or so, Sidney sensed soldiers rushing to where his legs intersected, like ants to a fallen cookie. He was close to the point of no return.

Looking down at himself, he almost laughed at the sight of his stiff pole jutting out of his gray dress slacks. It seemed so awkward, almost as if he were glaring at someone else—perhaps an actor in a movie.

His delight faded when he realized he had failed to plan a proper landing spot for what was certain to be a deluge. The imminent torrent he had perceived a moment earlier retreated slightly as his eyes darted around the kitchen searching for a proper receptacle.

He spotted pink and white floral patterned paper towels suspended below a nearby cabinet and gauged their viability. But Sidney, who was standing in his kitchen with a pulsing rod in one hand, and an old porn movie jacket in the other, wrote that off as a tasteless and crude option.

Sidney realized the kitchen made a poor substitute for the bathroom, and in a fit of panic headed that way, DVD boxes in hand. He couldn't move faster than a quick walk, as his rigid tentacle swayed uncomfortably with each awkward step. He wanted to stabilize it with his hand, but couldn't risk the extra stimulation. He needed to be careful; he could not allow the little demons to be released until he had reached a safe place to deposit them.

Sidney wended his way toward the bathroom, all the while glaring with anxious anticipation at his purple-headed dagger. He felt like he was taking an overwrought pet for a walk, weary that it might relieve itself in the most inappropriate place.

Watching it swing back and forth, Sidney had a notion that it didn't look quite the same to him. He feared it looked smaller than he had been picturing lately in his mind's eye. When he reached a narrow wisp of mirror that extended from floor to ceiling in the living room, he paused to catch his profile.

It did appear smaller to him, which upset him considerably. He wondered if he had always overestimated its dimension, or if there were some sinister factor working against him that was responsible for this unanticipated loss of proportion.

His first thought was that the decline in its stature was due to underuse. He considered that its prominence might be determined by activity, like the muscles in his arms or legs. If that was the case, he was grateful it was as substantial as it was.

Maybe it was age taking its toll on his body, he thought. He had heard tales of older people and their diminishing volume of flesh and bones as they edged closer to the end. He hadn't given it any thought until now, but he suddenly realized that this curse could extend to genitalia as well.

A spark of inspiration came to him when it registered that he was still wearing his pants. The bulky fabric surrounding the base of his penis had to account for an inch or two, at least. This was the logic Sidney had been hoping to stumble upon, and the reason he had stopped to view himself in the mirror. His confidence revived, he breathed a little easier.

His appendage still upright enough and strong enough to serve as a towel rack for several washcloths, Sidney started toward the bathroom again. He had taken only two strides when he heard the racket.

Evelyn's voice was loud and whiny, and Lily was obviously doing her best to console and soothe. They were inside the house, only steps from the living room.

Sidney couldn't believe his luck. For all the years he had maintained his Puritan level of resolve, he had chosen this day to break free. As hopeless as the situation seemed, he had to try something.

To his left was the backside of the large leather sofa on which he'd been so content moments earlier. He dove quickly to the floor, extended his arms, and thrust the two DVDs he was holding through the four inch gap between the sofa and the rug. His receding erection was trapped between the floor and his pants zipper, expressing its anger with a biting pain. He tried to remain quiet, but a muffled groan escaped his mouth.

Evelyn spotted him first, after hearing his agonizing sigh. The shock of seeing her husband face down on the floor and in obvious discomfort caused her to scream.

"Call 911! Lily, call 911!" Evelyn shrieked, in a voice worthy of the champion that she was.

"No!" Sidney bellowed. "I'm okay! Don't make that call, Lily."

"What's wrong Sidney?" Lily asked, calmly. "Why are you on the floor? Did you fall?"

"No, no, it's nothing like that," Sidney responded. "There was…a bug, a very fast, very scary bug that I saw scurry under the sofa. I sort of landed on my knee when I dropped down to look for it, but I'm okay, so you ladies can move along now."

"Oh my goodness, a bug? Oh, I hope you got it Sidney," Evelyn pleaded. "Well, this is not helping my condition whatsoever."

"What condition? What's the matter, dear?" Sidney asked from his increasingly humiliating position on the ground.

"We had lunch at a new Indian restaurant," Lily answered for his wife. "It didn't go so well for Evelyn."

"Lily, promise to call Jen to let her know what happened," Evelyn begged. "I'll phone her tomorrow to reschedule our manicures."

"Of course I will, Evelyn. You lay down now; I'm sure the antacids will be working shortly."

"She is such a sweet girl," Evelyn proclaimed as she left the room.

"Do you need a hand, Sidney?" Lily asked, looming over the man.

"I'm good, Lily. Um, maybe you could fix us something to drink. I'll go check on Evelyn."

"That sounds great," Lily replied. "Be right back."

Sidney thought he had manufactured a brilliant diversion before remembering that the liquor was just on the other side of the room, stored in the highly polished mahogany bar. When he sensed that Lily had walked away, he rolled over and stood up.

With his back to her, he left the room to check on his wife, zipping himself up along the way.

When he found Evelyn, she was already in bed and close to sleep. He asked if there was anything he could get for her, and she waved him off with her hand. He turned out the lights to the room and then closed the door behind him softly until it latched.

"How's she doing?" Lily asked, handing Sidney a double shot of Scotch in a short glass.

"She's off to sleep, it appears," he answered groggily, one hand covering his bogus yawn. "I'm probably not too far from that myself."

"Oh come on now, Sidney. It's barely dinner time. What should we do?"

"Well, we could order a pizza I suppose. Evelyn is not a big fan, and I don't get to eat it too often."

"That's a great idea!" Lily's eyes brightened as she moved a step closer to Sidney. "We can do pizza and a movie!"

Sidney froze when Lily held up the two boxes he had hastily attempted to bury under the sofa. He didn't quite know where to direct his eyes, not sure if he should be staring at the films in her hand, or at her reflective teeth beaming from the center of her smile. He considered feigning shock and confusion at the sight of the DVDs, as if they had fallen out of the maid's apron while she was cleaning.

"Why did you want me to know about this?" Sidney asked, his voice quivering like dry leaves on a windy autumn evening.

Lily didn't speak, but took a drawn out sip of her raspberry-flavored vodka. Sidney matched her swallow for swallow with his Scotch. After setting the movies on a nearby end table, Lily advanced toward Sidney, her eyes focused on her target.

She was very close to him now. Her hands reached up and pressed against his chest. He could feel her breath as she gently sighed.

"I didn't want you to be afraid of me," Lily whispered in his ear.

Sidney wasn't sure he understood what she was trying to tell him. He was merely overwhelmed in her presence before. He had been afraid of himself and his wavering self-control more than anything. But now that he had seen where she came from, and what she was capable of, he *was* scared.

Lily stepped back from Sidney and slid out of her clothes—quietly, effortlessly, and professionally. She stepped forward again and wrapped her smooth arms around his neck, her bare breasts flattening against his torso. Sidney's hands remained at his sides.

"Lily…I'm a married man. My wife is down the hall."

"Don't you think I know that, Sidney?" Lily said, softly.

"I don't think she'd be okay with this," Sidney said, peering at the distant wall.

Lily's arms skimmed down Sidney's back, tracing his spine, and then his ribs. She gently massaged up and down as she leaned her head against his pounding chest. Her hands moved to his thighs, and as she rubbed them stiffly, he sensed where she was headed next.

Sidney was surprised that he hadn't already embarrassed himself by soaking her belly with his prowling liquid. He was sure it would have escaped by now if he were a younger man. He did feel something slowly draining from his body though—logic and common sense.

Sidney lacked the courage to peel his eyes from the wall and lower them to the beautiful creature that held him in a tight embrace. He conjured an image from the movie jacket, and he thought about Lily the porn star. He wondered what must be going through *her* head right now.

Sex couldn't mean the same thing to her, he thought; maybe she actually enjoyed it. Maybe she didn't consider it a waste of clean sheets.

Sidney told himself to go for it, and he placed his hands on her narrow hips.

"You may not understand this, Sidney, but I think the world of Evelyn," Lily said, with unquestioned sincerity.

"I do too, Lily," Sidney replied, dropping his hands and breaking toward his bedroom.

Chapter Twenty-two

"Hurry dear, we can't be late!" Evelyn barked at her slothful husband as she watched him struggle with a tie selection. "I'll check on Lily to make sure she's ready as well!"

Sidney was having a hard time understanding why his wife was so excited about this benefit concert. Aside from having ringside seats to opera's version of murderer's row, he didn't anticipate it being anything too special.

He, for one, was not looking forward to the evening. Normally, Sidney found these events coma inducing. After the last performance he attended, he upgraded them to death inducing. He wondered if his wife was excited because she had something special to say to Alicia Cavaloni—not that she would have access to her, or her delicatessen/dressing room this time.

Evelyn handed Sidney her car keys, along with another snippy remark about his new miniature vehicle, and they were off to the Scottsdale Center for the Performing Arts.

•••

The gray, timeworn usher escorted the threesome to their covetable seats near the stage. Once they were comfortable, he handed a letter-sized, sealed white envelope to Sidney. Evelyn eyed her husband suspiciously, as if he'd just been passed special instructions for a clean escape.

"What do you have there?" Evelyn asked, trying to summon her x-ray eyes.

"How would I know?" Sidney answered, tearing off the end and reaching inside. "Apparently, we've been given some sort of voucher—here, you tell me."

"Oh my goodness," Evelyn exclaimed after examining the printed card. "I had no idea!"

"Would you like to share with us, dear?" Sidney asked.

"It seems that the 'premium tickets' I purchased came with a bonus that I was not aware of. This card entitles the three of us to a post-show reception—on stage! Champagne, wine, and desserts included. It appears that I *will* get to speak with Alicia again!"

Sidney's initial assessment was that this bonus soirée was disposable—there was never intent to purchase it, and thus, it needn't be used. That was going to be his excuse, anyway. But when Sidney heard the part about Evelyn wanting to speak with Alicia again, he had second thoughts. He predicted something nasty might transpire, and he was anxious to take in the proceedings. Then it occurred to him how unsettling this encounter could be for Lily, who he was certain would break down when introduced to her parents' killer.

"That's wonderful, Evelyn!" Lily chirped. "I've never met a real opera star before. This is so exciting!"

Sidney kept his thoughts to himself, including the fantasy he was nurturing of his wine-soaked wife knocking the diva's block off—if she could figure out how to reach it.

The show began with a brief welcome and thank you from the chief of the Scottsdale Fire Department, who quickly turned things over to the conductor of the orchestra. The maestro thanked the crowd as well, then broke the seal on his large group of professional string, wind, and brass players. He piloted them with vigorous wand waves and emotion-soaked countenance through a well-rehearsed collection of Rodgers and Hammerstein's finest. Evelyn was surprised, yet very pleased to hear the orchestra leader announce that the entire show was dedicated to everything Richard and Oscar.

After the opening numbers of *Some Enchanted Evening, Getting to Know You,* and *Hello Young Lovers*, a troupe of a dozen fresh-faced dancers vaulted from the wings, their well-executed glissades, barrel jumps, fan kicks, and layouts choreographed faultlessly to the orchestra's professional renderings. Fluid and agile bodies crisscrossed the stage, stirring the crowd with impassioned renderings of familiar, classic show tunes.

Alicia Cavaloni eventually made her appearance after intermission. The crowd responded with adoration as she strolled with focused intent to her position and grasped the stage's singular microphone.

Sidney noticed something different about her immediately. Although she was still the size of a small cabin, he could tell she had lost some weight. He leaned across Lily, who was seated between Evelyn and him and whispered to his wife: "it looks like she's dropped a few pounds."

Evelyn didn't respond, but Lily turned toward Sidney and whispered: "you're kidding, right?"

Alicia's set-list consisted of many classics to which she had committed wholeheartedly with her fleshy, shadowy soul. The crowd loved her rendition of *Bali Hai*. Sidney smiled radiantly as she belted out *Climb Every Mountain* and *I Enjoy Being a Girl*. He tried very hard to suppress his laughter as she warbled with theatric sincerity through these songs. He wondered to himself if Sir Edmund Hillary would have dared to attempt such an awkward ascent as Alicia Cavaloni. He was confident that this was one mountain he would not care to tackle. Sidney looked around the audience to see if anyone else was getting the irony, but everyone just seemed hypnotized by her over-the-top vocal styling, oblivious to the humor of it all.

The performance ended with Alicia launching into a lively a cappella rendition of *Shall We Dance?* The full orchestra soon complemented her soaring voice, and then the entire troupe of animated dancers waltzed around the stationary songstress, their arms high in the air as she hit her final notes.

The curtain dropped, and the same gnarled usher that had previously seated Evelyn, Sidney, and Lily, appeared once again. He invited everyone holding the premium ticket vouchers to follow him to the reception. About two dozen stuffy, uptown benefactors followed the bent man to the stage where sapped performers lingered and the sound of popping corks gave accent to the buzzing swarm.

Alicia's eyes met Evelyn's almost immediately. Evelyn broke away from Sidney and Lily to advance at a faster pace toward the statue-still diva. Sidney's brow puckered as he watched his wife embrace Alicia, extending her arms hard in a futile attempt to reach around the singer's globe-scale waist. He thought at first, and even hoped, that Evelyn was preparing for a double-fisted swing at the larger than life star. Instead, he was witness to nothing more than a clumsy attempt at a hug.

A server approached Sidney with a tray of bubbling champagne. He took a glass and handed it to Lily, and then snatched one each for Evelyn and for himself. Before the server was beyond arm's length, Sidney had downed his first and reached for another.

"Come on, let's get this over with," Sidney said to Lily who was standing by his side.

Alicia wasn't focused on Sidney, but rather Lily as they approached. She reached out for her hand as Lily drew near.

"Lily, my dear," Alicia started, "Evelyn tells me you are the daughter of Iris and George—dear, dear Iris and George. I hope you can find it in your heart to forgive us for your parents' untimely demise."

"Us?" Sidney questioned.

"Alicia," Evelyn interrupted, "you remember my husband Sidney?"

"Yes, yes, quite well," Alicia responded, extending her thick right mitt toward the man. "You've changed hairstyles, haven't you? Well, I'm so glad you could all attend the performance this evening!"

"Excuse me Ms. Cavaloni," Sidney said, holding her hand weakly, "what do you mean by us?"

"It was a tragedy, indeed," Alicia replied. "The unfortunate sequence of your push and then my loss of balance…"

"Excuse me?" Sidney asked, his voice rising and his face filling with blood. "I was simply reaching for your…"

"Alicia," Evelyn interrupted once more, "you look just wonderful, doesn't she Sidney?"

"Sure Alicia," Sidney answered with a shrug after giving it some thought, "you look like you dropped a few."

"Sidney!" Evelyn shrieked. "Please forgive my husband's errant behavior, Alicia. Now—you seem to have recovered nicely. How are you feeling?"

"Yeah," Sidney chimed in, "how's your fucking ass?"

With that, Sidney grabbed Lily by the hand and led her away from the potentially explosive confrontation. He located the champagne man and filched two more glasses, handing one to Lily.

Sidney apologized incessantly to the young Hanover for his imprudent behavior, stopping only after she insisted that he was her hero and that she was proud of him for his comments.

Lily and Sidney snaked through the crowd of performers and guests, enjoying two more encounters with the bubbly before Evelyn caught up with them.

"It looked like you two were having a wonderful chat," Sidney mumbled to his wife, his lips hovering just above his glass.

"Yes, we did actually," Evelyn responded, finishing the remains of her champagne. "I invited her to come to the house on Sunday."

Evelyn quickly reached across a couple having a seemingly enchanting discussion with a violin player and removed a full glass from the passing server's tray.

"What was that?" Sidney asked his wife. "I thought I heard you say Songzilla is coming to our house."

"Yes, Sidney," Evelyn replied. "I decided to have a little party—a pool party. Alicia's only in town until Sunday evening, so we have to have her over soon."

"That sounds like fun!" Lily said, trying to soften the blow.

"Sidney," Evelyn said, rubbing her husband's arm, "let me do this for me…for Lily and for me. I think if I can get to know Alicia as a real person, maybe I can rationalize the grief I've been suffering."

"Who else do you plan on inviting to your little get-together?" Sidney asked. "It's kind of short notice, don't you think? And something else—make sure whoever comes knows that this is not a get-in-the-water pool party. I can't begin to imagine certain guests in swimwear."

"Thank you Sidney," Evelyn muttered. "I'll call some of our acquaintances in the morning and see who's available to attend."

•••

"Are you going to share, or do you have that thing reserved for a whole hour?" Sidney asked his wife, who looked busily relaxed, if there were such a thing.

"Here you go, Sidney," Evelyn responded, passing her husband the colorful glass bong. "It's lit—don't worry."

"Very funny dear," Sidney replied. "So, tell me again who's coming today—I'm confused."

"You know what Sidney? I'm confused too!" Evelyn laughed in response, her eyelids tapering into slits. "But, wait a second—I know…okay, um, Theresa and David Lauder—they said they'd be here. He's the artist from down the block?"

"Are you asking me?" Lily inquired of Evelyn who appeared to be staring straight at her, "because I don't know any of these people."

"Yes you do dear. Ha! I said do-dear! So, what was I saying? Oh right, the Dean's are coming. You know Mark and Lindsay."

"Oh good," Sidney interrupted, "maybe Mark Dean can slap some sort of lawsuit on Ms. Cavaloni."

"Sidney behave," Evelyn semi-pleaded, "Let's see—your board friend Brian Carlstein and his wife Beth—they said they would love to come. And Lisa and Jared…I can't think of their last name, but you know who I mean."

"They've been our next-door neighbors for five years, Evelyn. I think I know who you mean."

"And Alicia, of course," Evelyn added. "I do hope she doesn't forget."

"You're serving food, right?" Sidney asked.

"That reminds me," Evelyn said as she passed the bong to Lily, "Lena's should be arriving any minute to set up. Oh my goodness—what are we going to do with all this smoke?"

"I'm going to inhale as much of it as I can," Sidney replied. "Stop worrying about these things Evelyn. You worry too much."

Lena's Catering arrived promptly on time. The two chefs/servers immediately unloaded their van and began creating an outdoor café on the Banks' covered patio by the pool. Evelyn realized that Lena's people were too busy to notice or care that she was stoned, so she became even more relaxed—and more stoned.

Thirty minutes before the guests were scheduled to arrive, the doorbell rang.

“Ciao bella!” Alicia cried out to Evelyn as she opened the door. “Please forgive my early appearance, darling. Mwah! I wasn’t certain how long of a cab ride it would be to your beautiful home, and I didn’t want to be improperly late.”

“Nonsense!” Evelyn replied, suddenly realizing that getting high may not have been a great idea. “Please come in and make yourself at home. The caterers are setting up in the back, and the other guests will be here in a short while. Have a seat, please!”

“Mrs. Banks?” Marvin, the lead man from Lena’s asked. “May I have a word please?”

“Of course,” Evelyn responded, inching closer to the man and further from her guest.

“I was wondering,” Marvin continued, “how would you prefer that we serve the wine? Would you like it at the buffet table, or do you want us to serve when everyone is seated?”

“Oh, I think when everyone is seated would be fine—but would it be available at the buffet table too? I wouldn’t want anyone to have to wait to have a glass. Actually, what wines are you offering? I think maybe I should have a taste before the guests arrive—quality assurance, of course.”

“Yes ma’am,” Marvin responded. “We can set up a white and a red at the buffet and also provide refills at the dining tables. But, you know we didn’t bring the wine, right? We don’t cater alcohol.”

“Oh my goodness, I forgot!” Evelyn shouted, sparking a twitch from the opera giant seated behind her. “Sidney!”

“What is it dear?” Sidney wheezed after crossing two rooms to get to his wife. “Hello, Ms. Cavaloni,” he said, gesturing politely toward the sofa. “Please—don’t get up.”

“Sidney, apparently Lena’s did not bring any wine,” Evelyn half-whispered to her husband. “How much wine do we have in the house?”

“I’m sure we have a bottle or two. How much do you want?”

“Enough for a decent presentation, Sidney –what are we going to do?”

“Don’t panic, Evelyn—we’ll buy some. Why don’t you take Lily and run to the store? Our guests shouldn’t be here for some time,” Sidney said pointedly, shooting a sideways look at the depressed cushion of the sofa and the even more depressing lump atop it.

"I'd love to help!" Alicia sang out to the Banks, who then realized they were speaking louder than they thought. "Please tell me what I can do."

"That's very kind of you to offer," Sidney said bowing to the diva. "Evelyn, why don't you take Alicia instead? Lily and I will hold down the fort."

Evelyn reached for Sidney's arm and dragged him to the far side of the room.

"Sidney, I can't drive in my condition," Evelyn whispered. "And neither should you or Lily. What am I supposed to do?"

"Let Alicia drive, dear," Sidney replied. "She must be capable of doing that."

"I'm not going to tell her I'm high from marijuana, Sidney. I won't do that."

"I'll handle this, Evelyn."

Sidney left his wife standing alone and approached the imposing creature who now appeared soldered to the sofa.

"Alicia, I don't want to be a nuisance," Sidney said in a hushed tone, "but I would like to accept your offer of help. You see, Evelyn is nothing but a bundle of nerves at times like these, with company arriving and all. I don't want to make a scene, and I don't want to embarrass her—after all, she's been seeing someone about this problem for some time. I'm afraid she'd be quite a mess out on the road. I wonder if you wouldn't mind driving the both of you to the store."

"It would be my pleasure," Alicia replied in the softest voice Sidney had yet to hear her use. "Poor thing."

"Evelyn," Sidney called out, "Alicia would truly love to accompany you to the store. And she asked if she could be the driver."

"I don't own a car personally," Alicia chimed in, "but every so often I enjoy getting behind the wheel and shaking off the rust—if you don't mind."

"Oh, of course I don't mind, Alicia," Evelyn replied, her hand pressed flat over her heart. "That would be just fine."

"And if you ladies could do me a huge favor," Sidney

begged, "and pick up some of those wonderful lady fingers they sell in that bakery by the grocery?"

"Lady fingers!" Alicia shrieked. "Certainly, Sidney—that would be our pleasure."

Chapter Twenty-three

"There's a parking space directly in front of the grocery, Alicia," Evelyn said, pointing a well-manicured finger toward the spot. "We'll pick up the wine first, and then drive over to the bakery—it's down a few stores."

"Nonsense!" Alicia replied. "I will park here, but please allow me to shop for the lady fingers while you're browsing for the wine—I can use the walk, sweetie. When I'm done, I'll return to help you tote the wine. We'll save some time that way, okay?"

"I suppose that would be fine," Evelyn replied. "I'll have one of the bag boys assist me with the wine though."

Larry, Curly, and Moe would have appreciated Evelyn's ham-handed attempt at liberating Alicia from her seatbelt. Alicia was leaning forward and to her left as much as she could in order to provide access to the latch. Evelyn struggled at first to find the latch, and then fumbled around with it for the longest time as if it were a technical marvel of the future. Eventually, the two made it out of the SUV and onto the broad walkway that fronted the center.

Evelyn lingered by the grocery entrance, watching Alicia amble toward the bakery. She had no valid reason for observing her like this, but she was stoned, and she was also intrigued. She likened it to viewing a motorcar race or heavyweight fight. There was always a good chance disaster might strike, and as much as she feared that possibility, she didn't want to miss anything either.

Confident that her chauffeur had made it to the bakery, Evelyn inched her way into the market. Her senses were abruptly overwhelmed by the barrage of colors, sounds, and most impactful of all—aromas. She stood by the line of nested, chrome carts that hugged the front wall of the store, visualizing them as one massive silvery snake that diminished in size with every new shopper. One piece after another of its long, metallic tail was being amputated, bit-by-bit, by the store's oblivious patrons. After much deliberation she peeled one of the carts from the queue, and then leveraged it around and around until she had control of the beast.

The wine section was located toward the rear of the store. It was a challenge for Evelyn to navigate the rows of tempting foods without succumbing to a few of the seductive morsels and sneaking them into her cart. She stopped when she came to a display of large, pillowy marshmallows encrusted with crisp, brown strands of coconut. Her mouth watered as if she were a marble scupper crafted into the back wall of the Trevi fountain. She tucked one bag of these jewels into the shallower, far corner of the cart before trooping forward.

Her perseverance paid off when she reached narrow rows of thin metal shelves stacked high with scores of colorful, glass wine bottles. They stood perfectly at attention, begging to be scrutinized and purchased.

Evelyn wasn't sure what she was searching for other than appealing, pretty labels on higher priced bottles. She assumed this to be a reliable formula when seeking the best tasting wine. She filled two emptied case boxes with her diverse, attractive preferences and then proceeded to the checkout line.

While waiting her turn in line, a mature woman sporting a severely coiffed hairstyle, and wearing a six-button, ecru and pink Castleberry knit suit, peered down into Evelyn's cart and glared at the mass of bottled intoxicants. She then glanced up to check out the irresponsible party. The expression of disdain penciled across her face reminded Evelyn of someone, but she couldn't place whom.

Her world was spinning in a different direction now, and everything and everyone in it seemed so familiar and yet strange at the same time. It was as if she had moved to a new place, a new town—but that wasn't so. She was still in her town, her Scottsdale, where she had lived for years. Something had changed, but she could not put her finger on it.

A young man clad in a white butcher's apron pushed Evelyn's heavy cart to her parking space, and then carefully placed the single paper bag and two cases of wine in the far back corner of her SUV. Evelyn watched him lower the hatch until it snapped shut, and then handed him a five for his efforts. She peered down the walkway that served as a buffer between idling cars filled with slump-shouldered husbands, and the row of shops that held their just-be-a-minute wives, but she did not see Alicia.

It was a very warm day and Evelyn did not want to walk into her own party a sweaty mess, so she started her car and waited in air-conditioned comfort for Alicia's return. After a few minutes she became concerned and wondered if she had the plan all wrong. She had a strange feeling that maybe Alicia was still inside the bakery, waiting to be retrieved.

Evelyn placed her left hand on the steering wheel and gauged her ability to drive even a very short distance. She was feeling very paranoid, yet very mellow. There was still a foggy blanket shrouding her senses, but she could tell that it was lifting somewhat, and she felt confident enough to attempt a journey twenty spaces down the lot.

With her foot on the brake and the car in reverse, Evelyn checked the rearview mirror. Passing behind her was an elderly couple pushing a near-empty grocery cart, and they were moving exceptionally slow. They struggled with their cart, using what Evelyn assumed was their entire reserve of strength just to thrust it forward a few inches at a time. It seemed to her a pantomime of sorts—the sad-faced clowns leaning into an invisible wind.

An eerie feeling of déjà vu crept into Evelyn's body from her toes up. She wasn't sure if this reaction was due to the large amount of marijuana she had inhaled, or if she would have experienced the phenomena regardless. Mindful of her current state of nominal confusion, and in the interest of safety, she put the SUV in park and removed her foot from the brake.

Finally, the aged man and woman whose atrophied bodies had been battling the cart's veiled, sinister strength, wrestled the stubborn, rubber-wheeled ferry to the rear of their car, which was parked next to Evelyn's.

Evelyn looked once more down the broad walkway, hoping to see Alicia shuffling toward her. The opera star was not anywhere in sight. Deciding it was now safe to back out of her space and roll across the parking lot to the bakery, Evelyn once again placed her foot on the brake and shifted the SUV into reverse.

Evelyn paid close attention to the old couple next to her, peering at them through glazed eyes as they situated their two shopping bags into the trunk of their pristine twenty-year-old Buick. She imagined the weight of their bags, leaden from bunches of bright yellow bananas and jumbo-sized boxes of prunes, causing them to slip backwards. In a dizzying fright, she pictured the both of them falling into her path.

Once the couple had their freight on-board and their trunk securely fastened, Evelyn determined that it was safe to proceed. She glanced at the pair as they stood behind their car and noticed they were waiting for her to make the next move.

Evelyn was not about to take any unnecessary risks, and so she kept her eyes glued on the brittle man and woman as she started to back up. They had their eyes glued on her as well.

Evelyn could see fear sprouting across the old couples' faces as she rolled her SUV gently backwards. She didn't mean to scare them, but understood their uneasiness given their lack of mobility and speed. She smiled at them as she approached, hoping to offer some reassurance that everything was going to be okay.

When the back of her SUV had safely cleared the couple, Evelyn stepped on the gas just a little. She wanted to rid herself of this situation as quickly as she could, and she was sure the old folks were hoping for the same.

Evelyn sensed the back of her SUV abruptly rising in the air, as if a tow truck had snagged her rear axle in error. She stepped firmer on the gas pedal hoping to break free from the obscured obstacle and then felt the car lower somewhat. Her eyes had not left the faces of the anxious codgers, so she knew they were safe. Her SUV though was still off the ground and seemed to be struggling for purchase. Evelyn placed it in park and stepped out to determine the cause of the glitch.

Trapped in front of the seven-spoke, alloy rear wheels of the SUV, Alicia stared up at the sky, and then at Evelyn. Her head and neck, pressed flush against the black asphalt, stuck out from under the chassis, her body otherwise lodged under the Lexus like a mechanic searching for a leak with his toes. She looked as if she wanted to say something, her lips wriggling like tiny waves across her face.

In a fit of panic, Evelyn jumped into her SUV and drove it quickly forward, back into the parking space. She experienced the dramatic rise of the car as it passed over the formidable obstruction once again, and then she was back on level ground. Evelyn's heart hammered fast within her breast as she rushed to the fallen diva.

•••

"Have you heard from Evelyn?" Lily asked Sidney who stood nervously at one corner of the patio, away from his accumulating guests.

"Nothing," he responded. "They should have returned a long time ago. I'm certain she's searching every wine bottle on the racks looking for the prettiest labels. I should have gone myself."

"I'm sure you're right—she'll be back any minute. So, do you want to introduce me to your friends?"

"I…I would be happy to," Sidney replied.

"Lily! So glad to see you here!" Mark Dean exclaimed as he approached the young Hanover with a smile. "Sidney, you are one very lucky man to have such a beautiful and smart house guest. What happened to your hair?"

"It's a pretty hot look on him, don't you think?" Lily asked, patting the top of Sidney's head with her palm.

"Personally, I think he's a handsome devil either way," Mark replied with a smirk. "Sidney, do you think I could steal this dazzling creature from you for a moment? I promise not to keep her too long."

"I suppose, Mark," Sidney responded while edging away. "Lily, just scream if you need me."

"So, do you need me to sign more legal papers Mark?" Lily asked. "I'm leaving this week. I hope you brought them with you."

"No, no," Mark answered. "Nothing like that; you don't need to do another thing regarding your parents estate."

"Well, don't tell me I'm coming into some of their money now. I don't know that I'd want it. They weren't really parents to me, you know."

"Oh, they were your parents, Lily—biologically at least—you know that. But, sorry—no more money."

"What is it then, Mark?" Lily asked.

"When you went through your parent's house," Mark said, pausing to organize his thoughts, "do you remember when I told you to look through your mother's things and to take what you wanted?"

"Yes."

"I hope you found some interesting pieces of her jewelry, hopefully everything of value."

"Actually, I took one of her pins. Nothing else really appealed to me," Lily replied.

"I was wondering, because when I did my final walk-through of their house, it looked like nothing had been touched… hmm."

"What's wrong, Mark?"

"What about any of her clothes, or maybe accessories? Did you happen to take anything like that?" Mark asked, his fingers rubbing his chin.

"No, of course not," Lily laughed in response. "There was nothing like that of hers that I'd want. Why do you ask?"

"This is silly, of course," Mark stated, "but I purchased my wife a gift—a surprise gift. I really couldn't hide it in my home. My wife spends her days doing nothing but organizing that place; it's almost impossible to hide anything from her. I had asked George recently if maybe I could use his place—you know, safe keeping for this special surprise."

"Uh-huh."

"Anyway, I brought this gift over to your parent's house and hid it in one of the bedroom closets. It was a special, small…figurine. I had it shipped from Europe. I didn't even tell your father or mother what the gift was. I didn't want Iris accidentally spilling the beans. I had it in a hatbox of sorts. I'm wondering if you happened to run across anything like that."

"A hatbox, Mark?"

"Yes, a hatbox. A large, round box, with colored stripes and a big rope handle. Sound familiar?"

"Not at all, Mark. It sure sounds like a special box, though."

"Oh well, that's a shame then, a shame. I'm sure your mother must have thought it was one of her old hats and threw it away…or maybe she donated it to a charity. Oh dear God."

"Something wrong, Mark?" Lily asked, holding back her extraordinary smile.

•••

"Hey, I know her!" the third medic to arrive shouted to the two kneeling by Alicia's side. "She was in that show a couple nights ago—the singer!"

"Yeah, too bad someone so charitable had to get run over like this," one of the kneelers said, pulling a crisp white sheet over the body. "Jonny, do me a favor and secure the area, okay? SPD's gonna wanna take a look at the scene."

"What about her?" Jonny asked, pointing to a pale, drawn up Evelyn sitting on the curb.

"It was her car. Keep her inside the tape."

Evelyn watched as the medic covered Alicia with a sheet. She had just killed one of the most popular opera stars in the country; Evelyn Banks—murderer. A few minutes ago, she was merely a stoned housewife on an errand to pick up some party supplies. Now she was a killer.

Staring at the giant white mound twenty feet from her, Evelyn attempted to rehash what she had done. She replayed the incident in her head at least ten times, wondering how this could have possibly happened. She had backed up the car, and that was that.

Evelyn was too panicked to be remorseful yet. Her heavy buzz had worn thin, but she knew that she'd be arrested for murder *and* for drug use. She wasn't sure how they would test for the marijuana, but she was sure it would involve needles, urine, and some sort of strip-search. She couldn't check, but she strained her mind trying to remember what style of underwear she had on. If it were a pair that Lily had selected for her, she was sure she'd be hit with additional charges.

As she contemplated her fate, an unmarked police car pulled up to the scene—lights flashing, no siren. Two men wearing suits got out of the car, one of them much taller than the other. They slipped under the yellow tape and greeted the medics, who appeared to be doing nothing but waiting for these men.

One of the suited men bent over and lifted a corner of the white sheet so that he could have a look at Alicia's face. The group chatted back and forth for a minute, and then one of the medics pointed at Evelyn who was still hunched over on the curb, her arms tightly wrapped around herself like she was wearing an invisible straightjacket.

The two suits directed the medics to remove the body, and then they approached Evelyn.

"Mrs. Banks?" the shorter of the two asked. "Detective Dach, Scottsdale police. This is my partner, Detective Hollahan. We remember you—do you remember us?"

As Evelyn stood, the bitter, liquefied remnants of some earlier ingested morsel sought quick escape from her distressed gut, darted up her throat, and pooled inside her mouth. Her knees tightened, her legs convulsed, and all of her strength disappeared—gone, like her future.

Her immediate concern was whether these J.C. Penney suit wearers would throw her against their car before putting on the cuffs. She could care less who they were.

"I'm sorry, but no," she answered.

"We met you the night Ms. Cavaloni fell on your friends. We were there," Detective Hollahan said.

"Okay," Evelyn responded.

"Mrs. Banks," Detective Dach said, "We'd like to ask you a couple questions, alright?"

Evelyn nodded.

"How did you not see this woman behind your car? She must weigh four-hundred pounds."

"Actually, the EMTs at the theater said it was four fifty-two, remember?" Detective Hollahan asked his partner.

"What the fuck's the difference here, Larry? Four hundred, four fifty-two, the point is, the woman was huge!"

"I get the point, Jeff. I'm just trying to be accurate. You ever lift fifty-two pounds? That's some weight there."

"Yeah, I've lifted it. I made Detective, didn't I? I've lifted much more than fifty-two pounds."

"You made Detective because you're my brother-in-law, schmuck. Now get your facts straight before you recite them."

"Excuse me, please," Evelyn said, her weak voice trembling, "what are you going to do with me?"

"Did you not see Ms. Cavaloni walking behind your car, Mrs. Banks?" Detective Hollahan asked.

"Of course I didn't," Evelyn responded. "I would never want to hurt anyone."

"I believe her, Jeff," Detective Hollahan said to his partner. "Let's go."

"That's it?" Evelyn asked, color returning to her face. "You're done with me?"

"We thought Alicia Cavaloni should have been tried for murder when she fell on your friends, to be honest with you," Detective Dach replied. "She was recklessly obese—unfortunately, that's not a crime in this state."

"Will you be okay, Mrs. Banks?" Detective Hollahan asked. "Can we give you a lift?"

"I'll be fine, thank you," Evelyn answered.

"Hopefully, she didn't damage your car too much," Detective Dach commented as he surveyed the scene and wiped his brow.

Evelyn strained to hear the two detective's oily voices as they argued about some sort of nonsense that did not pertain to her. Then they gathered the yellow caution tape, got in their unmarked car, and sped away.

Evelyn's eyes remained focused on the detectives' car until it turned a corner two blocks down the road. She shook her head to settle her still caroming brain and noticed a large shopping bag standing upright two parking spaces over. She at first assumed it was left by one of the curious onlookers who had wasted part of their day straining to understand the white-shrouded mess on the ground.

Edging closer to the bag, Evelyn could tell it was from the bakery down the row. She considered simply abandoning it, but felt compelled to peek inside first. Stretching the limits of the cardboard-colored sack was a large, white box, secured by a thin piece of twine. She untied the fibrous cord and the lid of the box popped open. Inside was what appeared to be the entire inventory of the bakery's lady fingers. Outside the box and wedged against the bag were a few chocolate looking crumbs, along with two soiled pastry wrappers.

Evelyn picked up the bag by its two looped handles and set it down at the edge of the center's walkway. She wouldn't be taking the freshly baked treats home, but thought some unfortunate soul who was naïve to the day's tragedy might benefit from them. She glared at the bag for a moment as if it were a memorial of sorts then got into her car and drove home.

•••

"Sidney, could you come here please?" Evelyn whispered, extending her head out the sliding glass door adjacent to the back patio.

"Evelyn!" Sidney shouted, fighting the roar of the chattering crowd. "What has taken you so long?"

"Just come here, Sidney."

Sidney skipped to the house, relieved that his social director had finally arrived. Evelyn grabbed his shirtsleeve and jerked him into the dining room.

"You did get the wine, didn't you?" Sidney asked. "In another minute, I was going to break out some bottles of the hard stuff."

"Yes, I did get the wine, Sidney. It's in the car."

"What's wrong, Evelyn? Did something happen? Did our not so little friend get into a not so little accident with your car?"

"Something like that, Sidney." Evelyn lowered her head and started to shake. "I…I killed her."

"What! What did you just say?"

"Shh. I don't want the company to hear," Evelyn murmured. "I'm not in trouble. The police seemed kind of pleased, actually."

"Evelyn—what the hell are you talking about? You killed Alicia?" Sidney fell into a seat at the table.

"I didn't see her, Sidney. She walked behind my car, and I just didn't see her."

"You didn't *see* her? You've got to be kidding me."

"I'm not kidding, Sidney. She's dead. I killed her."

Sidney sat, his elbows resting on the table, his head propped by his hands. He scrutinized his wife's face, searching for something he couldn't find.

Starting as a low rumble deep within his chest, Sidney's mushrooming guffaw exploded, penetrating the silence of the room like a thunderclap on a calm night.

"You ran over Alicia!" Sidney spit out between gusts of laughter. "I've got to tell the others."

"Sidney, no!" Evelyn begged. "Please don't. There's no reason for anyone to know."

"Then just tell Lily. She'll want to know—okay?"

"I suppose."

"Are you alright, Evelyn? Let me send everyone home. I'll inform our guests that Alicia had an emergency and won't be here; that's the truth, right?"

"We haven't had a gathering like this in a long time, Sidney. Let them stay."

"There's wine in the car?" Sidney asked.

"Pour me a glass, would you?" Evelyn replied.

Chapter Twenty-four

"I want you to relax, Evelyn." Lily breathed the words inches from her friend's ear. "Sidney's reading the paper on the patio and the door is locked. Would you like another glass of wine?"

"If I had another glass, Lily, I'm afraid I wouldn't remember any of this later." Evelyn almost choked on her words as she fidgeted about, desperately searching for comfort on the king sized bed.

"You find me attractive, don't you?" Lily asked as she began to strip down, her pink, knit top already over her head.

"You're a beautiful girl, Lily," Evelyn said uneasily, her eyes darting around the room.

"Why don't you take off your robe, Evelyn?" Lily purred, her fingers toying with and stiffening her eager nipples. "Or would you like me to take it off for you?"

"No, that's okay, Lily," Evelyn replied. "I can handle this."

Evelyn struggled to remove the floral silk robe, a difficult task from her reclining position. Her shoulders wrestled with the shimmery fabric in a comical dance. She finally stood and unleashed her body from the uncooperative cover-up. Then she quickly returned to the bed, arranging herself deliberately on her side, knees slightly bent.

"What now?" Evelyn asked.

Lily stepped out of her white cotton shorts and shimmied onto the bed, spooning her body to Evelyn's.

"You're a beautiful girl too," Lily whispered, gently caressing Evelyn's thigh as she spoke. "Like I said—relax."

Lily rolled Evelyn onto her back, and then ran her palms up and down her well cared for skin, carefully avoiding the most sensitive and sensual spots. She wiggled one hand between Evelyn's clamped knees, prying lightly and sliding it closer to its objective. Evelyn's thighs were like a carpenter's vice, gripping Lily's hand tight before it got too far.

"Evelyn," Lily whimpered, "I promise you I've done this often. We've talked about this many times. What's wrong?"

“I…I have never had a…I have never been with another woman, Lily,” Evelyn admitted.

“Don’t you think I know that?” Lily replied, caressing Evelyn’s belly. “Why did you ask for this, Evelyn?”

“I’m a lesbian, Lily,” Evelyn responded. “I’ve known that for so long.”

“You’ve told me that—I know. But I guess I never asked you: just what makes you think you’re a gay woman? Explain to me, Evelyn.”

“Oh, there are so many reasons, Lily. When I was a child, I never liked boys. They were always so mean and so disrespectful.”

“They were boys, Evelyn.”

“Still, it was like they were my enemy. I never felt anything…sexual toward them.”

“Evelyn, very few girls do. But as you grew older, didn’t you allow yourself to fall in love? Didn’t you love Sidney when you married?”

“Of course I did. I still do. But I think it’s another kind of love…I loved your mother, Lily. She was everything I ever wanted to be.”

“You loved her—you didn’t make love *to* her. You admired her, Evelyn. You admired her and you respected her.”

“And then,” Evelyn continued, “there’s the issue of the…of the act itself. It’s never too comfortable. It’s never been enjoyable—it’s not as you’ve described to me.”

“What else?”

“Well—I’m a very neat person…and I love the arts.”

“Seriously, Evelyn?”

Lily crawled off the bed, scanning for the clothes she had recently and seductively peeled off, and threw them back on like a fashion-show model overdue on the runway.

“You’re not a lesbian, Evelyn,” Lily said as she stood at the foot of the bed. “You may need a little coaching about sex, but you are not a lesbian.”

Lily turned toward the sound of the suddenly jangling doorknob. She looked back at Evelyn who was still naked, but not overreacting to Sidney’s unexpected presence.

Evelyn slid out of bed, and with a furtive glance at Lily, unlocked the door. She reversed course and walked shoulder-slumped toward the bed as Sidney entered the room.

"Sorry to disturb you ladies," Sidney started, "but…what's going on? Evelyn, are you okay?"

"She's fine, Sidney," Lily answered. "She might have something to tell you, though."

"What is it, Evelyn?" Sidney asked.

Evelyn collected her thoughts before she spoke: "I know you've seen her naked, Sidney—it's okay."

"What are you talking about?" Sidney asked, color sprinting from his face.

"Would you tell him, Lily?" Evelyn asked.

"Your wife confided in me, Sidney. She's been confused about a lot of things—a lot of personal things. She knows she hasn't been a um, complete wife I guess. She asked me to help."

"Are you serious, Evelyn? Sidney screeched at his wife. "You hired someone to seduce me?"

"Oh my goodness Sidney," Evelyn responded, shocked at the comment, "of course not. I know you've been stressed about…"

"Sidney," Lily interrupted, "I love you…and I love Evelyn. I thought I could help both of you through your…difficulties. I'm not a professional sex surrogate. I'm just a person with a lot of experience. I actually make a pretty good living using that experience, giving advice. Of course, I don't claim to know much about real relationships. I advise film directors in the land of make-believe. But still, they want me—they need me. I like that…I like feeling wanted."

Lily looked at Sidney's vacant profile and then turned toward Evelyn. The Banks weren't saying anything—they were looking at each other. Lily pulled her pink top over her head once more and stepped out of her white shorts. She stood naked in front of the two most important people in her life. She had never felt this close to anyone before. She wasn't sure what else she could offer them.

"Do either of you want me?" Lily asked, her voice hovering above a whisper.

"Yes, Lily," Sidney answered. "You're very special to us."

Sidney turned toward Evelyn, and continued speaking: "Put your clothes on please, Lily. If you could wait for us in the den, my wife and I have something to discuss."

Lily reached for her things, but did not take the time to put them on. As she was leaving the room, she twisted her head and looked back with a smile—a bright, wide smile.

When the door latched behind the young Hanover, Evelyn stood and approached her husband. Without speaking, she unbuttoned his shirt and reached inside with her smooth palms. She rubbed his chest for a minute and then stepped back, her eyes never breaking contact with his.

"Do we have something to discuss?" Evelyn asked.

"No," Sidney replied, embracing her cooperative body with his hands before lifting her to the bed.

The End

www.ingramcontent.com/pod-product-compliance
Lightning Source LLC
Chambersburg PA
CBHW060210180626
46813CB00007B/2774